SEDUCED BY THE FAE

LAXMI HARIHARAN

1

Alice

"Eew," something wriggles down my spine. I scream, and the musty taste of the gag fills my mouth. I try to move but my hands are bound in front of me. I heave myself over on my side. My knees hit the stony floor. Pain shivers up my legs and the cords around my ankles bite into my skin. The thing sliding down my back brushes the waistband of my pants. Ugh! The fine hairs on my forearms rise.

I need to shake off whatever creepy-crawly has found its way under my clothes.

At least that's the only thing trying to get into my pants and not the man who kidnapped me.

I'd take death by insect over being touched by whoever ripped me away from the gathering where I had been.

One second I'd been walking on the beach trying to escape the alpha-hole who'd made me so angry that I'd wanted nothing more than to get away from him, and now I'd do anything to have him at my side. *Doc. Damn you, where are you now when I need you?*

A chuckle bubbles up, but it sounds like I'm choking. Awesome. Hysteria. If I fall apart I'll conform to the stereotype of a weak human female. A slithering sensation oozes down the hollow of my back and my belly lurches.

My biceps tense, my forearms flex, and the ropes give a millimeter.

I draw in my breath, then rear back. My body creaks with every move, and I roll onto my back with a thump. The crunch of tiny bones echoes through the space.

My stomach roils. Damn. This. Hell. I am getting out of here. I scream against the gag, my eyelashes colliding with the rag that's tied across my eyes.

I am human. I can't teleport or draw on telekinetic energy in a flight—unlike the Fae or the shifters.

But the manner in which my captor has trussed me up, you'd think I was the most dangerous person he's met.

It's not going to be easy to give him the slip, which, considering I can't even move to scratch the itch on my nose, is me being optimistic. But hey, when you are a human adopted by Fae and brought up in a family of exceptionally strong mortals, you learn to hold your own. No matter that I look delicate, or at least that's what Doc tells me. *Fucking Doc.*

Since the day I met that Alpha Fae, I haven't been able to get him out of my thoughts. He's gotten under my skin, and I am not sure why.

The man hates me; that's clear from the way he's gone out of his way to avoid me.

So why has he accepted my help around the infirmary?

Certainly not because he's been overwhelmed by the volume of work—he works all hours and never seems to flag. I've never met anyone as dedicated to his profession... Okay, that's professions, plural. He's both a doctor and a member of the Fae Corps. And he's managed to successfully keep his distance from me.

Until the day he took on the Dare and proceeded to use his hands to pound his opponent—those beautiful hands which are better off being used for healing and for surgeries, for touching, holding, caressing me.

Heat flushes my skin, and my thighs clench.

The thought of his big, rough palms on me...and I do recall the feel of his hands, for on just one occasion I managed to anger him enough for him to grab me and haul me close. His lips had descended toward mine, and I had been sure he was going to kiss me then, except he hadn't.

His skin had paled, and he'd behaved as if he'd seen a ghost.

He'd let go of me and stalked off and…he's not touched me since.

Had being with me dredged up unwanted memories?

I stiffen. Had there been someone else in his life? Or something that had scared him off intimacy? Is that why he's decided to pretend I don't even exist? He probably isn't aware that I've been kidnapped.

Tears prick the backs of my eyes. I have to find a way out of here; I can't stop fighting. All the time I've been one of the few humans among the stronger Fae and shifters I haven't stopped trying to prove myself and now…? Now I am exhausted. Defenseless…A sound bleeds into the silence. Every pore in my body goes on alert.

There's someone in here.

I struggle against the bonds that restrain me, try to move my face around, inching toward the source of the shuffling. The air in the space thins. The scent of mint and something earthy, tangy like cinnamon, fresh like the newly fallen snow flows over me. That scent? It's so familiar. *Nah. It can't be.* Is my imagination playing tricks on me?

Wriggling over to my side, I lurch to a sitting position.

Footsteps approach and the blindfold is torn from my eyes.

I blink. It's dark; I can't see a thing. But something looms in front of me. Something…someone…large enough to block out even the gloom.

I choke, try to take in a breath and find I can't… My lungs ache; my throat burns. This is it. This is how I die, scared out of my head.

A touch brushes my cheek, and I scream just as the gag is loosened and slips off of my face.

A light flares up, and gray-blue eyes blaze at me.

"Alice?"

2

Doc

"It's me, Alice." I rein in my telekinetic energy. The glow at the tips of my fingers switches off.

I reach for her and her shoulders tremble.

She tightens her jaw, snaps her head forward, and butts me in the chest. The breath whooshes out of me.

"The fuck?" I retreat and raise my palms faceup.

She blinks, and those green eyes of hers lighten until they resemble pale mirrors.

She looks at me as if she can see right through to my soul. I reach for her again, and this time she doesn't move. *Thank fuck.*

I fling the gag aside.

She swallows, then flicks out her tongue to lick her lips and my cock twitches.

I came to free her.

The woman had been taken and restrained. All tied up and waiting for my ministrations. My cock thickens. I want to yank her to me and plunge my dick into her wet pussy, thrusting into her until she comes all over my shaft. *Fuuuck.* I spring to my feet so fast that she rears back.

"Sorry!" I rake my fingers through my hair.

Not a second in her presence, and already I am apologizing. *Huh? Why does she unnerve me so?*

"Doc?" She swallows. "How did you get in here?" Her gaze darts around the space, then she stiffens. "No, don't tell me…your telekinetic powers?"

"Yeah." I drop my arms to my sides. "I heard your scream and ran out of the Dare—"

"Stupid Dare." She tosses her head. The woman had been taken and locked up, and yet she's full of fight.

"Seems you haven't lost any of your sass."

"Seems you are going to just waste time talking nonsense when you should be untying me." She tilts her head.

"Fuck."

"Language, Doc." She sniffs.

"Shut up, woman, and let me help you."

"That'll be the day." She snorts. "You help me? Ha!"

"Can you keep quiet for just one second while I try to figure out how to undo this cord?" I reach for the glowing cable that binds her arms to the pillar at the same time that she says, "Don't touch that."

As if she can order me around?

My fingers brush the top of the glittering rope, and sparks fly off of it. A jolt of energy hurtles down my spine. My body arcs through the air, and I hit the floor. My shoulders slam into the hard, stony surface. Pain sweeps over my skin. "Fuck." My head spins.

There's a ringing in my ears. I stagger to a sitting position and shake my head, but the ringing doesn't lessen; in fact, the sound echoes through space, ebbing and flowing, rising and falling… "It's a fucking alarm." I lurch to my feet.

"I warned you…" Her voice wavers. "You need to get out of here, Doc."

"The bastards rigged the cord. They were sure that one of us would come for you because you are—"

"Bait." She grimaces.

The realization sinks into my blood at the same time that footsteps pound down the corridor toward us.

"There's only one person who would do this, who'd want to lure the Fae Corps into a trap. Someone who was confident that we'd come to rescue one of our own."

"You need to get away from here before they take you prisoner, too." Her chin wobbles.

"The fuck you talking about?" I move toward her, and she shrinks back again. And it's that which stops me. The fact that she shies away from me, thinking that I am going to hurt her. And I can't stand the thought of making her uncomfortable, not even now when her life is in danger. When in a few seconds her captors are going to be upon us, and I need to get her free before that.

"No fucking way I am leaving you here on your own." I clench my fists at my sides.

"You don't have a choice, Doc."

"You always have a choice, Alice." I narrow my gaze.

"Doc." Her lips turn down.

"Alice." I drop my chin toward my chest.

"Stubborn alpha-hole."

"Headstrong woman," I growl.

"It doesn't help if you end up here with me. Who'd rescue me then?"

"Me." I toss my head. "I am the only one who's going to break you free, the only one you need."

"My point exactly." She flutters her eyelashes, and my heart, the bloody thing, thuds.

"Quit trying to play me." I thrust out my chest.

"Quit being so full of yourself that you can't see what's right here in front of your eyes."

You, I see you, is what I want to say, but no way am I going to let on that she is my weakness. Nope. "And what's that?" I snarl.

"That you need to leave so you can stay alive and return as my savior."

It should sound corny, it should but it doesn't. I want to be that and so much more for her, and *what does that say about me, eh?* Except that I am fucked. Abso-fucking-lutely fucked.

Besides, she's wrong.

I am no one's savior, not the kind of person who'd rescue anyone. Certainly not this beautiful curvy human whose lips are blue from the cold, whose shoulders tremble, from being so close to me. Chemistry had blazed between us from the moment she'd walked into my infirmary to be treated for her injured ankle

She had been brave then, not making a sound as I had bound her ankle, all the while very aware of her touch, her looks, the scent of her—like jasmine and fiery pepper—that had crept into my blood. I'd been instantly hard.

I should have turned my back on her, told her to never come back, to ask one of the other doctors to treat her, but the thought of anyone else touching her, holding her, caressing her, comforting her, had sent anger rippling down my spine.

I had helped her to her feet and packed her off for home. I'd decided I was not going to have anything to do with her. *How difficult could it have been, right?*

A woman who'd appeared so innocent that I knew she was going to drive me to make mistakes.

I stare into the eyes of the woman who has tempted me more than any female I have ever met.

Whose every glance calls to me, warning me this is different. What's between us is much more intense. If I smell her essence once more, I'll possess her, mate her. *Mate her.* A growl rumbles up from my chest.

She blinks at me. "You have to leave." Her voice is soft but with an edge of steel to it. She looks helpless but she isn't. She holds my life, my heart in her palms.

Is she even aware of it?

"Not without you."

"You must, Doc."

"Nolan."

"Huh?"

"That's my name."

The thump of footsteps clatters outside the cell. Her gaze darts to the door and the skin around her eyes tightens. "Go, Doc, before they find you."

"I don't take commands from anyone." *Except you. You could ask me to do anything...anything, I just can't leave you here.*

"This is not the time for your stupid macho alpha-holeness to surface."

"Say it." I fold my arms over my chest.

"You think you can hold the fact that your stupid ass is about to be discovered over me and threaten me into this?" She juts out her lower lip.

Fucking adorable.

"Just say my name once, that's all I am asking."

She tosses her head.

"Why is it so difficult?" Tiny thing. Yet she has such strong willpower. I can't wait to break her.

"So I'll say your name and you'll leave?" She bites on her lower lip and my cock twitches.

"I'll think about it." I drum my fingers on my chest.

"Arrogant alpha-hole."

She looks ready to stamp her little foot which, given she is all trussed up and on the floor, is a little hard.

I can't wait to see her all bound up and waiting for me. *No. Get rid of the thought.* The image of her wrapped up in silken bonds and nothing else fills my head. Her skin, pale and fair, would show the lashings of the ropes. Her flesh would quiver in anticipation, her pupils dilated with desire. That succulent triangle between her legs would be drooling with need, for me.

The door grates open, and she pops up to her knees. "Save yourself... Nolan."

My name from her lips. The sound of it coils in my groin, and I am instantly hard. *Fuck.*

"Go," she tosses her head.

"I never was good at doing what I was told."

3

Alice

He turns and races toward the new arrivals.

"Nolan, don't do this," I yell after him but he doesn't heed me.

He's the most lethal male I have ever met. Sure, the Fae Corps men are all alphas, larger than life, and dangerous, too. Did I mention possessive? Very possessive. No way is Nolan going to leave me behind. Hell, if our positions were reversed, I'd be doing the same, except I wouldn't have the brute strength to take on the five men who pour into the cell.

Nolan growls and my thighs clench. Why does the guttural rage-filled noise turn me on?

This isn't normal.

I am neither shifter nor Fae, just human…a female who has gotten herself caught in this strange mess.

I am used to staying on the sidelines, melting into the background. And trust me when I say that as a human female in a city of Fae, it's easy to do so. Most assume I'm a specimen to be studied. Many make fun of how defenseless I am when faced with the raw power of the Fae. Their bloodthirstiness, their need for violence, the way they're turned on by the need to punish, all of it so different from what I am. Human. Female. Nurturer. *Yeah, that's me.*

Maybe that's why I'm so attracted to Doc...I mean, Nolan...have been from the moment I walked into the infirmary and saw him.

He's part of the Fae Corps but also a qualified surgeon. Maybe it's the two completely opposite sides to his personality that intrigue me?

He's ferocious enough to be enlisted as a soldier, yet had been so gentle caring for my swollen, throbbing ankle. He'd seen to my wounds, and by the end of it, *yeah*, other parts of me had been throbbing with need. He's a big powerful alpha male but his touch is gentle. He's sensitive...yet arousing, his scent so calming...yet sinking into my core and promising everything dark and dangerous that I have always wanted, but never acknowledged. At that first meeting, all of it had rushed to the fore. That primal part of me I had hidden all of my life had raged forth, and I had almost thrown myself at his feet and begged him to take me, rut me —

"Fuck!" Nolan's voice cuts through the thoughts swirling around in my head.

He takes all five of the new arrivals down, then moves so fast he blurs. He springs back on his feet, hauls up two of the strangers, knocks their heads together—literally— then flings them aside. Bends and slams his massive fist into the face of the third, lifts his foot and crashes it down into the chest of the fourth. The sound of breaking bones rends the air. I wince.

The fifth man staggers to his feet.

Only Nolan is already there. He lowers his head and brings it up in a sweep that crashes into the chin of his opponent. The man sinks to the floor. Nolan stands there, his arms propped on his waist. His shoulders heave as he draws in a breath. He tosses his head and turns sideways. A smirk curls his lips. The light from the open door caresses his face, highlighting the nooks and angles of his chiseled body. He's all sharp edges and hard planes. My throat goes dry.

The men around him on the floor don't move. He cants his head, then peels back his lips, and his canines drop.

I gulp.

Heat flushes my skin.

Why do I find the sight of those sharp teeth so arousing? It's a sign of just how different this man is from me. It's not just that he is Fae and I am human, but how completely out of my sphere he is. Macho. Hot. Sexy. Alpha-hole, who could have any woman, and he came for me. "Why?"

"Why what?" He angles his head, not even out of breath after that flurry of violence.

I strain against my bindings. "Why are you here?"

"Why do you think?" One side of his lips curls in an arrogant smirk.

My belly clenches. A glance from him and I'll forget everything. Where I am, how much danger we're both in. Everything for his fiery gaze, one whiff of that heady scent of his, one touch of that hair-roughened skin of his jaw as it rakes over the inside of my thighs...

I swallow hard. "Answering a question with a question." I press my lips together, "Typical macho behavior."

"Let's get one thing clear, Red. You don't get to tell me what to do." He leans forward on the balls of his feet. "Ever."

He glares at me and I gulp. He has that whole dominant thing going for him and it's hot. Really hot. My sex contracts; liquid heat pools between my thighs. I lower my eyes.

He draws in a breath. "*Now* you choose to give in to me?"

He groans, and the rough intonation tugs at my nerves.

"You sure choose your moments, Red."

"Red?" I frown.

His gaze rakes over my features. "Your hair, it's dark, almost black, yet when the sunlight pours over it, I see the glints of..."

"Red," I say at the same time as him. "You noticed."

"I notice everything about you."

O-k-a-y. Did not realize that.

He takes a step toward me and my pussy clenches. So not the time to be thinking about how much I want this man. How at his mercy I am. Bound

here on the floor, ready for him to take me and fuck me and... The door swings open. A burst of red-and-white energy swoops down and smashes into his back. His big body shakes.

"Nolan..." I scream.

He looks down at his chest. I follow his gaze and gasp.

A flash of fire blazes out, burning through the shirt. Whatever hit him from behind has burned right through his torso. *No. No.* I try to breathe and find I can't.

The scent of burning flesh fills the air.

His breath hitches and that sound...that little note that escapes his lips fractures something inside of me. I swing my gaze back to his face. Color leaches from his skin. He lifts his gaze to mine.

"Red..." He opens his mouth, and blood drips from the side of his lips.

"No." I scream, then roll up to my knees and try to spring forward. My bonds yank me back. The energetic chains cut into my arms. Pain lacerates my nerves, shudders down my spine. "Nolan."

The sound of his name fills my ears, the sight of his body swaying fills my vision.

He turns toward the doorway and his shoulders stiffen.

He swivels back to me, takes a step forward, then collapses to his knees. He raises his hand and his features twist. Sweat shines on his brow. "Forgive me."

His body lurches to the side, and he crumples.

A man steps forward, clad in formal pants and a button-down shirt.

He bares his lips, displaying holes where his front teeth should be. "Hello, little Virgin. You are going to get me a pretty penny at auction."

Turning around, he raises his foot and brings it down on the fallen Nolan's face.

4

Alice

Nolan's dead, and all because of me. He came to save me and paid with his life. He should have left when he had a chance. But I had been too focused on talking to him.

I'd been selfish and occupied his attention. I'd distracted him, and they had taken him by surprise. They had overpowered him and killed him. My eyelids snap open and I take in my surroundings. Not a dream. I am still in the cell. My heart shatters, and I come upright from the floor. My gaze arrows back to where Nolan had fallen, to the splash of blood on the floor which is all that remains.

Soldiers had come and dragged away Nolan's body.

The man who'd shot Nolan had walked up to me and told me that tomorrow I'll be sold.

I'll be taken to the auction, where virgins are sold to the highest bidders from around the region.

I'm not an animal… I am human, at the bottom of the food chain in a hierarchy where Faes dominate and shifters are only a step below.

Everyone else is third, and humans? We don't figure. Except for the one thing I am which makes me of consequence, even in this messed-up order of things. You guessed it, I am a virgin, Go figure. I've been saving myself, for...for Nolan. There, I admit it.

So I have silly notions of wanting my virginity to be taken by the man who means something to me. Stupid romantic that I am.

I'd seen him, and my instincts had locked in on him and never let go. I had hoped...that one day...perhaps he'd be the one? The band around my chest tightens; the pressure behind my eyeballs grows. Tears slide down my cheeks. Stupid tears. *Is that all I have left?* The only man I have ever wanted is dead, because of me. I sniffle. I need to avenge him. I dig my nails into my palms.

I need to stay alive and find a way to hurt those who killed Nolan.

The sound of the door opening sends fear racing over my skin. I roll up to a sitting position. The bindings tear into my flesh, but I ignore the pain. Nolan faced this and more. At least he hadn't suffered much before he died... I think. A sob catches in my throat.

He'd collapsed, and his gaze had still been on me. His big body had shuddered, the cords of his beautiful throat had moved as if he were saying something. Then the bastard who'd shot him had stepped in the way.

As if my thoughts conjure him, the hated figure of my captor appears at the door.

He raises glowing fingers. The bands tying me shudder, and I look down to find they've dropped away.

He claps his hands, and the noise echoes in the space, "Come, Virgin."

Never before have I had hated myself as much as now. I should have lost my virginity much earlier. If I get out of here, I am going to...yeah, I am going to make sure I lose that piece of skin inside of me that proclaims me to be untouched.

"Chop-chop, bitch, don't want to keep the clients waiting."

I heave myself to my feet.

My knees stay steady. Progress. I take a step forward, and my stomach heaves. The taste of bile fills my mouth, and I swallow down the need to lean over and hurl. *Nolan.* I am going to get through this for Nolan. I force myself to put one foot in front of the other, to keep going. I cross the floor of the cell until I reach the man standing there. The heat from his body laps at my nerves, and I cringe. He fixes those dark eyes on me, and there's nothing behind them. Empty. Cold. As if whatever he'd once been has been torn apart and swallowed by the shell of the man who's facing me.

"Who are you?" The words spill from my lips before I can stop myself.

"Haven't you heard of the arch-enemy of the Fae Corps, the only leader who is fit to lead all the Fae."

"Boris." I breathe out.

Of course, it's the deposed Commander of the Fae, the one who hates our current leader, Dante's guts. Who is on a mission to wipe out the Fae Corps.

"Right answer." He claps his hands.

The sound shrivels my skin. I want to sink down to the floor and roll myself into a ball to shut out the sight of those hateful bloated eyes of his, but I don't. For Nolan. I'll get through this and live for Nolan. I pull myself up to my full height. "What's the hold-up?"

His gaze widens and he nods as a smile begins to form. "You still have fight left in you. The clients want that. Gives them some personality to latch onto. Most relish a fight before they take you."

My stomach lurches, and I am almost sick then. I bite down on the inside of my cheek and press my feet into the floor for purchase. "Whatever." I glare at him.

He chuckles, then lifts his finger and runs it down my cheek. "Such a pity Doc's not here to watch his woman being taken as she deserves, by a beast who's going to rip into you and tear you in two." He snaps his jaw, and the clack is so loud that I jump.

"Don't talk about him."

"You are hardly in a position to negotiate." He shakes his head. "The delusions we feed ourselves, thinking we are the masters of our destiny, but we are not. Your entire life depends on how merciful I am going to feel —or not..."

"Here I thought you were going to sell me to the highest bidder."

"I am, but behave, and you may just get lucky... I'll make sure you find your way into the hands of one who'll torture you only briefly before taking you. And kill you fast enough, so you don't suffer. Get me?"

Sure, I do, but damn if I am going to grovel in front of this creature.

The man who murdered my Nolan. I lean forward on the balls of my feet,
"Fuck off."

Boris' features darken, then he snakes out his palm and slaps me. My
head snaps back. My cheek throbs, tears spring from my eyes, and I am
sure my teeth have fallen out. I stagger back and would have fallen except
he grabs my arm.

"Come on then, let's get you to your rightful owner. You have a date
with death, and she doesn't have the compunctions that I do."

He yanks me along, and I half fall against him, managing to right
myself before more of my skin comes in contact with him. His grasp
squeezes into my upper arm as he steps up his pace. My arm feels like it is
being pulled out of its socket. We race up a long corridor.

Faces peer at us from the cells on either side. All slaves. The scent of
unwashed human flesh and sewage stings my nose. The images blur into
one another until my head spins.

I stumble and fall and he drags me along, my legs trailing behind us.
When he reaches the end of the corridor, he turns down another, then the
floor swoops up.

He pulls me to my feet, up a few steps, and thrusts me onto a raised
platform.

A floodlight shines in my eyes, and I blink. My stomach flip-flops,
sweat laces my palms.

He pushes me, so I move another few steps.

"Here's the prize of the evening. Presenting a rare treat for all of you: a
virgin human. Who wants to start the bidding?"

5

Doc

Fuck, am I dead?

I try to move, and my back screams in protest. My chest burns. My shoulders spasm, sending pain shooting down my spine. I crack open my eyelids and the pounding at my temples ratchets up to a screech. *Fuck me.* I pant. White pain coils in my chest, compressing my rib cage.

Sweat breaks out on my forehead; every muscle in my body protests. I push myself over to my back and scream as pain cuts through my side. *Fuck, fuck.* My mouth goes dry; my stomach heaves.

Bile rushes up, and I turn my head to the side just in time for the puke to hurl out of me. When the spasm passes, I lay back, struggling to breathe, limbs twitching.

The sound of clapping reaches me, then a voice speaking, fading in and out. I can't make out the words. I crack my eyelids open, and the glare stabs my eyes. I wince and look around; I am in some kind of enclosed space. There are tattered pieces of cloth lying around, some bloodstained. Clearly, it's some kind of holding pen, but for what? A scream whips through the area, and my muscles go on alert. The pain recedes, and every instinct snaps to attention.

"Alice." I breathe out her name.

Another scream is cut off. Did someone clap a hand over her mouth?

Alice...Boris hit me from behind. The images pour over me. My heartbeat catches up, and blood pounds in my ears. *Fuck, Alice, why are they hurting her?* How long was I out, and what did that asshole Boris, use on me?

Telekinetic energy, but of a strength that ripped into me with such force that despite my fast-healing powers, my wounds still throb.

Silence descends, and that's worse.

Whatever they're doing to her, she will not survive. Oh, my human is fiery, maybe too much. Bet she stood up to Boris, and bet that only made him angrier.

Why have they not thrown away my body?

Perhaps he wants to use me as a trophy or a negotiating instrument? Either way, that fucker is not going to get away with this. I am going to to...*what...?* Well, I'm not getting myself killed or wounded again, for one. I am going to find a way to get out of here and get to her.

The sound of a woman's voice reaches me. It's too far away to decipher the words. But the pitch of it, the tenor, that incandescent lilt to it, all of it is hers. *Alice.* I lurch to my feet, and the world spins.

I squeeze my eyes shut, press my feet into the floor for purchase. I manage to right myself—*I am coming, Alice, hold on.* I take a step forward, and my legs don't give way from under me. Progress.

Who'd have thought the man who faced down the monster who had turned his very childhood into a living hell, couldn't bear the thought of this little human being hurt.

My father had not only raped me, he'd used his words to hurt me, and when he'd gotten tired of that, he'd used his fists.

He'd tell me every day just how I didn't deserve to live. How I'd killed my mother at birth, how he'd never forgiven me for taking away the only person who'd redeemed him. He'd made me hate myself—my reflection, my face, my voice. Until I couldn't stand to see myself in the mirror.

Oh, he'd fed me, clothed me, provided a roof over my head. He'd also emotionally broken me.

He'd destroyed all pictures of my mother, so I've never known how she looked. Then, the day I'd turned fifteen, he'd gotten drunk and revealed that I hadn't been responsible for her death. It had been him all along.

He'd suspected her of being unfaithful, had known when I was born that I wasn't his just by the color of my skin. A darker shade than his own. He'd known then I was not his son. He'd decided I wasn't his and had killed her.

He'd gloated about how she had died, the love of his life, the woman sent to redeem his soul. He'd hacked her to pieces in her bed next to where I lay, a newly born child.

He'd taunted her that he'd never let her son go, that he'd torture her child so her soul would never find release. His eyes had rolled back, spittle flying from his mouth as he'd swallowed the last of the liquor, before aiming the bottle at me. But I'd changed...his words had ignited that spark inside of me that insisted I avenge my mother.

I had grabbed his hand and shoved it, bringing down the bottle on his head and smashing it into his nose, his chin.

His grasp had loosened. I had torn the bottle from him, then smashed it into his chest. Pulled it out and hit him with it again and again.

I hadn't stopped, even when it was clear he was dead.

I had kept going until the cops had arrived and separated me from the corpse of what had been my only parent. The coldness that had gripped my heart has stayed with me since. That strange calm that I had pulled over myself, knowing I'd have to live with the sight of those crumpled features, those sightless eyes, the lifeless form of my nemesis, will haunt me for as long as I'm alive.

Pain shoots down my back, my legs. It wipes away all of those images, all thoughts except one. Her. I need to get to her. The one person who pierced that fog of nothingness and brought me to life, and I'm not going to let her go.

I'm going to make sure she lives, even if I have to kill myself for it.

I curl my fingers into fists and push forward, one foot in front of another. Keep going. Don't stop. I reach the door to the cell and kick it open. My chest hurts, my legs ache, but I will not stop. I lurch through the exit, toward the sound of cheering.

Reaching the steps, I look up and spot her on the stage.

6

Alice

The light is in my eyes, and I can't see the audience. The sound of jeering assails me. I don't need to see them to sense the lust that rolls off of the assembled males.

And they are all men, I sense that by the sounds of their panting, the yells. That barely leashed need to rip into me, to mount me, to tear me apart and have me. These men are here for only one reason. To let their base desires hang out, to not pretend, and to give in to the beasts that reside within each of them. The need to hurt me, to show they are stronger, more superior genetically, the stronger sex. Men. Not all men are monsters though. Doc, he's different. On the surface, he may resemble another alpha-hole who won't hesitate to hurt to get his way, but he's also a protector.

He'd never take advantage of those weaker than him. He'd fight for the underdog. He'd cherish me, and not because I'm the weaker sex but because he wants to. Because regardless of what he said, he'd looked at me...like I'm his safe harbor. And I am...except he's dead.

Anger floods my blood, adrenaline spikes, and my breath comes in pants. I am done being the victim here. I have nothing to lose. I don't care about my virginity—if that's what they want, they can have it—but I am not going to give in easily. No way am I going to let him walk away after what he did to my man. And he is. Mine.

I jut out my chin. "I am going to kill you." My voice cuts through the space. "You think because I am human, because I am a woman, I am weak?" I walk forward, my hands tied behind me until I reach Boris. I raise my head and meet his gaze. "Prepare to be surprised."

The noise from the crowd swells. Anger radiates from Boris, and mixed with it is a seething rage. My stomach churns; my head spins. I am not going to be sick. I am not going to lose my nerve.

"You're right." He bares his teeth. "I was saving the surprise for later, but you leave me no choice."

The bindings that restrain me dissolve. I bring my arms to my sides. Blood rushes through my unused limbs, setting my fingers tingling. The sensation of pins and needles intensifies and I groan.

He whips out a knife and slashes it down, once, twice. My breath catches in my throat.

A breeze dances over my naked skin. I look down to see my clothes fall away to the floor.

A man springs up to his feet in the audience.

"I get first dibs on the virgin human. Name your price."

Sound swells from the audience.

A second man clambers onto the platform and lurches toward me. Lust rolls off of him, and his gaze bristles at my chest, over my breasts and exposed waist to the triangle between my legs.

My skin crawls, and a cold sensation fills the pit of my stomach.

The new arrival leaps at me, only to be tossed aside. A figure looms in front of me. Tall enough to fill my vision, broad enough to block out the sight of the audience. The scent of mint and cinnamon fills my nostrils.

"Doc?" I whisper, so low I am sure I didn't speak it, but he senses my intention.

He half turns and throws me a look over his shoulder. "You okay, Red?"

"You're alive...I thought you were..." I bite my lips, I can't bring myself to say that word.

"I'm here, aren't I?" He peels back his lips, and his canines drop.

His gaze shoots over to Boris standing next to me. His gaze widens, and I sidle away, but I am too late. Boris' arm snakes forward.

He grabs me by my shoulders and rotates me, so my back is flattened to his chest.

That dead-flesh scent of him crawls over me, and I gag.

"You didn't learn your lesson, did you, Fae? This time I am going to make sure I burn you completely." Boris raises his hand, the fingertips burning blue, the rays of energy sizzling toward Nolan, toward the man I cannot allow to be hurt again, not because of me.

I snap my head back and connect with Boris' chin.

He stumbles.

The beam of energy goes wide and misses Nolan. And that's all the opening he needs. Nolan leaps across the distance between us and jabs his fist forward. I duck to the side, still restrained by Boris, but giving Nolan enough of an opening to get in a direct hit.

Boris howls, and his arms drop away, releasing me.

Nolan grabs me and yanks me to him. I fall against his chest, and he winces. The side of my face comes away sticky. Blood. His blood.

"You're hurt." I gasp.

He bares his teeth. "Later." He moves around me as Boris raises his hand again, then grabs Boris' neck with both his massive hands and squeezes. "I am going to kill you."

Another man jumps up on stage and swaggers toward me, the third close on his heels. I turn around, my back to Nolan, and hold my fists up.

"Back off," I snarl.

The stranger laughs. "Come, little virgin." He pauses, his lips together. "Let me show you how it is to be tamed by a man."

I narrow my gaze. "Stay where you are, asshole," I snarl.

He tilts his head, and his gaze rakes over my bare breasts, down my waist, to that inevitable conclusion where it comes to rest on the flesh between my legs. His pupils dilate, and his breathing roughens. "Or what? Will you let me finger-fuck you before I rip into you, human?"

Anger fills my veins; red clouds my vision, "You wish."

The man darts forward, and I swing, catching him in the side of his face. Maybe it's the surprise that someone who looks as weak as I do can fight, or that I actually threw the first punch, but either way, the man reels back and crashes into the new arrival. Together, they topple over the edge. *Huh. Did I do that?* Pain shudders up my forearm, I shake out my aching fist only to find the man springing back on stage.

Uh-oh!

His eyes blaze with anger. "I am going to tear you apart, and your friend, too." He charges at me.

I shrink back and hit a solid object. "Doc... Nolan.... Ah, were you planning on getting us out of here anytime soon?"

"Yeah." He growls.

"I suggest you do it sooner rather than later." My voice trembles and I firm my lips to stop myself from squeaking in fear.

His muscles tense, then something crashes into the back wall, and the entire ceiling shakes. Light fixtures crash down on the stage.

A fissure tears through the platform and continues down to the floor, then the entire stage seems to tilt. The man coming at me loses his balance, and the stranger behind him stumbles over his body.

It shouldn't be funny, honestly, but there's a comedic touch to the entire proceedings. I chuckle. It comes out on a strangled sob. Perhaps it's that which gets Nolan's attention, for the heat of his chest envelops me from behind. His arms engulf me and he tucks me into his side. "Hold on, Red."

The air around me thins. The hair on the back of my neck stands up, and all the oxygen in the space seems to be sucked out. I try to breathe and my lungs burn. Then the world seems to explode.

Geometric designs flash over me, speeding up, and I am drawn into a vortex.

7

Doc

I stagger out of the vortex, and my legs seem to give way from under me. I stumble and almost fall, but soft arms grip my waist.

"We'll be safe here." I draw in a breath and my lungs burn.

"Where are we?"

"Somewhere in Belgrade." My ribcage hurts, my shoulder screams, and sparks of red bang through my head every time I move. "The fuckers took you half-way around the world to Russia." I grit my teeth. "This is the closest Fae Corps safehouse I could get us to."

"So he can't find us here?" Her voice trembles.

"There's a security net over the property that blocks its presence from the psychic plane. Even if he does track us here...which he won't—he won't be able to get past the security barrier without setting off the alarm." My vision wavers and I shake my head to clear it.

"You okay, Doc?" Her voice breathes over my skin, leaving little flickers of fire in its wake.

I am hurt…and I'm sure I am going to lose consciousness any moment, but tell that to my cock.

That sweet jasmine-and-pepper scent of hers swirls around me. It sinks into my blood, and my groin hardens. I am sure she can sense my arousal, and trust me, that is not what I want. Not right now, when I've managed to rescue her from that fucker Boris. I try to push her away, but she tightens her grasp.

"You're bleeding out."

Yes, I am. I am hurting inside—my chest burns, my muscles cramp and a twisting sensation tightens my ribcage. "Leave me alone, woman." I hear the harshness in my voice. I sound angry and I am not sure why.

The skin around her eyes creases. "You are wounded."

No shit. But not as much as what the sight of her does to me. *Don't look down at her breasts, don't look down, asshole.* My gaze flows over her trembling lips, to where her chin wobbles, to the flushed curves of her breasts, and *holy hell,* her nipples are pebbled, calling to me, and *damn if I don't want to touch them, suck on them, tease them to points of hardness that can graze my skin and dig into my flesh, and that wound in my chest has obviously messed with me more than I thought.*

Yup. Surely, that must be the only reason why my mouth is dry, why the pulse beats at my throat, at my temples, even in my balls, which grow heavier by the second. *The fuck is Red doing to me?*

Her breathing quickens, "You are more hurt than you are letting on."

I drag my gaze to her lips. Curvy lips, sweet as sugar, rounded and glistening, succulent flesh that will be so damn juicy to taste.

"Doc, look at me."

I shake my head to clear it.

I am trying to save her from me. I don't want to meet her eyes. If I do, she'll see how much she affects me.

My heart throbs. Another flash of pain coils in my chest and that telekinetic energy inside me stutters. Bursts of energy stab at my nerve endings. "Fuck," I grit my teeth. "I am going to flame out at any moment, Red."

"What do you mean?"

"Boris has access to concentrated telekinetic energy. It's throwing my insides into turmoil; my energy is short-circuiting, and I am going to burn out."

"Has that happened before?" She slips her arm around my waist.

The softness of her skin, the curve of her hips, the way she molds into my side, all of it calls to something primitive inside of me.

"It's not supposed to hurt so much." Only when she snorts do I realize I have said it aloud. "What?" I glower.

"You're allowed to lean on someone else."

Yeah. That's what she thinks.

She doesn't understand how it is to have the one person you trust turn out to be your nightmare.

Besides, Red is too small, too tiny, too fragile.

"I won't collapse if I carry some of your weight, you know."

"The fuck?" I grumble. "You trying to second-guess me?"

I take another step forward. Sweat pops out on my forehead. My legs tremble. I am not allowed to be this vulnerable. Ever.

"I can hear you think, Doc, and I promise you, I am not as breakable as I look. I may only be human—"

"A beautiful human." I rasp, then cough. There's a roaring sound in my ears and I shake my head to clear it.

"You think I am beautiful?"

"Seen yourself in the mirror, Red?"

"You must be out of it if you are showering me with praise."

"Stay close, Red, and that's not the only thing I'm gonna be showerin' you with." The fuck? *Did I just say that?*

"You coming on to me now, Doc? Now?" She huffs out a breath.

"Wassamatta wit' dat?" My tongue is thick in my mouth. The world tilts around me.

"I've been hinting at you all this time that I am interested, and you've pushed me away, but you decide to be open with your feelings now? When you're all but keeling over?"

"I am...not." I try to straighten my spine, but gravity, the fucker, is against me. The floor threatens to rush up to meet me and I widen my stance to steady myself.

"Don't collapse here. If you fall, I won't be able to get you to the bed. You're too heavy—"

"'s okay, you can leave me here," I grouse.

"Nope." She grabs my arm — *when had I placed that over her shoulder?* — and stumbles forward.

I am leaning my more-than-twice-her-body-size weight on her slender shoulders. I am marking her further, and hey, not that I am complaining about that, my fingerprints would only enhance the beauty of her pale skin. My groin hardens. I strain to enunciate my words, "I need to touch you, Red."

"Yeah, once we get you on the goddamned bed."

"Your curses turn me on."

The breath wheezes out of her. "If you don't keep walking, I am going to slap your ass, Doc."

I can't walk and talk at the same time. "Nope, only I get to do that... slap your ass, I mean. Whatcha think about that?"

There's no answer from her.

I turn my head and almost fall over, and it's not because my body is on the verge of blacking out, but because her gaze locks with mine. Her green eyes dilate until they resemble dark pools of water. Hmm.

"You'd like that, huh?"

"You'll have to recover first." Her cheeks redden.

She's so fucking beautiful when she is flushed. I lower my head to hers until my breath raises the hair on her forehead.

She tosses her head, then urges me forward.

I follow like a fucking lamb.

I even allow myself to lean some of my weight on her, only because I am bemused. *Yep, that's all it is.* I'd never thought Red would...ah... welcome the kind of edgy build up that fuels my need. I'd take her any which way, except...she's human...and a virgin. *A virgin.* My breath catches.

I'd be her first...her only, and no way can she take the barbaric mating practices of the Fae. *Mating? Whoa, hold on there, back up, motherfucker. What are you thinking about?* My knees hit the edge of the bed, and I topple, facedown.

8

Alice

I rake my gaze over his broad back. The tattered remains of his shirt cling to his shoulders. I should strip it off of him so he's more comfortable but no way am I going to be able to move his weight. The hard planes flex, and my gaze darts back to his face. His eyelids have fluttered shut, the eyelashes a dark fan against his cheekbones. His shoulders rise and fall. His breathing deepens.

Even asleep, he's a vital presence that sucks up all of the oxygen in the room. His massive body takes up too much space. All unforgiving angles, and ruthless planes. The air around him is saturated with testosterone that seduces me to creep closer...closer.

Restless energy drags at the edge of my nerves. Heat tugs at my belly, the need for him a heavy ache between my legs. I squeeze my thighs together. *What's wrong with me?* The man is out of it, exhausted. He's injured.

He took a shot in his back for me. The Fae heal fast, so I haven't seen any evidence of open wounds. He's still wearing the same shirt, bloodied and dirty, but it covers his torso, clings lovingly to those powerful shoulders, the arch of his back that stretches the remnants of the fabric, before narrowing down to his lean waist.

It's only when my fingertips rub over the cloth that I realize I have leaned in close and am trailing my fingers over his back, down to where the shirt is tucked into his fatigues.

I want to dip my fingers into his waistband and trace the curve of his butt. That very tight, delicious male butt that makes my breath catch. My sex clenches, and small pinpricks of heat tug at my fingertips.

I am not averse to worshiping the male figure.

So what if I have never seen a man naked before? Yeah, there you have it. The bulk of my experience. I am a fucking virgin… Uh, okay, an oxymoron to use those two words together in one sentence. They do not go together. And I don't belong with him.

He is strong, experienced, and has been with many women, no doubt.

Anger burns a trail down my spine, and *why does that make me jealous?*

I already hate every one of those females he's fucked.

He's a strong, virile man. A soldier of the Fae Corps, no less. And a doctor to boot. Accomplished. Gorgeous. So fucking sexy that it makes my heart ache. And I am using those four-letter swear words again. Me, who has never sworn aloud in my life. That sheltered human that I was. Protected by my Fae family, who'd made sure to keep bullies away from me.

My childhood was as idyllic as it could be, given my adoptive Fae mother had found me crying near the body of my dead human mama on a trip to Bombay. My birth mother had died in an attack when the berserkers had raided our city.

The Fae had been called in as a last resort and had joined forces with the mayor of Bombay to help beat them off.

My adoptive mother had been sent in by the Fae Council to help.

She'd always told me that she'd seen my little two-year-old body, grimy with soot, crying my eyes out next to the burnt-out corpse of my dead mother, and her heart had broken. She said that she had fallen in love with me right then and had decided to take me back with her.

Her mate and son had welcomed me into their home and their hearts. They told me that I completed their family. I had lucked out enough to never miss my original birth parents. Perhaps had even enjoyed the fact I was different from the Fae. More fragile, one who could be easily broken...so human.

And still a virgin.

It's what started this entire misguided adventure, why I had been kidnapped, and almost sold.

I lean over and place my palm flat against Nolan's back. Through the remaining shreds of his shirt, the heat of his body reaches out to me. His breathing deepens. His body twitches then settles into that unmistakable stillness which indicates that he is deep in slumber.

He senses I am close to him, that it is me touching him, who drags my palm up over his shoulder and rests it over the nape of his broad neck.

I play with the strands of hair that brush the collar of his shirt. Baby-soft hair, the texture so unlike the rest of him, which is hard. Heavy... throbbing. I gulp. The need to see him strip off his clothes, to run my fingers over the warmth of his back, over the ridges of his body, around to the front and under the jut of his pelvic bones to grasp that hardened shaft of his.

A moan whines out of me.

He's not even awake, and I am turning myself on simply thinking of the sight of his body. His beautiful, luscious, body that I want to see naked. Speaking of which, I look down at myself. *Yep, naked.* The dress I had been wearing had been ripped off of me by Boris. I should look around for something to wear. I glance around the room, and spot the closet in the far corner of the room. I might find something there... *On the other hand, what if I stay this way, and see what happens when Doc wakes up? Hmm.* Live dangerously and all that. I am with the only man I ever want to be with, and when I leave this room I am making damn sure I am no longer a virgin. No more leaving things up to chance. Time to take things into my own hands.

I snuggle down next to him.

He is so broad that I can just about throw my arm over him. My other arm is tucked between us. I bring up my leg and loop it about his waist. The heat from his body cocoons me. My muscles unwind; my shoulders relax. He is fast asleep and still hurt, but I am confident that nothing can touch me when I am with Doc.

He will always fight off my worst enemies, my nightmares, and keep me safe. Safe. My breathing evens out to match his.

My breasts are flattened against his thick bicep, and my chest rises and falls in synchrony with his. The stress of the last few days bleeds out of me, leaving me limp. I close my eyes and let sleep engulf me.

A noise reaches the edge of my unconscious mind, and I push it away.

Something tickles me under my chin, and I grumble. Then the heat enfolding me lifts. Cool air blows over my flushed cheeks. My eyes fly open and are caught by bright-blue ones.

Glittering pupils deepen in color until they seem almost indigo. A storm rolls in them then fades away. Gorgeous blue eyes that I can drown in. They seem to mirror all of those unspoken questions in my heart. They reflect back the uncertainty that wavers in my chest. The skin around his eyes creases. I allow my gaze to roam over his features. His nostrils flare and I gulp. He cants his head, the slight movement so animalistic that it draws my attention to his ears, to where the tips elongate.

My mouth parts in surprise.

Of course, he is not human. Not even a shifter. He's a beast. A blood-thirsty Fae. One clothed in the civilized veneer of a doctor...but he's closer in nature to the Fae Corps he is part of. The kind who can take, ravage. Break. And I want him to do all of that. *What am I thinking?*

He peels back his lips, and his canines drop.

Goosebumps pepper my skin. *Why do I want to feel the razor-sharp edge of those teeth on my skin? Why do I ache for the friction of that whiskered jaw over the skin of my inner thighs?* I nibble on my lower lip, and his gaze darts to my mouth. His jaw tics.

Fascinating. I've never been this close to a Fae male. Well, other than the ones in my family, and Doc himself, and that was either when he was in the role of a health professional, or earlier when we'd been in the middle of that crazy fight with the Fae who'd been set to auction me off.

This is different.

We are in a strange house, in bed, and he's looming over me. His big body shuts out the sight of everything else. All of my attention is focused on his face, his neck, the low rumble of sound that snarls from him. The hard planes of his chest heave as if he's aware of exactly what I am thinking now. Something inside me shatters. I want him...need him. Hell, I was his from the moment I set eyes on him. Everything else has been fore-play leading up to this moment. Just me and him. This. I raise my palm, and he snakes out his hand and grabs it.

"The fuck you playing at, Red?"

9
_____

Doc

Heat. Sweetness. That honeyed scent of her arousal is thick in the air. It seeps into my skin, and my groin hardens. Is she aware that I can read her, scent her, all but taste how turned on she is?

Her big green eyes dart to my ears, and she gulps. The tips of my ears tingle, they must have extended farther. I flick them back for effect, and the color washes out from her cheeks. Clearly, she is afraid of me—an alpha Fae male who'll rip into her and divest her of her innocence. My cock lengthens. *Why does the thought of messing her up, of stripping her of all those romantic dreams that she harbors, of breaking her, putting her back together, then ruining her all over again…why does that turn me on so?*

She opens her mouth and a moan escapes her lips. *Holy hell.*

"I am not one of your puny boyfriends who'll kiss you goodbye and leave your virtue intact."

"I'm betting on that," she breathes.

The sound hitches from her lips, just a mumble, an almost whisper. So soft that I shouldn't have heard it. But hell, when my ears are extended and my canines are pushing through my gums with a vengeance, not to mention that muscle between my legs throbs, aches, and threatens to tear through my pants...well, every instinct of mine is on alert. Every part of me is tuned in to her. My vision tunnels. My breathing levels out. My biceps bulge and I can't stop it.

"Do. Not. Mess with me." My voice comes out hushed. Yeah, another thing I forgot to mention. When I am turned on, and other than the very obvious outward signs of my arousal, like my dick extending in preparation of the upcoming penetration, the elongation of my ears amplifies every single sound made by the object of my attention.

The tips of my canines drawdown so I have no choice but to part my lips so they can jut out.

So they pick up the changes in the environment.

My senses hone in on her. I can track the change in her breathing, the drumming of her pulse at the hollow of her neck. The hammering of her heart as it flutters against her rib cage. Yeah, I can track every single change in her biochemical constitution, so I can use it, manipulate it. And not just to my own advantage. It's so I can pleasure her, ravish her, rut her. I want to bring her to climax, then take her. Mark her...knot her. I'll shatter her illusions, snuff out her innocence, take the most important part of her, her secrets. Her core. Her.

My chest burns. The tips of my ears pulse. Even my fucking balls ache. Any minute now, I am going to turn her over, and thrust into her from behind, again and again. A low growling reaches my ears. *Oh! Wait, it's me.* This creature who can't control himself, who can barely hold back from claiming this woman is me. *And I can't take her for my mate.*

I shove back from her so fast that she yelps.

Somehow, I am standing at the foot of the bed, my chest on fire, and fists balled in front of me.

She scrambles up to a sitting position, then scoots back until she is flattened against the wall.

Her eyes widen, the skin stretches over her cheeks. Her chest heaves.

Don't look there.

Don't.

My gaze drops to those creamy breasts, the curves trembling, dark rosy nipples calling to me, to suck on them and mark them. The sinews of my throat strain, my biceps bulge, and I curl my fingers into fists.

"Wha...what's happening, Doc?" She swallows, thick waves of fear spool off of her.

Yeah, we are back to being Doc and Alice. Nolan and Red is a fantasy. A sick, twisted, warped dream conjured up by a mind that wants more. Wants a dream that doesn't exist. A dream that cannot exist. Needs the comfort of her innocence to live, to feel. *Yeah, she makes me fucking feel. That's what's wrong.* "Everything," I rasp. "Everything is going to hell."

"I don't understand." She frowns.

"You were trying to seduce me."

She blinks, and her gaze skitters away. "And if I was?"

"No one taught you what it means to fuck around with a Fae male?"

Her shoulders tremble, then she draws up her knees, so she covers the sight of those beautiful breasts. "No one taught me how to fuck around, period." Her chin quivers.

And isn't that the honest truth and what's getting me really horny even now as we speak? A growl rips out of me, and she shudders then buries her head against her knees. Her shoulders squeeze down. She throws her arms around her folded legs and rocks herself back and forth. *Ah! Hell.* I didn't mean to shock her...okay, maybe I did.

Maybe I wanted her to see exactly what kind of beast I am. Even half out of my head with pain, even wounded as I am.

My heart thuds.

Pain thrums against my rib cage.

I bring up my arm to rub the skin over my heart, and honest, that square inch of space literally vibrates with hurt. With an ache, I can only describe as craving. I need her. I want to be inside of her. I squeeze my arms at my sides, then force myself to glance away. "I didn't mean to scare you, Alice."

10

Alice

His voice is harsh and growly. His biceps bulge, his shoulders expand, and his very persona seems to amplify in front of my gaze. The force of his dominance weighs down on my shoulders, pressing in on my rib cage. I gasp. This...this version of the male I am seeing is different from the Doc I know.

The man who's kept his distance from me all these months since we met. The doctor who'd taken care of my ankle and put my fears to rest. Who'd carried me home that day, so that I would keep my weight off of my feet—he'd said. But he hadn't needed to see me home. He could have sent one of his staff with me if he had been concerned. But he'd left the infirmary in the middle of a working day and made sure to escort me back.

My breath catches in my throat.

Come to think of it, since that day I had seen him around often. Everywhere I'd turned, he'd been there. He'd even agreed to let me assist him, learn from him. He had shared the codes to Tristan's place so I could get in and help

Jess—not that the two of them are fighting anymore. Last I saw, they had made up and mated up and were all loved up, with eyes only for each other. He is a considerate man, Doc…Nolan is. He'd seen right through Tristan's bluster, had known how much he was hurting and that he needed Jess to soothe his spirit. Doc had helped the two of them find each other. *Who's going to help him?*

I raise my head and meet his gaze. "You didn't scare me." I rub my cheek on my knee to brush away the tears.

His gaze grows hooded, and he stares.

"I wasn't crying because I was afraid of you."

"What then?" He drums his fingers on his chest, and it's my turn to survey him.

He looks better than when he'd stumbled up on stage and proceeded to bash up the men who'd tried to get to me.

His color has returned, but despite the power inherent in his massive frame, Doc is vulnerable. Both physically and emotionally.

Why did it take me this long to realize that?

I sniff away the last of my tears. "Guess, the enormity of everything I've been through sank in."

He rakes his fingers through his hair. His shoulders hunch forward. "Did those men hurt you, Alice?"

Alice? I miss him calling me Red. I mean, not that I can demand it, but I miss that sense of intimacy that facing a combined enemy together had brought out. I am going to find a way to get him to call me that again. I bite the inside of my cheek.

"Tell me." He leans forward on the balls of his feet, and his big body seems to tremble. *No.* He's too strong, Doc, nothing fazes him, not even when that monster had shot him with that bolt of pure energy. But then, once he'd teleported in, he'd confessed he was on the verge of a burnout. Yet, he still had not allowed me to help him. Typical alpha male behavior. I huff out a breath and his forehead furrows. "Answer the question."

"He didn't hurt me, not that way." The words spill out.

"You hiding something from me?"

His blue eyes bore into me, probing the depths of my spirit, my soul, and a melting sensation suffuses my chest. Something heavy inside of me loosens and a tingling grips my limbs.

"I am still a virgin if that's what you are asking." My voice doesn't shake, and I am proud of that.

Color sears his cheeks.

"That is what you were...asking about, right?"

He glares at me and a shiver runs down my spine. *Why am I so nervous?* "I am not as experienced as the other women you've been with, but I have learned about the proclivities of Fae males from—"

"From?" His voice is hushed.

My belly flip flops. I didn't do anything wrong. *So why are my palms damp?* Ridiculous. I flick my tongue out to lick my lips and his gaze latches onto my mouth.

"From my friends." I gulp.

"Friends?" His left eye twitches.

He seems angry. *Why is he angry? Is there some underlying meaning to this conversation that I am not aware of?* I bite the inside of my cheek.

"Yeah... you know... friends..."

His gaze narrows. A vein throbs at his temple. Tension radiates off of him. *Huh?* He is working himself up to a fine rage. *Why? What?*

"What kind of friends are these, Red?" His voice lowers to that gruff pitch that hints at the edge of darkness that rolls just below the surface. His ears pull back, *oh! Oh!* They are definitely more pointy than they were before.

"Answer me, who exactly has been coaching you in the needs of Fae males?" The tendons of his throat stand out, a dull redness flushes his neck and that's when I realize...

"You're jealous?" I blink.

He pulls himself up to his full height. A nerve tics at his jaw.

Definitely jealous.

"Answer the fucking question."

"Girlfriends." I squeak, "Just, you know, girl talk, Doc." I drag a trembling hand through my hair, "I mean, you hang out with the other Fae Corps guys and shoot the breeze. Right?" He frowns.

No, of course not.

They just get together and fight during the weekly Dares to blow off steam, or else meet and strategize on how to protect the rest of the city, and put plans in place to grow the economy, and all that fun stuff.

He watches my face, drinking in every single expression that dares reveal itself on my features.

"Doc," I venture, and he doesn't reply.

His jaw hardens; his chest rises and falls.

"I am really fine. Honestly. Nothing permanently injured." I raise my arms at my sides and flap them around. *Wow. That should look appealing, because blabbering like a nervous fool wasn't enough. Besides I am not trying to seduce him, right?*

I am just trying to calm him down from wherever in his mind he's retreated.

He's still trying to get over the near death experience we've been through. That's all. I shuffle my feet.

The silence stretches a beat, then another.

My nerves strain; my hackles rise. I've never been good at these silent faceoffs; I much prefer to overshare and talk things out. A part of me warns me not to speak until spoken to, but dammit. I can't stay silent while he glares at me. Bet he's plotting how to spank my backside, where he's gonna mark me, how he's gonna fuck me, and it's so hot. My nipples pebble and I gulp. *Say something, anything to break this impasse.*

"You...you okay, Doc?"

Brilliant. That was such a clever remark. I hunch my shoulders and he draws in a breath, "Yeah." He cracks his neck; his joints pop. His gaze is still fixed on my face. He seems to be memorizing my features. *Nah, that's my imagination, that's all.* "Yeah, I'm okay."

Tension whips off of him in dense waves, saturating the space between us with so much testosterone, so much male dominance, that my thighs tremble. My toes curl.

He doesn't look okay.

He looks anything but okay.

He feels too wound up, too stressed out...too everything. He's at the edge of his control, and not just because he is still hurting from the wound inflicted on him. No, this is more, much more.

He seems to be on the verge of having a breakdown. Like someone who is holding in too much feeling, too much emotion...too much hurt. Someone who wants...no, needs me so much that it's tearing him apart.

He widens his stance, and my gaze is drawn down to his thighs. To the evidence of his arousal that strains against his pants. I gulp. Heat radiates over my skin. Curling down toward my belly to tug at the flesh between my thighs.

"You need me, Doc."

He peels back his lips and his canines drop.

Oh...those...those sharp teeth. Feral. Wild. He's so different from me. Fear crawls over my scalp. My fingers tingle.

His nostrils flare. *Damn it,* he's sniffed out just how out of sorts I am. I need to distract him, say something, anything. *No, not that. Anything but that.*

"You want me because I am a virgin."

Every part of him goes solid. "You don't know what you are saying, woman."

I tilt my head. "Don't I?"

His shoulders flex, and he winces, then rubs his chest again with his hand.

"The thought of being my first turns you on so much that you can't stop yourself from wanting to throw me down and tear into me."

"You're pushing me." His hands clench at his sides.

"You think it's wrong to lust after me. Because I am human and you are Fae. Because I was kidnapped precisely because of this damned virginity. But guess what? I'd prefer to be rid of it. It's this stupid idea of saving myself for the 'one' that got me into this mess. I'd rather be divested of it completely."

"Shut the fuck up," he snarls.

The harsh sound chafes my sensitized nerve endings.

"I am not nearly done yet." I don't stop the slow smile that curls my lips. I have never felt this strong, this powerful. I am playing with something way beyond my control. Something I don't fully understand. Something my instincts say I should trust and see through because the alternative...is not one I can live with. I want him. Need him. Now. I don't question it.

I drop my arms, straighten my legs, and slide them apart.

His shoulders go solid. Every muscle in his body tenses.

His gaze rakes over my breasts, my stomach, to come to rest on the flesh between my thighs.

The urge to cover myself up, to squeeze my legs back together is so damned strong, but I resist. I curl my fingers, dig my nails into my palms, and thrust my chest out instead. "I have news for you, Doc. It's not you who scares me, but the other way around. You are afraid of what being with me will mean to me. You don't want the responsibility of being my first, yet the thought turns you on. You don't want to be burdened with taking my virginity. Yet you want to be inside of me. The need to rut me is written in every angle of your body. You want to fuck me, Doc, admit it."

Silence.

He doesn't move. Doesn't take his gaze from the source of his focus, my pussy, which is now drenched and drooling for him. The inner walls of my channel contract. Liquid pools between my lower lips. I've never been this turned on, this ready. He could take me now, and I'd...welcome him.

A breath shudders out of him. He raises his gaze to meet mine, and I gasp. Gone is that burning blue gaze. His features are shuttered. He's pulled back every last inch of emotion inside of him and built back those walls he likes to wear.

"You thought wrong, Alice. I don't want you."

He turns around and stalks to the door. At the exit, he stumbles, then grabs the doorway and straightens himself. "You may want to wear some clothes, by the way." He shoots me a gaze over his shoulder. "Whoring yourself out doesn't suit you, human."

11

Doc

I shove away from the door so fast that my head spins. Sweat breaks out on my forehead. My chest hurts, and it's not just the aftereffect of being burned by Boris.

This is something deeper, more complex.

Something that strips away the veneer of civilization I have fought so hard to cultivate all these years. One word from her, and I am ready to shred it all to pieces. The thought of her close to me, within reach, near enough to run my hands over her flesh, squeeze those breasts. Mark that butt, slap her, whip her...and if I show her my true nature it's only going to make her hate me. Which is the entire point of this charade.

It's why I'd called her a whore and hurt her.

Everything I'd done had been to put distance between us. Physical, emotional. *So why am I having second thoughts?*

I lurch toward the doorway of the safehouse—in my weakened state, it's a miracle that I've made it even this far. At least I'd managed to track her to the auction in St Petersburg. If I hadn't gotten there in time... My heart squeezes.

As long as I am alive, nothing can happen to her.

A growl rips out of me. The thought of anyone else touching her, scenting her, marking her... "No!" I growl and the sound echoes in my head. My body trembles, and it's not from anger. It's lust, pure lust that squeezes my rib cage, that pushes down on my shoulders until my legs grow heavy.

Admit it...it's a fucking turn-on that she is untouched, that she's been saving herself for the right 'one,' *but can that be me?* The boy who killed his father, the man whose warped, depraved sexual tastes have made him turn away from any relationship. To take refuge in pain. Find pleasure in hurt. A chill shudders down my back.

Walking to the door, I fling it open.

I need to get away from her before I do something I will regret. I stumble out to the landing, toward the steps, miss the first one, and go crashing down. Rolling down the next one and the next, I tumble onto my back at the bottom.

The world tilts and sways.

I push my elbows into the ground and try to sit up.

Whatever Boris did to hurt me also burned away all of my resistance. Perhaps its poetic justice that it should happen now, when I am alone with the most beautiful, vulnerable female I have ever met. The only woman I've ever felt anything for, whom I should protect.

I dig my fingertips into my hair and pull at it. Pain slides down my neck and my back, coils at the base of my spine. It only heightens that sense of vulnerability that grips me. Me? Vulnerable? And last I checked, I had my balls.

My skin crawls with pinpricks of lust; heat and goosebumps rake over my skin.

I'd had the sense of something shifting, something pulsing inside of me the moment I'd laid eyes on her, and that had convinced me to put distance between us. I'd turned her away, and she'd pursued me, insisted on crawling under my skin.

When she'd been kidnapped, I'd gone after her. I hadn't hesitated, hadn't sent any of the other Fae corps soldiers.

No.

No one else gets to be near her.

No one else gets to protect her.

No one else gets to ruin her.

No one else but me.

"Nolan?" A touch on my shoulder makes me shudder. I spring to my feet and reel away from her. "Don't come near me."

12

Alice

He plants his feet wide apart. His jaw tics and tension radiates from him.

"You're hurting." I narrow my gaze.

His back curves, the planes of his wide back ripple. He is in more agony than he's willing to admit.

I sidle closer to him, and he stiffens.

"Stay where you are, Alice. I mean it."

His voice is harsh, rough, but there is something else. Beneath is pain, and that white noise of hurt, that plea for help that had touched me. That had called to me even as he had left, even as he'd called me a 'whore.' I pause. He'd insulted me, said whatever had come into his head. *He didn't mean it. Did he?*

"Let me help." My voice is soft, coaxing.

Physically, Doc's so much bigger and tougher than me, but that thick exterior doesn't fool me. Not one bit.

"You can't." He wheezes. "No one can." He takes another step forward, and his big body shudders. He hunches his shoulders, and his head drops forward.

"I can."

"Oh yeah?" He chuckles and it's not a nice sound.

He sounds nothing like the Doc I know. Not the closed-off harsh man who's rejected me at every turn.

He's in pain and unable to hide the true nature of his feelings for me. He's vulnerable and so open. If I lose this opportunity...? No, I can't. This is it. I have to act now. Now, when it's just me and him and he's so close to breaking. Push him. I just have to push him over the edge. *Do it.* "Yeah."

My voice comes out firm, despite my anxiety. I swallow, then straighten my shoulders. "Yeah. I am the only one who can help. Admit it. It's why you are running away from me."

His body goes rigid. "What did you say?" His voice is soft. Hushed. Dangerous.

I gulp. My stomach trembles. He's past rage and in that space where just a touch, and he'll tip over. *Don't say it, don't say it.* "Didn't take you for a coward, Doc."

He clenches his fingers at his sides, then straightens his head. "Think very carefully what you say next, Alice. Your opportunities to leave unscathed are decreasing by the second."

My pulse rate speeds up. *Holy hell, why does the threat of hurt that laces his voice turn me on?* Why is it that the calmer he gets, the angrier he is? That something inside of him is about to erupt, and when it does, there will be no escape. *I don't want to escape.*

I inch closer. My bare feet slip on the pebbles, and the noise seems too loud in the silence that shimmers between us. His shoulders rise and fall, but he doesn't turn around, doesn't look at me. I raise my hand, and he jerks his head.

"Touch me and don't complain then about what happens next."

I jump. I want to withdraw my hand; I should just turn from here and leave, *and then what? Wait for him to come to me?* Find clothes for myself and cower under the sheets and pretend nothing happened between us?...which is true. Nothing has taken place, and yet everything has changed. I don't want to save myself. I want him, only him. He is 'the one.' *So what if there is no future for us together? So what if we are so different?* I am tired of justifying what I am. Tired of always being the weaker one. This once, I am going to take my fate into my own hands. I am going to choose him. I reach out and touch him, and he swivels around.

I gasp.

His pupils snap vertically. So different. So hot. So damned sexy. My toes curl.

"You are Fae, but your eyes, they resemble those of a dragon shifter."

"Dragon blood." His voice is hoarse and gravelly. "A throwback to an ancestor who was a dragon. It wasn't enough to be born Fae. Nature decided to fuck with me by stitching dragon genes into my DNA." The blue swirls in those irises, deepening with flecks of indigo. "You know what that makes me?"

Breathtaking. Gorgeous.

"Fucking dangerous." He peels back his lips, and his canines drop.

Lethal.

"Cruel."

Beautiful.

"A monster. A beast who takes what he wants."

The hair on the back of my nape rises. The sharpness of his teeth...they could hurt me. They could slice right through me. They could rip me to shreds. And I want that. I want him to tear me apart and destroy me, so I can reinvent myself all over again.

I thrust out my chin.

He flicks back his ears, and I gulp again. Of course, he's a predator. But just how feral he is sinks in. I half angle my body, poised on the tips of my toes.

The skin around his eyes tightens, "Run away, Red. You still have a chance."

I should go. I should. I shake my head. "No."

He flattens his lips. "No, what?"

"No, I am going to stay."

"You'll regret it," his jaw tics.

"I won't."

A growl rumbles from within him. He leans forward on the balls of his feet, and the force of his dominance shoves at me with such an impact that

I'm literally forced to take a step back. I stumble and almost fall, except he grips my shoulders and rights me.

His touch sears my skin; I am sure every finger of his has left an imprint on me.

"I want." The words bleed out of me.

Those vertical eyes hone in on me. He holds my gaze, and I can't look away. Mesmerizing, hypnotizing.

"What?" He bends his knees, then peers into my face.

His face is so close that his hot breath settles on my cheeks. That scent of his, mint and cinnamon now laced with the very faintest of dragon smoke, teases my nostrils.

"What do you want?" His voice curls around me, pulling at me, sinking into my blood.

Awareness skates down my spine. Anticipation tugs at my nerves. All of my brain cells seem to melt together. I can't think. Can barely form the thoughts that swirl around in my head.

The breath dribbles out of me. "You, I want you."

13

Doc

Her words sweep over my skin, arrowing straight to my groin. My dick twitches. The tips of my ears tingle. The burning in my chest intensifies. I don't have much longer before the beast I have hidden all of my life surfaces. "You don't mean it."

"Don't profess to know what I do or do not want."

She thrusts out her lower lip, and my gaze drops to it. Pink, glistening, succulent. Her mouth, I want her mouth.

I need to taste her, just once. The yearning crawls down my spine. It's only when my lips almost brush hers, I realize I've leaned forward so close there's barely a millimeter of air separating us.

"I have every right, considering you've lost your sense of self-preservation." My voice whips out, and she winces.

My stomach twists. My dick lengthens. I haven't even touched her, and I am already hurting her, *and hell, if that doesn't turn me on?* I drop my hand to my side and take a step back, only she follows me, mirroring my footsteps. I move back farther, and she follows.

"Don't do this." I clench my jaw.

When did this little curvy human become a temptress, a seduction which I have no ability to withstand? It should be laughable, really. Me, a grown-ass, lethal alpha Fae trying to put distance between myself and a woman half my size. A beautiful, gorgeous, out-of-this-world, pint-sized bundle of delectation who's going to be my downfall.

I pause so suddenly that she crashes into me. Her breath bounces against my chest. Through the remnants of my shirt, the softness of her curves burns an imprint.

"I am doing this... I am long past trying to save myself, can't you see that?" She raises her head, and I clench my jaw.

"I don't do relationships Red."

She blinks, then huffs out a breath. "Tell me something I don't know."

Huh? "I've never had a virgin before."

Her lips form an 'O' of surprise.

Yeah, me too, Red. Didn't mean to share that little piece of information. Didn't mean for my groin to harden right now either, as I ache for the heat of your mouth around my cock.

"Guess we both have firsts here, huh?" She flutters her eyelashes and I stare.

Fucking beautiful. *So she knows how to exert her feminine charms, eh?* I wipe my hand across my face.

"You are going to regret having anything to do with me."

"You kidding me?" She waves a hand in my direction. "I mean, I am just an average-looking woman—"

"False modesty doesn't suit you Red."

She pouts, then raises her shoulders and lets them fall. "What I am trying to say is that you are way out of my league. You...you..." She blows out a breath.

"I..?" I frown.

"You are this delectable hunk of masculinity who can have any female he wants."

And I want her.

"I'll ruin you."

"Says who?" The breath hums from her lips. "You have no idea what I want. If you did, you wouldn't waste time talking."

"Protecting." The word wheezes from my mouth. "I am protecting you." I turn my back on her.

She steps around me, then stabs a finger in my chest. "From what?"

"Me. The man who can bring you to heights of ecstasy but who will make you ache, cause you so much pain, make you experience the highs and lows which will rip you apart, Alice." I crack my eyes open, and she gasps.

My vertical pupils should scare the hell out of her. I peel back my lips, making sure she gets a load of my canines.

My very sharp teeth, which I want to sink into her neck, graze over her arteries, and draw on her sweet blood. Saliva pools in my mouth. I tilt my head, and the tips of my ears tingle. My scalp tightens. My groin throbs. Every part of me comes alive. And it's because of this curvy little woman who stands in front of me, looking at me with those big green eyes.

She extends her hand toward my cheek, and I snap my teeth.

She pales but doesn't flinch.

She lowers her hand slowly, slowly, bringing it down to hover over my mouth. Then, as if soothing a wild beast, she trails her finger over my lips. The fine hairs on the nape of my neck rise.

She stays right there, hand raised and all but plastered to me from toe to thigh to chest. My groin tightens, my cock hardens, lust fills my blood, and *what the fuck am I fighting?* Everything I have always wanted is right here in front of me, and I am trying to shove it away, and *why?* Some misplaced sense of doing right? Me? The one who's spent my life in pursuit of pain is denying myself the pleasure this will bring. Being with her, touching her, taking her, slaking my thirst in her, burying myself balls deep in her. There. I've let myself think of what I want. The pleasure it will bring me...something inside of me shatters.

I open my mouth and wrap my tongue around her digit, and a moan slips out of her. She pants. The woman fucking pants, as if she cannot get enough of me, as if she wants more, knowing what I am. Doesn't she understand how I could hurt her? How completely I would consume her, and not just in the way of a normal Fae mating?

I tilt my head, and she drops her hand to her side. She raises heavy-lidded eyes to mine.

I can't stop the growl that bleeds from my lips. She trembles. Her body shudders. The sugary scent of her arousal wraps around me, and fuck if I can stop myself now.

"Last chance. If you don't leave now, then I won't be responsible for what I do to you next."

"What?" Her breathing goes ragged, then she squares her shoulders, "Tell me what you want to do to me, Doc." She clasps her fingers together in front of her, "Tell me what you want from me."

Alice

"I want to fuck you." He fastens his gaze on me.

The breath whistles out of me at his words.

So, I knew it… I mean, it's not a secret what he wants from me, or what I want him to do to me, but to hear him state his intention in that emotionless voice, the threat of his dominance lacing the tone, his intent writ clearly in every move of his body, sends a primal thrill racing down my spine.

"And?" My voice cracks, and I clear my throat.

His gaze darts to my mouth, and my chin wobbles.

"What else do you want to do to me?"

R-i-g-h-t. What am I trying to do? Trying to unhinge him and send him over the edge?

I flick out my tongue to absorb every last bit of moisture that clings to my lips. His shoulders bunch. His biceps seem to swell. He doesn't move, but every part of his body seems to tighten, stiffen… Harden.

I only have to glance down at his crotch to see the kind of effect I have on him.

My nipples tighten.

I am not a seductress. I've never known what it is to touch a man, caress his rough skin, run my fingers over his bearded chin and tremble when the whiskers dig into my flesh. Lean in and lick his mouth, his beautiful corded throat, drag my fingers over the crevices of his chest, and worship those hard planes that tremble with tension.

"Tell me." My breath hitches.

The promise of things to come, the threat of what he is going to do to me has my insides melting. Heat flushes my skin, and on its heels, chills race down my spine. My body is as conflicted as my mind.

"I want to whip your ass."

"Excuse me?"

I swing my gaze to his face. He meets my stare. His pupils blink vertically. Just once. Enough to hint at the beast that prowls inside of him.

"Is that...uh...a dragon thing?"

"What? The kink I like?" A smirk curls his lips. "I could say that and that would be the easy way out. I could give many excuses to justify my behavior." He cants his head, and a considering look comes into his eyes. "Is that what you want? To explain away my actions? To find some basis for what I like? Because, really, there is none, except for the fact that it's how I am built."

"How...how are you built?" I am echoing his words, mirroring his posture as I shuffle my feet apart and plant my hands on my hips.

"For pain."

"Huh?" I stare.

"I want to see you hurt, Alice. I need to see you writhe before me, under me. I want you to cry out as I slap the flesh of your curved butt, as I pinch your clit and tweak your nipples, as I whip the backs of your thighs, the soft skin of your inner legs, as I manacle your wrists and tie you to my bed, as I bend you over my whipping post and part the cheeks of your ass and—"

"Stop." The word trembles from my lips. My thighs clench, my toes curl, and liquid lust pools in my core.

"I am not done yet." His lips twist.

He's mocking me, throwing back the intensity of what I am feeling at me and...I am taking it all in. Absorbing it. Every pore in my skin stretches open, aching, yearning for him. The heat from his big body pours over me, and I gasp.

It's a mere foreshadowing of things to come.

My thighs clench. Saliva pools in my mouth. The thought of him doing all that to me, hitting me, causing me pain, should send me screaming. Should make me want to run away from him right now. If I had even one iota of self-preservation, self-respect, any sense of self, I should try to leave, and then what? Find my way back to an existence that is safe.

Boring.

Without him.

When had he become such an intrinsic part of me, that the idea of being without him makes the rest of my life stretch out in front of me?

A long line of endless waiting, waiting for him. Is that why the thought of everything he can do to me has me aroused? Has me trembling? Has my hips jerking forward as if trying to seduce him to hurry up? Hurry up. When had I become such a perversion of myself? Since I met him and a part of me had responded to that cruelty of his gaze. The way his eyes narrow at me, gauging my reaction. The way he stalks my every move, follows my every breath, waiting for me to say something. Anything.

"What...what else?"

"I want to find your limits. Test them. Push them. I want to take you over the edge into that space where nothing exists except pain. So much pain that it puts you out of your mind, releases you of the trappings that hold you back. You ready for that?

My throat goes dry.

Everything he says is different. Words packed with yearning, a hushed determination. A deep need for something that is so wrong. All wrong for me. So wrong that it seems right. *Is it wrong that I want everything he says he can do me?*

Excitement crackles over my skin. My instincts scream at me to leave. Warn me that once I taste every forbidden delight he has to offer, I'll be spoiled forever. I'll never want another the way I want him. There is no future for us. My heart stutters. Perhaps it's precisely that thought that loosens the conflict inside of me.

I straighten my shoulders. "You're right."

Color fades from his face. His features twist in a semblance of pain. The kind of pain he'd said he wanted from me. The pain that would have filled the hurt inside of him. Two parts of a whole.

He squares his shoulders. "Okay then." He swivels on his feet and begins to walk away, his back straight, that hardened butt of his flexing with each move under his clothes, his powerful thighs unfurling with each step that he takes forward.

"Aren't you forgetting something, Doc?"

He pauses but doesn't turn. The muscles of his back go solid. "What?"

"Where's the pain you promised me?"

Doc

Her voice sweeps over me with the force of a storm. My chest tightens, my muscles bunch, and my shoulders go solid. "What did you say?" I turn on her.

She gulps. Color burns her cheeks.

"Tell me, Red."

"I want to find out what you can do to me. How far can you push me before I break?"

"What if you can't bear it? What if it is too much for you? What if it makes you hate me?"

"You won't hurt me."

A breath rushes out of me. "In case you missed it, that's what this entire conversation is about. The pain I can cause you, remember?"

"That's different." Her gaze skitters away.

"Look at me, Alice."

She raises her chin.

"How is it different? Tell me." *I need to know.*

Can she have read between my words? Can she have gleaned what I meant? Known what I have been trying to communicate to her all along? *Nope, not possible.*

No one has seen past the harshness of my tone, the implied threat of my dominance, the absolute need to possess that hides what I really want. The need to be turned on with that raw edge of emotion that only comes alive with the pain of another. *Yeah, I am a bastard.*

The kind of man your ma warned you about.

The most perverse kind of filth, the one who gets off on the yearning of another. The only women I have been with so far are those who are professional pain seekers.

The kind who wants more...more. The more I inflicted my demands, the more they wanted. The more fake they became. All fake. Unlike her.

This pure, giving woman who stands in front of me meets my gaze, sets her jaw, and tells me, "I trust you, Doc. Don't you see that? I trust you with my body, my soul, my emotions, my feelings." She squeezes her eyes shut. "What more do you want me to say?"

"Nothing." I tuck my elbows into my sides. "The fact that you can give yourself so willingly, that you want to put up with everything I can do to you, that you don't even question the kind of perverted man I am..."

"A sadist."

"What?" I snap open my eyelids.

"I've heard about it, you know."

"You have?" I scratch my chin.

"There are women who get off on the perversions of Fae males."

"Oh yeah?" I frown and lean forward until I tower over her. "And what do you know of that?"

"I may be a virgin—"

"Don't remind me," I growl.

"But I am not innocent." She sets her jaw. "You don't grow up with a Fae family and not hear about the out-there tastes of alpha Fae males."

"And what have you heard?" I want to scoop her up and take her back to the bedroom and tie her down, butt in the air, curves exposed and quivering, and waiting for me. My groin throbs, and I pull my thoughts back to the now. To her. Her face, her lips, her cheeks that grow rosy as I arch my eyebrows at her. "Tell me, Red."

"About the pain sluts, the groupies who hang around Fae haunts in the hope of finding a master. One who'll take them on as submissive and teach them the meaning of pain, of heat, of love—"

"Who are all Fae. I can't hurt them with my perversions, the way I could hurt you." I lean forward on the balls of my feet and her gaze widens.

"So all this...this fuss is because I am human?" She sets her jaw, "You think I am too weak to bear the consequences of your demands?"

I glare at her and she gulps, then mimes zipping her lips. *Hmm, sassy.* Definitely, need to spank *that* from her. I flex my fingers.

Her gaze lands on my hand and color floods her cheeks.

"Besides, there's nothing romantic about what I want from you." I crack my neck and my joints pop.

She raises a trembling hand to smooth her hair. The scent of her fear bleeds into the air and my vision tunnels, focusing on her. Elevated breathing, dilated pupils, pulse fluttering at the base of her neck. A calmness descends on me. This is what I yearn for. Her giving in to me. Her wanting everything I can do to her. Her ready to submit. To me.

She squares her shoulders and peeks up at me from under her eyelashes, and my groin hardens. The blood drums at my temples, echoing the throbbing of my balls. *The fuck?* My throat closes. The scent of dragon smoke seeps into the air.

I was mistaken.

Holding back with her is impossible. I thought I could make her give in, to break her and reveal her soft core? It is I who is close to revealing what I am. A perversion among the Fae. One who has the genes of my dragon ancestors sewn in with my Fae compulsions, which makes me unsafe, dangerous for her. "What if I don't just mark you, but go further?" I rake my gaze over her face, her breasts, over the curve of her waist to where her thighs squeeze together. "What if I push you to the point of no return?"

The scent of her arousal rends the air and wraps around me, and my heart…the stupid fucking thing, stutters. My chest hurts for her. To be inside her. To squeeze her flesh and absorb her cries of pain. Yeah, it comes down to that. The need to see her come undone in my arms.

"What if it is too much for your body? What if I break you completely?"

"You're forgetting something."

"Huh?" I lean forward on the balls of my feet.

"I trust you."

Trust. Did she just reveal exactly how vulnerable she is to me? That she would lay herself wide open for me, bare her heart. Hand over her body, herself, her emotions to me and ask me to show her what it means to be completely at someone else's mercy.

"You have no idea you are saying." I close the small millimeter of distance between us, bend my knees so I am at eye level. "No fucking idea."

My voice rasps through the space between us.

She flinches but doesn't back down.

"I do."

"Oh yeah?" I reach out a finger and trail it over her cheek. Just a touch. A gentle caress to soak in the warmth of her skin, to sense her anticipation, smell her excitement, revel in her fear.

Just a glimpse of what I can offer her.

Of what I can do to her, of how it could be between us...should she choose to take things further.

"I understand that you can cause me pain." She holds my gaze, "that sometimes my body may think it doesn't want it, but that what I hate may be exactly what I need."

The breath whooshes out of me. *Fuck me.* I stare at her. "And how exactly did you learn all this?" My voice is hushed. Any of the women I've commanded before will tell you that's the calm before the storm. That's the casual voice I use just before I go all Dom. That's the warning that my true nature is about to be unleashed, to wreak a whole swathe of pain on my unsuspecting slave.

"Tell me, Red."

Her breath stutters.

"I...I followed you to the club you frequent." She gulps. "I may have even crept inside and seen you whip some of your subs."

"What else?"

Her chest heaves; her breasts tremble, "I saw you leave with women and I hated them."

"Is that right?" My tone drops another notch. I can't stop my lips from curving in a satisfied smirk. *Hey, I am allowed, okay.* She's the one who confessed to stalking me, prying into what I did.

"Yeah." She gnaws on her lower lip, and the scent of blood seeps into the air. *Fuck. Fuck. Fuck.* Not good. She shouldn't have done that. Pain. Blood. The kind of stuff that's a siren song to my senses. Combine that with her vulnerability, the fact that she trusts me and...well, it's a potent aphrodisiac. The kind that makes me realize that I can't back away now.

Not when she says, "I wanted to be them." She sets her jaw, "I wanted to take their place. I wanted to kill them all, so you'd see no one else but me, feel nothing else but my skin, do to me whatever you were going to do with them, instead."

"And now?" I allow my chin to drop forward. "How do you feel now when I've told you what I intend to do to you?"

I keep my tone at an even keel, when inside, blood pounds at my temples.

"Answer me Red."

"Now I am sure that there is no one else I want for my first time but you."

14

Alice

I should turn and hide. Beg him to take me back home.

I wasn't lying when I said I wanted him to be the first. I've known I wanted him since the day he looked into my eyes and told me he would make the pain go away. Now the same man who took care of my ankle is promising me a world of pain, an entire sea of possibilities I haven't contemplated before now.

I had been truthful when I said I'd hated every woman he'd been with, and nothing gave me the right to be that possessive of him.

Especially not when he's making it clear that there can be no possibility of a relationship between us—not in the conventional sense, at least. He's promising me what? Something different, kinky, something that more than arouses my curiosity. It arouses me, period.

Makes me want to delve into my true nature and explore the hidden parts of me, find out what exactly I am. Not just human. Not a virgin... more than that. I sense there is something more, and I want to find out how he will react to me. How he will inflict more than just pain, reveal what I haven't been able to discover on my own. Yeah, there's that pain word again. I should be terrified of it. I should be scared of it, but I'm not. All it does is turn me on. "Please."

Right now, I am begging him. I have all but bared my soul to him, stripped myself of everything. My self-respect, my needs. I have handed over my trust to him. What else does he want?

"Please what?" His gaze is steady.

Is this what he meant, that he would push me beyond my boundaries? That even after I have given him everything, he will make me dig deeper, pull on reserves buried deep inside?

"Please show me what it means to experience true pain. True pleasure. True everything. Show me what it means to truly belong to you." My voice hangs in the space between us. The words sound so hollow, that I wince.

It's not easy. Giving up so much of myself. Stripping myself of every single barrier I have built up against the world to survive so far. Will I survive this? Survive him? And if I don't, will it be so bad?

"Once I start, there is no stopping."

"So if I wanted to, I couldn't back out?"

"You need to do all your thinking now, before I take the first step…the first slap, my first…taste of you."

I swallow. "Okay."

"We do this as a test."

"A test?"

"Just for two days." His voice is gruff, and I expect him to smile. But he doesn't.

He simply speaks with those canines protruding from the sides of his lips. "I am not completely heartless, you know?"

"No, you're just scary."

"You afraid of me, Red?" He flicks back his ears and my gaze darts to those lengthened tips.

"Yes," I reply honestly.

"Good." He straightens. "You should be afraid. It keeps you alert. Heightens the anticipation of what is to come."

"It also makes me wet."

He sucks in a breath, "You little tease." His eyes glint. "I know what you are doing, little Red."

I stare, and he smirks, and that wicked curl of his lips sets goosebumps unraveling over my skin.

"You are trying to provoke me, taunt me. You are forgetting one thing, though."

"Wha...what is that?"

"In this relationship, I am the Master, and you are my...?"

I open my mouth, and the word sticks in my throat. *Say it, do it.*

He raises an eyebrow, and that's all it takes. The force of his personality crashes on my chest; my breathing grows labored. My thighs clench, and it's as if he's drawing out the words, pulling on my response, tugging on every inch of my skin to say, "Slave." I mumble.

"I didn't hear you."

Jerk. Sadist. Yeah, he's all that and I still want him. Which makes me what? A masochist. It makes me his..."Slave."

My voice sounds strong. Like I am aware of what I am doing. Not. Not that it will stop me. I'm his to command, and he knows it. He can tell me to jump off a bridge and I'll do it...I can give up my life for him if he asks me, and he hasn't even touched me yet. The thought fills me with a strange satisfaction. The fact that I am his to do with as he wants. "I'm yours."

He nods.

"Your slave," I repeat. *See? That was easy.* My voice didn't even tremble.

His lips pull back, giving me another hint of those long, sharp canines. I gulp and draw in a breath. *Okay, it's gonna be okay.*

"And you'll do as I say for the next forty-eight hours."

The hushed tone in his voice books no argument.

He's asking me to put myself at his disposal, to allow him to do as he wants with me. It goes against everything I have tried to stand for in my life. To hold my own against the stronger Fae who have surrounded me for so long. Yet there's also a strange poetic justice to it. I have wanted to be one of them, wanted to fit in, and here it is. The chance to allow myself to be subsumed by the most masterful of them all. My own Alpha Fae. My Master. My Dominant. Mine.

"You have no safe words. You can't back out. You allow me to inflict what I deem necessary for your pleasure. You let me draw out your needs, your desires." His gaze surveys my features, "You also can't speak."

"Not at all?" I frown.

"Well, in between our sessions, yes, though I plan to make sure you have no strength left to do much more than sleep and recover."

O-k-a-y.

At least he's telling me now, and not after this forty-eight-hour...what, torture? No...orgasm-inducing-interval in my life has started. "And during the sessions?"

"There are no rules."

"Huh?" I blink, trying to focus my attention on what he's saying.

"Did you hear what I said?" His voice is harsh, with an undertone of need. An answering lust licks at my veins. My pulse pounds at my temples and spots of black pepper my vision.

"Alice?" He snaps his fingers and I start.

"You're not listening to me." The words growl out of him and I drop my gaze to his mouth. Thin mean upper lip. Pouty lower lip. I want him to kiss me with it. Lick me all over, bite down on my nipples, between my legs. I clench my thighs. Take me. Mount me.

I wheeze out a breath. "No rules, you said?" I wet my lips, "What if... ah I wanted you to stop?"

"You said you trusted me. Did you mean it?"

Damn it, I knew that would come back to haunt me. I do trust him with my life, but can I trust him enough to be completely dependent on him?

I may have followed him to the BDSM club and spied on what he did to those women but I have never been at the receiving end of those whips, slaps...those kisses. My belly clenches. My nipples pebble. I want to find out what that feels like.

"Do you Red?" His hushed voice ripples down my spine, leaving little pinpricks of anticipation in their wake.

I shiver.

He has that entire 'I am in charge' thing going on here...not that Doc didn't have that going on earlier. Only, he's turned it up a notch.

He's just stopped pretending and shown more of himself, and...I am not sure what to make of it. *This is what I wanted, right?* Doc vulnerable and not hiding his emotions anymore. He won't hold back now and I am responsible for that. My scalp tingles. What if...what if he was right to have been cautious?

What if I can't take it?

What if it's too much for me?

What if...it's everything he promises it to be? He's the only man I'd want to use my body however he sees fit. He's the only one I want to be with. A sizzle of anticipation lights up my nerve cells.

"Y...yes." I stutter.

"Yes, what?"

"Yes, I do trust you to understand what I need."

He glares at me and my breath catches.

My palms grow damp. "Anything else?"

"I decide when to stop. I decide what you need. I decide when you can orgasm. What you eat, when you can breathe."

One side of his mouth twitches, in what I am coming to see as Doc's evil smile.

"You are saying this just to shock me." I pout.

"Am I succeeding?"

Yes.

Yes.

"No." I clench my jaw.

"Excellent." He rubs his palms together. Long fingers, thick digits, the girth of each one is about the circumference of my cunt. And I am sure he means to have each one of those inside of me, all at once. My toes curl.

"In that case, you wouldn't mind if I told you that I plan to make sure various parts of you are teased out, that you are filled up to the point that you can't move, can't whine, can't do anything except ask me to stop. Beg me to cease...and when you can't even do that, you will submit to me."

Omigod! Did he read my mind? Did he say that just to see the effect his words have on me?

His eyes gleam; his lips purse.

Bet he thinks I am going to turn around and run away screaming, conforming to the stereotype of the fainting human virgin female. And if I had any common sense left, I would do just that, except...my gaze drops to the front of his pants and the erection tenting his crotch. It's massive. Huge. About the size of my forearm. I gulp.

He's going to cram that...that monster dick inside of me?

My pussy quivers. Moisture gushes out from between my legs.

"Agree, Red?"

15

Doc

Her pupils dilate, and she darts out her tongue again to lick her lips. A groan tears out of me. I am trying my best to rein myself in, but this woman insists on testing me, pushing me to the furthest extent of my control. She knows just what to say and do to entice me.

"Yes." She lowers her chin then peers up at me from under her eyelashes.

Coquettish, and yet, seductive. Innocent, yet such a tease, and all mine. *Mine.* I get to be her first, to introduce her to the pain that waits for her. It is I who will initiate her into an entire new world of experience, at every level. My cock thickens.

"Yes, Alpha." I harden my voice.

She pouts, and my gaze falls to her rosy mouth. A mouth that I intend to make full use of as I thrust into it. I intend to stuff my dick down her throat, make her suck on my shaft, lick it, swirl her soft tongue around it, and make her swallow every drop of my cum. A vein throbs at my temple.

Get your head back in the present; focus on her. This is about her, how she responds to you. How much can she take.

I need to coax her into my world. Small steps.

Just one thing at a time, you don't want to overwhelm her, do you?

"Yes, Alpha." The repeated words tremble from her lips on a sigh. She hunches her shoulders and lowers her gaze. Her chin rolls forward, and she folds her fingers together in front of her, just the right blend of supplication in every angle of her body.

"You don't have to do that, you know."

"What?" She tilts her head.

"I prefer it when you challenge me. You don't have to comply with everything I say."

"You want me to question you?"

"Try." I pinch her chin so she raises her head and meets my gaze. "That's the imperative word. I want you to stand up to me, to go toe to toe with me. I want you to push back, not suppress."

"I am confused... Alpha."

Heat sears my veins.

"I need you to go with your instinct and ask me to stop, to cry out in pain, to whine with need and not pull back."

"I thought you want me to submit?"

"Only when it feels right. Only when you have accepted me as your Master." I peer into her eyes.

She blinks, "You want me to not hold back my natural responses. You want me to give you a chance to—"

"Prove that I am worthy of you."

"That's strange, I never thought of it that way, Alpha."

The sound of her voice calling me by that title, *fucking hell,* my dick twitches, tenting my pants. I need to be inside of her now.

"Let me show you." I drop to my knees and grip her thighs.

She stiffens; her muscles clench, and her legs instinctively squeeze back together. I raise my head to meet her green gaze.

"Let me." I massage her curves, and she allows me to slide her legs apart.

In this position, I am eye-level with her chest. That's how tiny she is. I lower my gaze to her breasts and her gorgeous flesh trembles.

I lean forward and curl my fingers around her nipple. Her body tenses.

I pinch the hardened flesh, and a moan wheezes out of her.

The sweet scent of her arousal drifts around me teases at my nostrils, and my cock thickens. My back twinges and my chest burns. Outwardly, I have healed. My wounds have closed up—there are no scars left, but my insides ache.

Is it because of being burned or due to another kind of heat, this nearness to her that sweeps aside all my defenses and exposes me to her? Does she realize how vulnerable she makes me?

She's agreed to give herself to me over the next forty-eight hours. She's put herself in my hands; she trusts me.

It's a big responsibility she's given me. Opening her eyes to the fact that sometimes what her body doesn't want is just what she needs to be aroused. How will she react when she discovers that? Only one way to find out.

I lower my head and fasten my lips over her clit.

16

Alice

A whine shrieks out of me. No warning, nothing. He simply fastens his lips around my pussy and sucks. Heat sizzles up my spine. I rise to the balls of my feet, straighten to get away from him, but that only pushes my pelvis closer to his mouth.

His beautiful, gorgeous, torturous mouth that licks through my lower lips, and slinks into the crevices between the folds of my cunt. Too much. Too soon. *Oh!* The stirrings of a climax ripple up from my toes. *Omigod. Oh my! No. Not so soon.*

I cannot be on the verge of a climax already, not when he's only just begun to tease me.

But then everything, since we'd set eyes on each other, was but foreplay leading up to this moment. This instance when he grabs my hips and angles me up so I am riding his mouth.

His tongue plunges into my wet channel, and my knees buckle.

Once again, he doesn't hesitate. Simply sweeps me up close to him. He drags his arm under one of my legs, hooks his palm under my knee, and wraps it over his shoulder. In that position, I am open and vulnerable and spread for him. His tongue plunges inside my drooling channel again and again. A shudder runs down my spine, to meet that sweet spot of torture in my groin. Blood thuds in my temples, my heart thumps and its every throb is echoed by the beat in my core.

He bites down on my pussy, and I scream. I hunch over him, plunge my fingers into his hair, and hold on for purchase. I am going to come. Going to come. I can't hold on, not any longer. My vision swims, my breath catches, and that's when he pulls back.

He's gone. And I am empty and throbbing. Again.

"Open your eyes."

The hushed command in his voice laps at my already frayed nerves. I crack my eyelids open to find he's completely naked. *Uh!* When had he lost his clothes? I rake my gaze down those demarcated pecs, the hard eight pack that flows down the concave stomach to meet the heavy weight of his shaft...his beautiful, angry, throbbing cock that points in my direction. Everything I had guessed about its size was wrong. It's bigger than I imagined. It's a monster of a cock. Even to my inexperienced eyes, it's clear that his dick is a work of art. The muscle in question extends and thickens as I stare. I gulp. He'd been right about one thing. It's gonna hurt, doesn't matter where he sticks it in me, he's going to fill me up and stretch me and change every perception I had about making love. And that's what this is. It's the physical expression of what he feels for me. Doesn't matter what he calls it, or how much he denies it. Doc cares for me. He knows what I need and won't hesitate to give it to me. My heart flutters and my breath catches.

He makes a low sound in his throat and I jerk. My gaze flies to his face and those glittering blue eyes lock on mine. They hold me, consume me, draw me in. His body is larger than life, massive, overwhelming, but his gaze...his gaze sears me to the bone, sinks into hidden crevasses, probing, stretching, preparing me for the intrusion that is to come.

His pupils blink vertically, and my sex clenches.

He bares his teeth and the sight of those sharp pointy canines... I gulp. Moisture floods from between my legs.

He flicks back his ears, and it's animalistic and feral and so different from anything else I have ever seen. Okay. I admit it. That's sexy as hell.

It's an outward sign of the emotions roiling inside of him. The fact that even though he pretends he is in control, he isn't. That thought sends me over the edge. All my muscles go rigid, my spine bows, I thrust out my breasts, and the breath shudders out of me and...

"Don't you dare come, Red." His warning tone cuts a swathe through the sexual haze in my mind.

I open my mouth to speak, and he shakes his head. *Oh! Okay.* So apparently our sessions have already begun, and he doesn't want me to orgasm. *Hmph!* I pout, and his eyebrows lower.

I flutter my eyelashes, and he tightens his grip over my ass, squeezing the flesh so tightly that I gasp.

"Focus, Red. You need to be present, with me, here."

Where the hell else does he think I am?

I widen my gaze, and he clicks his tongue, "I don't want you in your head, I want all of your attention to be on me."

Huh, then how do I come if I am supposed to look at him?

"Exactly." His features resolve into a look of satisfaction. "If you have your attention on me you won't come without my permission."

Should he be telling me that?

I mean isn't that like a trade secret or something?

He tosses his head, "It's the only way for me to monitor your reactions, make sure you are safe."

Safe? I'll never be safe as long as I am near him, with his face between my legs, with his lips gleaming from the evidence of my cum. My arousal all over his mouth. He licks his lips and a shudder teases my skin.

Little flickers of heat pinprick down my back.

Ah! Hell, he knows how to get me off.

He frowns, "You may be thinking that is a contradictory statement, but trust me on this, Red."

Okay. I nod.

His blue eyes flare; a nerve throbs to life at his temple. His gaze rakes over my features as if he's seeing me properly for the first time. Is that good? Or bad? I mean, I've done what he's asked so far. I allowed those mesmerizing eyes to lock on mine and tether me to him, right? I had not come despite the fever pitch to which he'd aroused my body, too. So what else can he want?

"I want all of you. I am not going to stop until you fall apart under my lips, hmm?"

Still holding my gaze, he leans close once again until his breath sears my weeping pussy lips. Until my lower belly quivers, and liquid lust dampens my core. A moan whines out of me, and I shudder.

A nerve flexes above his jawline. He's trying to control himself and almost succeeding. Not fair. I've agreed to be his for the next forty-eight hours. I've offered myself up to him willingly. I can't wait to see what else he can do to me. He could play my body like it was his, but I could tease him just a little, too, right? He hasn't said anything about not doing that.

I tighten my grip on his hair and tug. A shudder runs down his spine, one he can't hide. A fierce satisfaction grips me. I am having as much of an impact on him as he is on me. I pull at his hair, and a growl rips from him.

"Next time I am going to bind your hands."

He thrusts his tongue into my channel again. He twists it inside of me, sweeping over my trembling inner walls.

He squeezes my hips and pulls my pelvis toward him.

He tilts me at just a slightly different angle, just right for his tongue to curve inside of me. He hits a spot that sends shivers of heat skittering over my nerves. Adrenaline laces my blood, and my heart pounds so hard it shoves away all of the thoughts inside of my head. My eyelids flutter; I so want to close them, to focus inside, on the turmoil he's putting my body through, on how he's drawing my emotions from me, making me want to come…come. I need to come.

A groan trembles up my throat, and color brightens his cheeks.

He's pleased with the reaction he has wrought from me. My hips buck forward, and I have nothing to do with it. He's controlling my body, willing it to come and yet hold back. I stay poised on the edge of that precipice that calls to me to take a step and go over. *Please. Please.* I repeat the words in my head, my lips moving to form them. He shakes his head, his tongue thrusting in and out of me. He drags one hand forward to pinch my clit, and I howl. Tears run down my cheeks. A wave of tension grips me. More moisture bubbles out from between my legs, all swept up by his mouth. He tears his mouth from my pussy, and those eyes of his flash vertically, sending another ripple of lust down my spine. *Now. Now, it has to be now.*

"Not yet."

Bastard. I snarl, the sound frustrated and as animalistic as him.

There is no change in his expression. He watches me as if I am a clinical specimen or his newest creation. I am his plaything. His.

What have I let myself in for? Barely ten minutes into our scheduled forty-eight hours, and I am not sure how I am going to survive. I am in so much pain…pleasure. Both. Neither.

He plunges three fingers inside my pussy at the same time as he slaps my ass cheek with his other hand.

The pain whines over my sensitized nerve endings. All of my brain cells seem to fire all at once.

"Come for me, Red."

17

Doc

Her cheeks grow fiery, her chest heaves, and a keening cry emerges from her mouth. I have never seen a woman come apart so beautifully on my tongue. She throws back her head; her nails dig into my scalp. The pain rips down my spine, arrowing to my groin, and my dick hardens. I welcome the lust that laps at my nerves. The need to take that unfolds in my belly. She arches her back, her nipples thrust up, and moisture gushes out from between her legs. I lick it up, all of that sweet honeyed essence of her. All of it is for me. Only me. I shove my tongue into her wet cunt, and she shudders. Her shoulders jerk.

She opens her mouth, and a moan drips out.

Fuck me. That keening cry of hers, the way she's pleading with me to take her and put her out of her misery…oh, not through words.

I hadn't been kidding her when I told her that she should not speak in our sessions. I hadn't told her that it was because she didn't need to. Because I can intuit each nuance of her body, I can sense her every want, read her actions, which, by the way, do speak louder than words. Sometimes what she wants is not what she asks for. What she craves is not what she'll request.

Nothing like words to pollute the sheer purity of the body's need, and that's all this is. Lust. Hunger. The need to satiate that greed inside of me. For her. Just for her. I have never felt this needy with anyone else.

I've never wanted anyone to submit to me more.

Never has someone held me in their power as much. Yeah, it sounds all wrong…but this is not only a power exchange.

This is not a give and take. This is all about her.

I am her Master because she chooses to submit to me. She follows my rules because she chose to agree to it. I have control because she believes I deserve it. I punish her, I mark her, I use her, for she allows it. I own her. The fact that she has me in her grasp. That I will adapt my body to her needs. Bend my perversions to accommodate her. For in gratifying her, in pleasuring her, is my true fulfillment. She has me in her power and she isn't even aware of it.

She chose to give herself to me and trust me when I say that I take my obligation to pleasure this woman seriously.

A scream tears out of her, and her entire body shudders. She slumps, her breasts grazing my hair as her head bows.

My dick hardens; blood rushes to my groin. The burn in my chest deepens. Blood thunders in my head. Her legs give way under her, and she slides down, her slick skin, slipping over my shoulders. I swallow, and the sweetness of her fills my mouth, the scent of her surrounds me, teases me, tugs at me to throw her down and rip into her and knot her. *Knot her.* My vision narrows on her.

Everything else fades. All other thoughts empty from my head. *Mine. She's mine.* I am going to take her, and no one can stop me from claiming her. She belongs to me.

I rise to my feet, my arms cradling her as I hold her close to me.

She's tiny enough to huddle against my chest. Aftershocks rack her body, and her breasts twitch. The outline of her still hard nipples strokes my chest.

Another shiver of lust tears through me. My balls grow heavy; my dick hardens to the point that I am sure that I am leaking precum.

A growl rumbles up my chest, and she whines, the sound so hungry I forget she's human. Fragile. She is mine. My mate. Mine to take and please. To command as I want. To fulfill and knot and...*do it. What are you waiting for?* I stride up the stairs and into the house, to the bed, where I lay her on her back.

I shove my much bigger body between her legs that fall apart to grant me full access.

The scent of her arousal deepens. Her chin wobbles. Her lips move, but no sound emerges. She's talking to me in her head, but no words leave her mouth. Even now she obeys me. Such a fucking turn on. My cock lengthens. I bury my elbows on either side of her head and bracket her in.

"Look at me, Red."

She trembles and her eyeballs move behind closed eyelids.

"Open your eyes." I infuse enough command in my voice. Those green eyes of hers dilate, the black of her pupils filling her eyes until only a circle of sparkling emerald remains.

"I am going to take you, Red."

She groans.

"You hear me, Alice?"

She swallows.

"Nod if you understand."

She jerks her chin.

"You want me to fuck you, little human?"

Her gaze widens, and she nods. The open trust that laces her features...*fuck that's my undoing and my aphrodisiac all at once.* "You are aware that Fae are built differently than humans, right? Fae males extend out farther and—"

The woman reaches between us and grabs my dick and positions it at her entrance. The wetness of her cum bathes the head of my shaft. The liquid heat of her luscious pussy calls to me, tugs at me, and something inside of me shatters. *Holy fuck!*

"You are definitely getting bound the next time."

She juts out her chin, and that defiant gesture sends me over the fucking edge. I thought I'd tamed her? *Nope. Nah, not even close.* But she will submit to me by the time I am done with her. My balls tighten. I grab her thighs, pry them even farther apart, then tilt my hips and plunge into her.

18

Alice

Too big. Too thick. I'd expected it, but the physical reality of having his dick in me, it...*Omigod, he's splitting me in half!* My eyes roll back in my head. He stops, allowing my body to adjust, allowing my soft pussy to shape around his girth. His cock pulses and every ribbed callus of his shaft scrapes over my inner channel. Heat saturates my blood and all of my brain cells seem to fire at once. More. I need more. "Please..." the words stick in my throat.

"Take me, Red. Take what you need from me."

He thrusts into me with such force that my body moves up the sheets.

His cock breaches the tender skin of my barrier, and I howl. *Ow, ow! That hurts.* My breath comes in pants, my entire body goes rigid, and my back arches off of the bed.

My body quivers. It's only when he leans his weight on me that I am aware I have cringed away from him. Tears leak from the corners of my eyes and he bends his neck and licks them up.

Somehow, that's even more intimate than him burying himself balls deep inside of me.

His dick thickens, pinning me down so I can't move. Not that I am even trying…to move, that is. I can barely draw in a breath, for the force of his dominance holds me captive.

He tilts his hips and his girth stretches me further.

"Let me in." He growls.

What the—? How much deeper is he going to sink into me?

"I'm not even halfway in, Red."

Gah! No way.

"Eyes on me."

When he commands me in that voice of his—I gulp—I can't refuse.

He clicks his tongue, and my gaze veers to his face. His features come into focus. Harsh. Hard. Those planes and angles of his cheekbones can cut me up.

Those blue eyes hold my gaze.

The force of his presence is all around me, pinning me down with as much assuredness as his dick has me pierced to the bed.

I gasp my chest heaving. A moan wheezes out of me.

"You in pain, Red?"

What do you think? I open my mouth to snap at him and he shakes his head. Just a jerk of his chin, that's all it is, but I get him.

I can interpret his every signal as if he's already getting through to me, training me…and he is. Of course, he is.

He slides out of me, and I whine. *What the hell—?* He's only been inside of me for a few seconds, and already I miss him. My core clenches, seeking out the hardness that had impaled me a few seconds ago. I need more of him. Want all of him inside of me.

He has to fuck me again. *Now.* My nerve-endings crackle with anticipation. My skin feels too tight for my body.

I wriggle my hips, and his lips draw back, exposing those canines. I gulp again.

This close, they seem even sharper than I had expected.

A drop of liquid shimmers at their pointy edges. His eyelids blink, and like the well-trained human I am, I drag my gaze back to his.

His pupils blink vertically, just for a second. His irises—blue, violet, indigo, so many colors infusing and fading away. So. Hot. My mouth goes dry. I can't stop staring.

"That's it, look into my eyes, Red. Use it to ground yourself. Let me guide you."

What's he talking about?

My head whirls, and I am yanked into his penetrating gaze, losing myself in those searing indigo depths. He's consuming me with that hypnotic stare, looking right into my soul and reading all of my deepest, darkest secrets.

A white noise pulls at my subconscious, tugging at me. A warmth steals over my limbs, pulling me down, down.

"Stay with me."

He plunges into me, and the jolt forces my awareness back into my body.

Red and blue flashes ignite behind my eyes, and I scream. *It hurts. It hurts. More than before.* And...every pore on my skin pops open. I have never felt so alive as with his dick throbbing inside of me anchoring me to this plane. He was right. He's forcing me to feel every breath, every gasp, every brush of his skin sliding over mine. I have never felt as one with my own self as in this instant. I have never been this alive.

He drops his head and closes his mouth over mine. He sucks on my lips, as his cock expands in my channel, holding me captive.

He tilts his hips and thrusts.

His shaft plunges even deeper, nudging my cervix.

I try to shove him away but I can't. He's too big, too intense, too much. He's all around me, absorbing me into himself, forcing me to absorb him. Heat from him pours over me, his scent fills my senses, familiar, reassuring. His knot throbs, filling my channel.

He locks his shaft behind my pelvic bone...*ow!* The pain, the pain that lashes through my body is so intense that it shoves me over the edge.

Tight on its heels, a deep shudder tears up from my toes, grips my thighs, sweeping over my belly and my chest, to crash over me.

Starbursts of blue and green splash behind my eyes, followed by a darkness that envelops me.

When I come to, he's still inside of me. His gaze narrows; his lips flatten. "You're back."

I swallow and nod. *Am I allowed to speak? What just happened? Did I blackout from the pleasure?*

"Did you orgasm, Red?"

Yes.

Warmth sears my cheeks, but damn if I want to admit it. To do so will, no doubt, only feed his already swollen ego.

A smirk pulls at his lips.

His dick lengthens inside of me, and I gasp.

"Yeah, I'm still hard. I've been waiting for you to awaken. Wouldn't want you to miss what I am going to do to you. When I come inside of you for the first time, I want to make sure you are conscious, that you can feel every inch of me as I knot you."

Wait, knotting? He's never mentioned that before. I am aware that Fae males knot their women, *but isn't that reserved for mates?* I open my mouth to ask, and he slaps his palm over my lips.

I bite down on his flesh, and his shoulders heave.

"It turns me on when you fight me, Red."

He surges inside of me, and his shaft, that thick, throbbing muscle rams into me, sliding through the liquid that pools in my core and eases his entry. I sense his muscles tense; his flanks coil under my calves...*uh? When did I wrap myself around him?* I dig my heels into his waist...*wait. I want to push him away, right?*

So why am I clinging to him and tilting my pelvis up, just that little millimeter more so his dick jolts in even farther, going deeper than where anyone else has been? A moan trembles up my throat and crashes against the barrier of his palm. Color burns on his cheeks.

"You're mine, Red. Only mine."

He rams himself in so hard that his balls slap against my sensitive flesh. He's possessing me, filling me, pinning me to the bed.

A scream boils up, only to be shushed against his palm that gags me. Pain, so much pain, the white edge of it tears through me, pushing me up, higher, higher, urging me to reach for something that's just out of reach. So near, yet so far away. It shoves me straight into that zone that's always existed just a little out of reach.

A trembling grips me; my entire body is one writhing mass of need, lust, all of it mixed together to form a tapestry of longing, of just needing him to finish what he started. I grip his waist harder with my legs, throw my arms around him, and dig my nails into his shoulders. A burning sensation throbs at my temples, and my vision wavers. *What is he doing to me?*

His gaze burns into me.

"I am going to fuck you now, Red."

What the — ? What's he been doing so far?

My heart bashes against my rib cage, and adrenaline laces my blood. My entire body trembles and I want to tear myself away from him, but I can't. For he's holding me immobile with his gaze, his dick, the weight of his presence that pushes me to stay where I am, to take the pain he is giving me, the pain he is going to deliver to me.

I try to speak and tell him that I am not sure I can take any more of this, this brutal fucking, this edge of pain, the fierce pleasure that hovers right there just out of reach, killing me with the suspense. But all that emerges is a gurgling sound.

His entire body tenses, his dick grows even thicker — *is he going to rip through me?*

He takes his palm from my mouth, then locks his arms under my knees. He yanks my legs up, only to loop them around his neck so my shoulders are flat on the bed.

The angle lets him slip in even deeper.

He brushes his lips over mine. "Hold on, Red."

19

Doc

I feel myself extend. The hard flesh inside of my dick slides out.

I should have warned her of what is to come, how savage it is when Faes mate... I didn't. I want her to experience it without flinching. I want to absorb every single gasp of pain, every whine of pleasure as I sink into her hot, tight, cunt.

Does that make me a bastard? Yes.

Am I selfish? Probably. I revel in the searing heat of her virgin pussy as she tightens her muscles and clamps down on my shaft, pulling me in.

I lock my extended cock behind her pelvic bone knotting into place.

Her body goes rigid. A scream boils up her from her lungs, her throat. I lock my lips over hers, absorbing every last sound she makes. I yank her close, so her breasts are flattened against mine, swipe my tongue over the seam of her lips, suck on her, taste her sweetness. The scent of her sinks into my blood. Each wave of the aftermath of her climax ripples over her, over me. She shudders and digs her nails into my shoulders, then drags her other hand up and curls her fingers into my hair.

She tugs on it, and I tear my lips from hers.

My balls draw up, my knot contracts, and I shoot hot streams of cum, filling her up, marking her.

"You're mine, Red, you understand?"

She moans, and her eyelids flutter.

"Look at me, look at your Master."

She cracks her eyes open, and her gaze widens.

What must she see? A beast who has lost control? Who won't stop until he has taken her over and over again? The tips of my ears tingle and I flick them back. I pull back my lips, and her gaze drops to my mouth.

She shudders, and all color fades from her cheeks.

"You belong to me."

A fierce need grips me. It's not enough that I knotted her, that I came inside of her, I need to mark her in a much more visible way. Claim her, mate her. Blood thuds in my temples, and my vision narrows. The scent of dragon smoke fills the air. I drop my head and bury my teeth at the curve of where her shoulder meets her neck.

A scream rips out of her, and her body thrashes underneath me. Moisture gushes from her pussy and her cunt tightens around my shaft. Heat lances up my spine and my groin hardens. A fierce satisfaction fills me...I raise my head then hold my lips to hers. "Open your mouth."

She parts her lips, and I kiss her again. Thrust my tongue into her mouth so she can taste me, taste her blood. I reach down between us and swipe up some of our joined cum. Lifting my mouth away from hers, I drag my fingers over her lips. She swirls her tongue around my digits and licks them clean.

"Rest now, little human."

Her eyelids flutter down, her chest heaves once. Then her breathing deepens. Her body twitches as she falls asleep.

Her legs loosen around me, her arms slip down my shoulders, and her little body goes limp.

Her face is flushed. Strands of dark hair stick to her forehead. I lower my nose to her throat and nuzzle her. She smells of my cum mixed with that sugary scent of her arousal laced with jasmine and that hint of fiery pepper, and *mine...all mine.* She moans and cuddles closer; her nipples graze my chest and fuck me if my cock doesn't jump again. *You are still knotted inside her, asshole.* I claimed her without telling her what it means. I mated her, and she can never leave me.

And isn't that what I wanted?

A way to keep her close, to make sure I never let go? And when she awakes, will she hate me?

I will not allow that. I need her to give in to me. I need her sweet caresses to soothe the beast inside of me.

She settles me, even as she incites the need to possess. To protect. I must keep her hidden away from everyone until the mating bond is consolidated. Until our soul bond is strengthened such that there is no doubt to whom she belongs. I have another day and a half before I take her back to Singapore, and I am going to make full use of that time.

I bend down and lick her lips. "Wake up, sweet Red, I have a surprise for you."

20

Alice

His voice whispers over my skin, and I turn my head toward it. A touch over my lips makes me moan. I open my lips, and his tongue sweeps in. Sweet, so sweet. His caress flickers over my shoulders to touch the throbbing pain point at my throat. I groan and crack my eyes open. "Doc."

My throat hurts. *Have I been screaming?* Strange, considering he had told me not to speak and I hadn't uttered a word, not counting the moans I had swallowed. The word I had been repeating to myself...his name...*yeah, I had been saying it over and over again.* I try to open my mouth, but all that emerges is a sigh.

"Shh!" He feathers his knuckles over my jawline. His touch is so gentle, that I blink.

I tilt my head, and he nods.

"It's fine to talk."

O-k-a-y. Apparently, I had been waiting for him to give me his go-ahead. He's reached into some part of my psyche that he's tamed and commanded and brought to heel...how had he managed that?

"What happened?" I try to move, and my muscles protest.

"You had another orgasm." Those beautiful lips draw up in a very satisfied smile.

His shaft thickens inside of me, and my pussy quivers. "You knotted me."

His eyelids grow hooded.

"Isn't that what Fae males do with their mates?"

He tilts his head, not confirming, not denying it. His features tense, and all expression is wiped from his face. I can't read him, *dammit*. I hate it when he does that.

"So…this." I contract my inner muscles and wince. Slight shivers of pain radiate out from my pussy. *Ouch.*

His dick thickens in response, and I gulp. "You're still hard."

He tucks his elbows into his sides.

"You don't seem happy about it."

A vein surges at his temple, the tendons of his neck swell.

"You going to speak or let me do all the talking?" I peer up at him.

"You're doing fine on your own." He growls, and the sound is so harsh, so full of intent that it grates over my already sensitized nerve endings.

"Please don't do that." I swallow.

"What?" His tone is hard, but he lowers his voice so it's barely above a whisper.

"When you infuse that dominance into your voice, I want to jump and obey your command, but I am so very tired."

"You should be, Red. What I did to you wasn't right."

"Huh?" I frown. "What's this? An apology?"

"I am laying out my intention, something I should have done before I took your—"

"Virginity?"

He nods; the skin around his eyes creases.

"Being a virgin is overrated. I am better rid of it. Besides, I chose to give it to you, Doc."

His shoulders go solid. "I knotted you Red. I should have warned you, but…"

"You thought it might scare me?"

"You are strong; your capacity to experience the highs and lows of pain are more extreme than you could have imagined."

I frown and survey his features. What's going on in the mind of this very complex man? How do I respond to his unspoken question?

"It was not what I expected." I manage.

"I told you I liked to inflict pain." He sets his lips.

He wants my pain, but he worries about hurting me. He wants to protect me, be my savior, but he's worried about getting too close to me. Yet he wants to experience the most intimate connection on the physical level. He craves the kind of closeness that only bonding on the most instinctual level offers.

The man is a contradiction of so many different emotions. Tension manifests in his stance, writ in every angle of his rigid body. How do I bring him down from whichever corner in his head where he is trapped?

"I am not angry, Doc."

I raise my hand to his cheek, and to my relief, he doesn't move away.

He lets me feather my fingers over that hard jawline.

"You're not?" He frowns. "So you didn't hate it?" The cords of his throat move.

"I didn't love it." I peer up at him from under my lashes. *Uh, how is he going to react to that?*

"Sometimes what you love is not what you need." He angles his hips, and his shaft chafes against my pelvic bone.

"That…you being so deep inside of me, Doc…it's just…so different."

My hand falls to his shoulder and I dig my nails into his skin.

"I am different. A Fae with the blood of a dragon running through me. I am the kind of monster you should have run from as soon as you saw me."

"Never."

He frowns again. "You are a strange woman."

"Look who's talking." I snicker.

"I am still knotted inside of you, woman." His eyebrows lower.

Not only.

He's stripped me of all defenses, torn away that semblance of protection I had worn around me and exposed what I am. A woman who likes depraved things, flawed things, men who can hurt me and make me come and give me the most incredible orgasms of my life. Yep, I confess that. I drag my palm down between us and brush it over where his dick joins us.

He growls, and his shaft thickens. "What are you doing to me, Red?"

"Making the most of the fact that I can still speak."

"I am going to shut you up next time, and it won't be with a gag."

"Promise?"

21

Doc

Did she just say that?

Her eyes gleam. She is going to be the death of me. "Don't bait me, Red."

"I wouldn't dare."

"You do realize I am going to punish you again, right?"

I move inside her, and she stutters. Her pupils dilate, and she moans. Moisture pools between her legs, and fuck me if I don't want to come right now.

This is not how I want it to be. She is not the one in control. I am. I cup her breast, and squeeze the trembling flesh. Her nipple pebbles and she groans.

"Do you have any idea what you just did?"

"Wha…what?" She pouts, and my gaze drops to her lips.

"You can't bait me that way."

She frowns and inches closer.

"Not without facing the repercussions."

She pushes her breast into my palm. Her flesh thrums with an inner fire. She's vital, this woman. I need her fire, and I am the one with dragon blood, go figure. I drop into myself to tap into my telekinetic energy, but I am still empty.

I need to recoup my energy to get us out of here. And she...she needs to rest. I let go of her flesh and drop my elbows on either side of her shoulder. "You need to recover from my ministrations."

I move away and she snakes her arms around my shoulders, "Don't go." She flicks out her tongue to wet her lips. My gaze falls to her swollen mouth, down to where streaks of red mark her creamy skin. "You are not used to being used so harshly."

"I... I have a confession."

My shoulders lock, my muscles tense.

She blows out a breath. "You hurt me and...I"—she squeezes her eyes shut—"I...I want more."

"What?" I blink.

She swallows, then opens her eyes and locks her gaze on mine. "You asked me to take what I need from you Doc. This...this is what I need. The pain, it pushed me to the end of my tether, into a zone I have never been before."

"The high that comes from the endorphins released by the pain." I firm my lips.

"I felt completely in my skin for the first time." Her breath quickens and her pupils dilate as if she's reliving the climax. She doesn't need to. As long as I am here, I intend to bring her to orgasm again and again, until she begs me to stop, and even then, I'll wring more pleasure from her body. But first, "You need to get back your energy, Red. I should leave you alone for a little while." My dick throbs inside of her.

"Uh...but your...your..."

"Cock?" I supply helpfully.

Color flushes her cheeks. It's the single most enticing thing I have seen. My dick thickens, stretching her further, and she gasps.

"Say it."

She shakes her head.

I glare at her and her breath hitches.

I raise an eyebrow and she gulps. "Cock" she sputters, and the color flows down her neck, spreading over the trembling skin of her breasts.

She's a fresh canvas spread out before me and I want to mess her up so badly. She'd take every single depraved thing I do to her and reflect it back to me. She is the culmination of everything I have faced in life. My redemption. My salvation. My mate. *Not that. Everything except that.* I can't allow my darkness to taint her. But I can take her to heights she's never experienced before.

She jerks her chin toward my crotch, "Your cock has other plans."

"What can I say? I am an alpha Fae. My sexual appetites are beyond that of humans. Mix in my dragon blood and that makes me needier than shifters…and I am horny for you, Red." So not a good idea to say that aloud. My dick thickens further, tightening in the tiny space of her channel.

Her pussy clamps down on my flesh in reflex.

My hips jerk and my shaft slides deeper into that sweet heat of hers. My groin hardens; my balls draw up. "Ah, fuck, I am coming, Red."

I drop my forehead to hers, and my cock twitches with such force that I wince. My flanks contract and I shoot streams of hot cum inside of her.

Her arms come around me, and I am aware of her holding me, rocking me. *How strange.* I am the Dominant, the one supposedly in control, the one who caused her pain, yet here she is soothing me. She runs her delicate fingers down my spine, and I shiver.

What is Red doing to me? My thigh muscles uncoil, my shoulders relax, and just for a second, I allow myself to taste what she is offering. Unrestrained comfort. Softness. A delicate sense of warmth. It's like coming home…and the thought constricts my heart. She is everything I need, and I shouldn't get used to it.

My knot loosens, and I move back, sliding out of her.

The mixture of my cum and hers gushes out from between her legs.

"Let's get you cleaned up."

22

Alice

He rises to his feet and pulls me into his arms. He carries me as if I don't weigh anything...and while I am human, I have curves. Baby fat, I've always thought. Maybe it's the kind of extra pounds that will come off when I get older? To my dismay, the curves have only rounded out, given me an hourglass figure that has attracted male attention. It's the bane of my existence. And my breasts...they seem almost too big for my body.

I hunch closer to him, trying to support the ample roundness against the planes of his chest.

"Whatcha doin'?"

I sense him peering down at me as he walks toward the door at the far end of the room. "Ah, nothing." Blood rushes to my cheeks. It was almost easier when I didn't have to talk. It took away the onus of having to justify my tastes. It took away choice. My shoulders sag. I want to hand over control of my body to him. Let him decide what I want, what I like, what brings me pleasure, how much pain I can take.

Maybe that's why he wants to gag me next time? So I can simply focus all of my attention on him?

"I can hear you think, woman."

"Right," I grumble under my breath.

There's no hiding anything from this man, and strangely, I don't mind. I mean, I should be angry, right?

I should, at least, put up a token protest at how he'd simply taken what he wanted from me, commanded my body into the positions that best suited him, inflicted the kind of pain I had never experienced before, only to deliver the kind of orgasms which...*uh!* My body still remembers.

I rub my thighs together, and liquid pools between my legs.

"Hmm, you curious about what else I can do to you? How many orgasms I can wring from you before we leave here?"

Yes.

Yes.

"No. Of course not."

"Liar." He chuckles, and the sound is so rich, so male, so damn confident that it's a turn-on.

My nipples pebble and my breasts are squashed against his chest so I am sure he feels it. He grasps me closer, then steps through the entrance of what turns out to be a bathroom. There's an old-fashioned tub under a large window, a shower cubicle on the other side, and in between, a large sink. Oh, yeah, and towels and soaps line the shelves. "Do the Fae Corps have many of these safehouses?"

"We have eight of them spread around the world in strategic locations."

"And we are definitely safe here, right? You did say that there's a security net around the space, but what if he manages to infiltrate that?" A shudder runs down my body. Boris had snatched me from a gathering where most of the Fae Corps were in attendance. Then he'd almost sold me. My throat closes.

"Look at me, Alice."

I raise my gaze to his.

"He can't get through the security system without my being aware of it."

Doc lowers me to the side of the bathtub. I can't stop staring at him.

The fact that he'd almost died sinks in. The thought of losing him... My shoulders tremble. He makes to straighten, and I grab hold of his arms.

"Hey." He squats in front of me. "You are safe with me."

I nod. And that's the problem. I feel safe *only* with him. Everything that happened in the last few days has brought home the knowledge of just how woefully inadequate I am. How weak I am...a human in this world filled with Fae and shifters and monsters like Boris.

He snaps his fingers, and my gaze darts to his face. "You are not listening to me."

Hell, that dominating tone of his voice. So commanding, so sure of himself, I want to throw myself at him and ask him to take care of me and protect me always.

Does that make me weak? Maybe.

Am I wrong in thinking this? Probably, but for just the time we have here, why can't I give in to him? Let him command me, allow him to protect me, and I want that. So badly.

I take in a deep breath.

"Yes, Alpha." I bow my head.

I sense him start. *Huh?* He's the one who told me to call him that, right? And it felt correct to do that just now. It felt good to acknowledge that he is my Master. And it doesn't feel degrading to acknowledge that. It is I who give him permission to be in that position of power. I place my trust in him and wait...wait. The moments tick on. A drop of water plops from the tap, and the sound echoes around the space, tugging at my already stretched nerve endings.

I don't dare raise my eyes, don't want to break whatever this is that has us cocooned in its heart. This strange intimacy formed in the aftermath of what he's done to me. Taken me and slapped me into submission, knotted me and made me come. I had fallen apart in his arms. Had responded to the dominance in his voice, his need to see me break, to mark me, claim me...and he had. The wounds at the base of my neck tingle, and I sneak up a hand to touch the furrowed flesh. *Ow!*

"It hurts, eh?"

Of course, it does... Only I don't mind it. The pain keeps me anchored, allows me to focus on myself, on him, on his touch that feathers over my skin. Every part of me vibrates with a strange energy. Every single pore on my body is open to receiving him, to sensing him, to him. Just for him. I take in a deep breath, and that dark, edgy scent of his fills my nostrils. My head spins, and I sway.

"Hey." He grips my shoulder, and I tremble. "You're shaking, Red."

No kidding.

He hasn't expressly forbidden me to speak this time, and yet I prefer not to. I can say 'No' to him anytime, but I haven't. I don't want to resist him…or refuse him any longer. The fact is, the way he had taken me had surprised me. He had used the pain to get through all of my defenses and give me the singular most intense orgasm of my life…all of that crashes over me.

I am not ready for this.

Not ready for how vulnerable it makes me feel. Like I have exposed myself, stripped of all my defenses, to him. Shown him what I am. Someone who wants to be possessed. Owned. Broken by him. Joined to him. My thighs spasm. My shoulders jerk. *No way. I choose now to have a meltdown?* I open my mouth, and a gasp escapes me. Tears knock at the backs of my eyes. *What's wrong with me?*

"Hey, babe, stop." He rises on his knees and wraps his arms around me and pulls me close.

He tucks my head under his chin, rubs my back in slow, soothing circles, and I hiccough. He's big and massive and solid.

His heat curls over me, the touch of his skin so soft. The planes and muscles that coil under it so hard. I bury my nose in the crook of his neck. The scent of mint and cinnamon, laced with an edge of darkness that is uniquely Doc, fills my senses.

He drags his fingers over my hair, tugging at the strands. My scalp tingles, and a wave of lust coils in my belly. *Damn.* All of the emotions come crashing over me again, and I sob in earnest. *Nice one.* I am falling apart in his arms, conforming to the stereotype of an ex-virginal, weak, helpless, human female. Everything I have striven not to be.

Maybe I fought too hard.

Maybe what I am inside is someone who wants to be taken, protected, fucked, and knotted.

Maybe that's what I have been fighting—my true nature. Another sob wrenches out of me.

I curl my fists against his sides, wrap my legs around his waist, and let the tears fall. I cry my heart out, and he lets me. I am not sure how long we stay that way. When I stir, he loosens his vice-like grasp from around me. "Feeling better?"

His voice rumbles up his chest. The vibrations sink into me, soothing, calming. His rubs his cheek over my head, and his touch is so gentle that my heart stutters.

I nod, not trusting myself to speak. If I do, I might have another break-down, and that's not what I want, not right now at any rate.

"Let's get you in the bath then."

He shifts his weight back, and I refuse to let go.

He rises to his feet and carries me with him. I cuddle closer, allowing myself to bask in his warmth. In that secure feeling that comes from being carried.

This man had caused me pain, he'd torn into me, penetrated me, knotted me without telling me exactly how different that experience could be, and now he's the only one who can soothe me.

He places me in the bath then leans over, supporting my weight with an arm around my waist. He reaches out with the other, and I hear the water run in the bathtub. He straightens and hums under his breath. The vibrations that resonate through his chest warm my skin, heating my blood. The steam from the water shimmers against my back. Some of the tension drains from my shoulders.

"I am going to step in."

He slides into the tub behind me, in a smooth move that leaves me blinking. His entire body submerges into the tub and some of the water spills over the side. He lifts me up and turns me around then settles me over him so I am straddling him. Then scoops water over my back, whis-pering his touch over my arms, my hips, the curve of my butt. His fingers brush against my aching core, and I groan. My muscles clench.

My pussy quivers.

I am still sore.

He'd split me into two and put me back together again. It sounds really sadistic when I put it that way, but I enjoyed it. The thought of Nolan taking me and knotting me again…a shiver of anticipation tugs at my nerves.

Moisture pools in my core.

Yep, he was right. I am more masochistic that I thought. Apparently, my body likes the pain he can inflict on me and craves the pleasure that is sure to follow. I am getting addicted to him, and it's wrong. He's going to spoil me for anyone else, and I am going to worry about that later.

His fingers brush the cleft between my butt cheeks, and I shiver. He drags his palm to my pussy, swiping the edge of it over my folds. A lick of fire sears my core. Another moan wheezes out of me.

"That whine of yours, Red… I could almost forget that you are human."

Is that a compliment? Not sure. And honestly, I don't care. Just as long as he touches me, caresses me, smacks me again.

I rub my melting core into his groin.

His muscles tense, then he takes a breath, and his shoulders relax. "I know what you want, Red, and I am going to give it to you."

Please. Please. My chest heaves.

"Just not yet.'

What the hell? I try to turn, but his arm is heavy around my shoulders, holding me in place.

"When you are ready, that's when you get what you deserve."

Huh? I am hurting inside already. I am sore yet needy. I am horny and aching and —

"Not enough, Red. If I always give you what you want, as soon as you ask for it, it just spoils you."

So what's wrong with that?

"That's not what we want."

There is a hushed tone to his voice, that tinge of dominance that makes goosebumps pop on my skin. That alerts me that he is back in his Master mode and I am his slave. His property. His to take. And he's right. I don't deserve it yet…but I want it, I do. I whine, not caring that the sound that escapes me is closer to that of an animal in heat. Maybe it's him, his presence, his nearness that brings out every primal instinct in me.

I tighten my thighs around his waist, and he lifts me with his arm under my hips. Cold air hits my butt. A second before he slaps my ass.

"Ow." I cry out. *What was that for?*

He spanks my left butt cheek, then the right, the left, the right.

Ow, ow, ow. That hurts. My skin tingles. The moistness of my skin only amplifies each touch. Makes each slap singe and sizzle and—*oh! So that's what the bath is about? Taking it up another notch, is he?* And I'd thought he was being considerate for my welfare—*ouch!* He smacks me again, and my belly flutters.

Moisture gushes from between my legs, and I moan. I can't possibly find this exciting; I mean, it hurts, all right? So there's no way it should turn me on, but tell that to my body, which writhes in his arms. Tell that to my pussy, which quivers and weeps to be filled by him. Tell that to my heart, which yearns for his touch, his kiss. Is it possible to want someone to ravish you so completely? To have him break you even as he tenderly soothes you? *Please. Please.* I say the words over and over in my mind, drop my neck until my forehead is pressed to his chest. The water level laps up between us to wet my breasts, and I shiver.

He rubs his big palm over the stinging skin of my butt, and my core shudders. I swear there's a direct connection between his touch and that secret core of me that aches for him. For his turgid flesh to sink into my melting pussy and fill me with his cum.

He drags his thumb down to my clit and tweaks the bud. I moan and raise my head only to hurl it back down against his chest. Why doesn't he just take me and put me out of this misery? *Why is he torturing me?*

"Shh."

He thrusts his thumb inside my channel, and I all but come apart right then. He slips in a second finger and a third and…*oh! Damn.* My belly clenches. I dig my fingernails into his thick shoulder muscles. It's too much, too little. Not enough. I lean back and sink down onto those fingers. His thick fingertips brush that sensitive part inside of me, and I groan. Moisture gushes out from between my legs.

A quaking starts at my heels and works its way up. My back arches, my breasts shudder…*damn, I am going to come.* That's when he pulls out his fingers. I cry out, raise my head and lock my gaze on his.

He smirks. "Glad to see you are back to your feisty self, Red."

23

Doc

She bares her teeth and snarls at me. How cute. This little human shows me her true colors. I knew there was a feisty female underneath that shy virginal façade she's been holding on to all along. I peel back my lips and snap at her, and she blinks, then her lips turn down in a pout. I want to lick those pink rosy lips, and bite down on her mouth. I want to eat her up, consume her whole. I want to absorb her into myself, merge my skin with hers. I want to break her, rut her, protect her...*the fuck?* "What am I going to do with you?"

"You can feed me for one thing, you jerk." Her stomach growls on cue.

"So back to speaking now, are we?" I smirk.

"Thought you wanted me to shut up and play the role of your willing slave." She flutters her eyelashes and the skin above my chest throbs.

Huh?

How is it possible that I have a visceral reaction to something that's so blatantly a feminine trick?

She wrinkles her nose, and I can't stop myself from bumping mine with hers. "You're a handful, you know that?"

She frowns. "You mean I am not what a virginal human is supposed to act like?"

"I was going to say a submissive pet, but that, too." My lips curve up, and I don't stop myself. Okay, so I am going to seem smug and satisfied, but *hey, I am allowed, right?* At least for the next day. My throat closes.

I rise to my feet so suddenly that she squeaks and grabs my shoulders for support.

Water flows down and sloshes over the side of the tub, but I don't care. I step over, still cradling her—*fuck, but she's tiny, yet such a handful and so right for me.* She deserves a home, a family, warmth and laughter, none of which come naturally to me.

Being a soldier of the Fae Corps is all I know. The heat that comes from taking on an opponent in a fight is the only time I have let myself feel. The adrenaline rush of a surgery well done when I save a life…is the only time I am allowed to feel alive.

This gorgeous, sensuous woman in my arms? She brings out my protective nature, yet invokes the darkness inside of me.

When I am with her I want to act out every depraved fantasy I have ever carried inside of me. I want to break her and find out what makes her tick; want to kiss her, seduce her, fuck her and consume her. I want to rip out every single barrier I have built around my heart and show her just what she means to me…*and you corrupted her.*

It's what I do best. Mark everything that I encounter with my own brand of degradation.

I reach behind her for one of the folded towels on the shelf. Grabbing it, I drape it around her.

"Get dressed."

Her forehead creases in a frown, and she opens her mouth to speak. I shake my head, narrow my gaze. She bites down on her lower lip but doesn't say anything. *Thank fuck.* If she had, I might have lost my battle with that part of me that insists that I throw her down and rut her all over again. The band of skin over my heart twitches again. I rub my chest, and her gaze drops to it.

She reaches out to touch me, and I pull back.

I lurch away from her and her confusion is so intense that I sense her discomfort coming off of her in waves. I almost turn then, to reassure her...almost.

But if I do that there is no telling what is going to happen next.

And you weren't thinking of that when you were slapping her ass, or when you marked her throat?

If I tear off the towel and turn her around, I'll see that gorgeous reddened flesh of hers, feel her wince as I trace my fingers over those lashings. *Fucker. Get out of there before you take hurting her to the next level...*not counting the ways in which I have already changed her...taken her virginity, introduced her to my perverted world of kink, where there is no justification for my actions, except that I enjoy it.

That I get off on it.

That I want her to feel every inch of my flesh as she comes.

The scent of her arousal seeps into the air, and I quicken my steps.

"Doc, why are you angry?"

The fuck if I know.

I don't turn. Walking to the open closet I grab a towel and dry off, then fling it aside. It hits the wall then plops to the floor. I am making a mess of the place, but whatever. No doubt the Fae Corps will be sending someone along to check up on us. They'd have tracked me in my crazy headlong rush to get to her, then here. Which means I have very little time left. *Yeah, asshole, so you already reminded yourself.*

There's a strangled sound from behind me.

I turn to find her standing at the entrance to the bath still wrapped in the big towel, her dark hair in wet strands around her pale, heart-shaped face.

Her pupils are dilated, her breathing harsh. Color floods her cheeks, and *fuck*, my dick twitches. My balls harden.

Bending, I drag on a fresh pair of pants.

Not bothering to towel my hair, I walk to the exit. "Get some clothes on before you catch a cold."

"Doc, wait."

Don't turn around. Don't stop. I pause at the doorway. "What's up?" I glare at her over my shoulder.

"You're acting like a bear with a sore head."

"Something is sore, and I promise you that it's not my head, at least not this one." I rap my knuckles against my forehead.

She snickers. "Bet you are nowhere near as sore I am."

"If you are asking for sympathy, you're not getting any here, considering you all but begged me to take your virginity."

"I did, and you know what...?"

I straighten my spine.

This is when she says that she regrets it, that she should have never asked me to fuck her, that I should have warned her just how brutal I was going to be with her...speaking of which, why hadn't I? Had I meant to scare her away? Probably. Had I succeeded? Maybe. Only one way to find out. I turn around and glare at her.

"What?" I wait for her to say it. *Say it.*

"I don't regret one second of it."

I stare, then a chuckle cracks out of me. "You should be scared of what else I can do to you. I thought I could rein myself in, but obviously my control is nowhere near as good as it should be." My gaze drops to the broken skin on her neck.

She raises her palm to touch the wound and winces. "Are we going to talk about this?"

No.

"I warned you about what it meant to give yourself up to me."

"You did." She drops her arm and tucks it against her side, favoring it.

Fuck this, I hurt her and in a way I hadn't planned for. What was I thinking about claiming her? I hadn't been thinking at all, not since I'd met her. I'd been too carried away in the heat of our coupling. I had told her she could trust me and I had betrayed her.

I rake my fingers through my hair.

I shouldn't feel sorry for her. I shouldn't. I take pleasure in hurting, remember?

I want my slaves to beg for release...but with her I need more. I need her for my mate. Need to tie her to me, hide her away forever, so no one else can come near her again. And that's so fucking wrong. She deserves a man who is capable of giving her the love, the tenderness she needs, which she's not getting from me.

I initiated a fledgling mating bond, but there's still time to break it.

"This is all you are going to get from me, Red."

Her gaze widens. "You mean—" She gulps.

Why does she have to look so stricken? She knew the score. She knew what she was getting into. Hell, I thought I knew what I was getting into.

Just another Master-slave relationship, just a way to get off on my kink, to indulge my need for pain, that's all it was. So why am I sure that my world just shifted? That nothing can be the same again? Why does my chest throb like my heart is breaking into many pieces... because I've decided to let her go?

Because I tasted her sweet essence, buried myself in that hot, succulent pussy and felt complete fulfilment. I knotted her so deeply that it changed not only her, but also me? The thought of pumping her up once more with my cum, filling her up with the evidence of arousal and making her climax again and again, sends a surge of primal lust raging through my blood. *Fuck.*

Her glance drops to my crotch, and she swallows. "Ah...you're, you're..."

"Horny."

"So why not just make love to me again?"

"I didn't make love to you. I fucked you. I knotted you."

"You claimed me, Doc." She wraps her hand around her throat, covering the evidence of the wound that gapes at her neck.

Fucking hell, she is going to scar, and those won't fade, for she isn't Fae or a shifter. She's human. It's clear for all to see that she belongs to me. Only to me.

And I must let her go.

My chest burns. I slap a palm to the skin above my heart and sway. I fucking sway. My legs weaken, my thighs spasm, and a searing weakness grips me. "The fuck?" I swear and grab hold of the doorframe for support.

"What's wrong?" I hear her voice as if from a distance.

Guess I am not over whatever that bastard Boris hit me with, and the mating bond I initiated is reacting with the poison that still lingers in my system from the hit.

I stagger against the door, curl my fingers into fists so my nails dig into my palms. Pain slices up my hands, and I use it to center myself. There's a touch on my shoulder, the scent of jasmine that floats in the air. She is here, next to me. I swerve away from her, so her hand falls away. She stiffens. I've hurt her…again. But it's for the best.

"Stay where you are."

She obeys me, *thank fuck*.

I take another step forward, and another. My chest aches once more, before the pain recedes to a dull throb. I straighten my spine and walk up the corridor. "Get dressed and come to the kitchen."

I stalk up the corridor on legs that are almost steady. If you don't count the thick shaft that strains between them. My cock is not happy to be separated from her for even a second. I crack my neck.

"You sure you're okay, Doc?"

Her voice is hesitant, and I sense her lingering in the doorway. "I won't be if you make me wait any longer."

24

Alice

"Don't make me wait, Red. Turn that way, Red. I want to whip your ass, Red." *Gah!* Bossy is too tame a word to describe the man.

He's a force of nature who blew into my life, ripped me out of every single innocent fantasy, and plunged me headlong into the kind of sinful experiences I hadn't ever thought could be real. The smarting skin of my backside confirms the truth.

I blow out a breath as I examine the contents of the closet. There's only men's clothes. *Of course!* And all of them are in just one color. Black, light black, darker black, bluish black, oh, yeah, a pale, worn-out...you guessed it, black.

I pull out a pair of boxers—okay, it might almost make do as shorts.

He hadn't worn any underwear, had he? *Hmph.* Guess he was worried about poking his way through the cloth when he extended. *Ha!* Did that happen to Fae males when they masturbated? Or did they only extend the way he had when he was inside me, knotting me? A trickle of liquid creeps down from my pussy, and I squeeze my thighs together.

Not good, don't think of that particular part of the Fae anatomy, but hell you could forgive a girl for being inquisitive, right?

You wouldn't begrudge me my curiosity on how he looks fully aroused, fully extended as he runs his big palm over his cock then cups his balls with his other hand, right before he grips my head and yanks me close and pushes his turgid shaft between my parted lips. Saliva pools in my mouth.

He'd taste salty and musky and laced with that dark edge that is Nolan. Funny that only when I think of being in such an intimate situation with Doc do I think of him as Nolan. Perhaps it's because I don't know him at all. I am aware his perversions, and the taste of his cum, and how he can fill me up to the brim, and the sting of his palm as he whips my ass...I am intimate with the man in the carnal sense, and my instincts say that behind all that kink is a man who cares, perhaps too much.

Beneath all that dominance is a sensitive soul who's been hurt, enough that he needs pain to feel again. Yeah, and I am the woman who's going to redeem him, eh? That's the classic mistake committed by females who are attracted to alpha-holes.

We think we are the ones who can reform them, that by giving ourselves up to them, we'll somehow soften them up enough to make them want to...commit?

But he claimed me, right? Doesn't that mean something? *Holy hell, he claimed me.* The breath wheezes out of me.

The wound on the junction between my neck and shoulder burns on cue. *What does that mean?* That I am his mate? Can a human be a Fae... well, a half Fae, half dragon man's mate? And...he came inside me. He pumped me up with his cum, so I could be pregnant?

My legs weaken, and I grip the door of the closet for support. *Okay, stop. Take a deep breath. And another. No use getting ahead of yourself.* Obviously, everything that happened—the kidnapping, the almost being sold off, giving up my virginity to the man I wanted to...all of it is taking its toll. And on top of that, pun intended there, this discovery that I have a kinky side to myself, that I am turned on by Doc's sadism...*well, admit it, that's a lot. A freakin' lotta stuff to take in.*

My heart thumps. My pulse rate surges. "Get ahold of yourself."

The sound of my voice echoes through the space. I dig into the closet, pull out a T-shirt and shrug it on. It slides down almost all the way to my knees. Then scrounge around and yank out a pair of pants, then another. Okay, this pair is closer to my size. In fact, they're small enough to belong to a woman. *Huh?*

I step into them, and they're still loose at the waist. I bend and fold up the legs, and it's not a bad fit. *Has he had a woman here? Why had I assumed that he's never brought any other female here?* Or perhaps it belongs to someone else who'd stayed here on another mission. After all, this is a safehouse used by all the Fae Corps. Either way, I need to find out.

Adrenaline laces my blood. I slam the closet shut, then swivel around and cross the floor. He'd better not have brought another female here.

Hell, he's not going to look at anyone else, no woman, that is, except me. A part of me warns that Doc won't appreciate my being this possessive... his rule that I cannot make any demands, remember? But no, this is different.

This is about showing him that I am not a pushover female.

I am his, and I want him to acknowledge it. But how do I do that? Maybe to begin, I try to understand what exactly makes Doc the way he is. This seething mass of contradictions that annoys me, and yeah, intrigues me.

I've never met anyone who turns me on this much.

Who infuriates me until I want to fling myself at him and shake some sense into him, and yeah, lick him from head to toe. My belly spasms, and my pussy trembles. No winning with him, is there?

Even when he's not with me, the dominance of his presence surrounds me, pulls me, tugs at me, makes me miss everything he did to my body.

The fabric of my pants brushes the skin of my butt, and pinpricks of pain dance over my skin. Little sparks of lust go off in my brain, and my scalp tingles. Clearly, whatever he did to me has conditioned my body into wanting more...more of what he did to me.

My breath comes in pants, and I hurry my steps. I need to see him. *Now.* Must go to him. *Now.* By the time I reach the door, I am already running.

I sprint into the corridor when a crash from the other side of the house reaches me.

25

Doc

"The fuck is wrong with me?" I glare at the dishes scattered around me.

Okay, so I am not handy in the kitchen. I've known enough to get by over the years, had picked up the basics from one of my foster moms, the only one who'd been somewhat maternalistic with me.

Then, her husband had changed his mind and become envious of the bond that had sprung up between her and me. He'd dumped me back at the home where I'd met Tristan. Protecting Tristan, who had been younger than me and weaker, had given me purpose. I have always been big for my age, growing into my almost seven foot height by the time I'd turned twenty-one. Guess the dragon genes had to manifest themselves in some form. I can't shift, never have developed wings or sprouted scales, or claws for that matter.

My Fae genes are more dominant, so I have all the outward appearance of a Fae male—ears extending, canines elongating when experiencing high emotion. The Fae Corps has tried their best to modify our behavior by teaching us techniques to control the outward signs of stress. None of which have worked. The only way I can relieve tension? Pain. And it's not the kind inflicted on me either.

It's the sound of a woman groaning, screaming, begging...no, not just a woman. Her. Her whines. Her moans, her asking me to take her, to let her come, to fuck her. And I hadn't. I'd held out, allowing her the relief she'd asked for, but not seeking my own. And I am paying the price.

Every part of me aches.

My chest hurts, and it's not just from the wounds recently inflicted on me. The fledgling mating bond writhes against my rib cage, reminding me of what I've done.

I've initiated the mating connection, and does she realize what that means? How long before the bond locks into place, becoming permanent in the way of mates? *Is this what I want?* I raise my hands, not surprised to see they are trembling. It's why I had dropped the dishes in the first place. "Fuck."

I kick the pan on the floor, sending it crashing against the wall. I drop into myself, looking for that curl of telekinetic energy that will reaffirm what I am—a powerful Fae male.

The man who had been unable to stop her from being kidnapped. I'd saved her, only to claim her.

I'd knotted her, and she had withstood every one of my demands.

She had submitted beautifully, but she hadn't hidden just how different the entire experience had been for her. How often can I subject her to my perversions? I had asked her to trust me...fact is, I don't trust myself to hold back the next time.

Every time I look at her the need to protect her overwhelms me.

If something were to happen to her, I'd never forgive myself. It's why I need to do the right thing and return her before the mating bond locks into place.

I should take her back with me and walk away.

I'll make sure to bury myself in my world of singular focus—the surgery, the missions with the Fae Corps, and the occasional pain-slut who'll weep for me, in whose tears I'll find redemption. *Not.* I'll never find the peace I crave. The sense of completion that had swept over me when I had knotted her, balls deep in her with my dick extended and locked behind her pelvic bone and filling her up with my cum, even as I bit down on her neck and tasted her blood and claimed her over and over again.

Once more. Just once more can I taste her?

"Doc?"

I stiffen. Every muscle in my body goes on alert.

She shuffles closer and the mating bond twangs. The damn thing writhes under my rib cage.

"Nolan?"

Her voice is closer, just behind me. If I turn, I'll see her face, those beautiful eyes, those plump lips that I want to caress, right before I plunge my tongue into her mouth and sip of her essence. Absorb her into myself, meld with her, fluid bond with her all over again when I make her climax, then bury my dick balls deep in her.

"You okay?"

Her voice is soft; a tinge of worry laces it. She shouldn't care for me. That will only make it all worse when I break the bond between us, when I leave her.

My jaw tics, my shoulders bunch. "Stay away, Red."

The scent of dragon smoke rends the air.

Fuck.

Her presence excites that hidden part of me that has always been buried deep inside. The tips of my ears tingle, and I am sure if I had a mirror my reflection would throw back an image of an out-of-his-mind-with-lust male. *Control? Ha, what's that?* When she's around, I want nothing except to slap her butt, then stuff her asshole with my dick, fill her to the brim, and make her come again. *Is that the way out?* To bring her to climax, satisfy myself, but *not* knot her again? *Not* complete this compulsion to seal the mating bond I initiated? I scowl.

"Are you hurting?"

I chuckle, "You have no idea."

"I can help, you know."

"No." I set my jaw.

"You're so stubborn." She walks around me to pull out a fresh saucepan.

"What are you doing?"

"Making us breakfast...or is that lunch?" She glances through the window to look outside. It's dull, gloomy, and dark clouds cover the sun. *Wonderful.* Just the kind of weather I like.

"I told you I was going to feed you and I'll do it, woman."

I stalk to her and reach for the vessel, and she turns around at the same time. Her chin collides with my chest, her breasts flatten against my waist…she's tiny. Just a handful. Just the way I like. I can maneuver her body into every position I want. Expose the parts of her I want to take, lick her, make her come, make her submit. My groin hardens. My dick leaps forward, and she squeaks.

I lean back then bend my knees so I can peer into her eyes. "Are you blushing?"

"No." She swallows. "Jeez, can't a woman just be allowed to think without you getting all in her face about it?"

Her gaze skitters away, only to come right back to my groin.

Hmm. So she is as obsessed with my body as I am with hers. Thank fuck. It settles something inside of me, and it shouldn't, not when this situation between us is temporary. I grab her shoulders, then jerk my chin over my shoulder. "Sit."

She sets her jaw, her lower lip thrust out. That sexy pout…I can't stop myself. I grab her and toss her over my shoulder.

She yelps, "What are you doing?"

"Making sure you obey me." I slap her butt, on the right cheek, on the left, right, then left again.

"Ouch, ouch. Please. Stop."

Blood thuds at my temples. The sound of her voice, her soft curves writhing against my harder body, brings out the contrast between our bodies. She fits me. She was made for me. Her scent saturates my senses, replacing the pain that coils in my chest. A pleasant numbness sweeps over me. The sound of my palm hitting her ass—through the fabric of the pants which have to go—heats my blood. The feel of her curves shifting, her flesh pulsing, her thighs twitching… This, this is what I crave.

Being able to focus on something outside of myself, watching her react to my ministrations, seeing how she responds to me. Making her ache for me. This is what I want. I slap her butt one last time.

"Nolan, ow, it hurts."

Need to gag her, too. After she eats.

I stalk back to the table, hook my foot around a chair, and pull it out, then dump her on it.

She grunts in pain, then turns those big green eyes on me. She opens her mouth, and I frown at her. She subsides. Not that she's going to stay quiet for long, "You need to be taught a lesson, Red."

Her gaze widens.

"Yeah, exactly that kind of a lesson." I prop my fists on my hips, "and it's only going to get more painful the longer you take to learn to obey, you get me?"

She bites her lower lip and my cock twitches. I want to feed her only one thing, and it's not the food. Heat races through my blood. Best get her to eat before I lose track of the reason I'd let her out of the bedroom.

I point at her. "Stay."

26

Alice

How can I refuse him when he's back in that alpha-hole Dom mode?

Maybe I am getting used to his commanding ways, because I lean my chin on my hand and prepare to enjoy myself. Watching him is no hardship. He's a beautiful hunk of a man. I let my gaze run up those tight flanks, the roll of muscles that move as he stalks forward, that massive back with planes that undulate under his skin, which is surprisingly soft to touch. His sweatpants rise low on his hips, showing off that crazy 'V' shape of his. He hasn't bothered to pull on a T-shirt. Not that I am complaining or anything. I can't think of a better way to pass my time than by drinking in the sight of those massive shoulders which seem too massive for his trim waist. Those thighs...powerful and lethal weapons, built for speed, and he can use them to hold me down with barely any effort.

There's something primal, almost otherworldly about how he is built. He's one heck of an alpha, and so far out of my league. I lean forward in my chair, "What am I doing here Doc?"

Only when I hear my words do I realize I've spoken aloud.

"No talking." He snarls.

Really? I huff out a breath.

He glances over his shoulder, and I frown, entreating him with my eyes to just answer me for once.

"Right now you are here to eat what I cook for you."

I pout. *Please, give me a little more credit okay?*

His gaze takes in my features, and the planes of his face seem to soften. "You know why you are here. I was hurt, I knew I was running out of power, and I needed to get you to safety. I chose the nearest location I could get to in the condition I was in."

"You are still in pain."

He glares at me, and the tightening of the skin around his eyes promises punishment for the fact that I did not shut up as he'd asked. I gulp, then press my lips together.

A vein throbs at his temple.

That can't be good. My throat closes. *Guess my response didn't satisfy him, huh?*

"To answer your question" he grumbles, "I am almost recovered."

What a grouch. A brooding hunk of a man whom I want to throw my arms around and hug tightly. Don't think he'd appreciate that though, not in the mood he's in.

He rubs his chest, then turns back to the task at hand. "I am getting stronger by the second."

Is he trying to convince himself? Is there something more I can do to help him? Something to take the edge off...that is, if he'd let me.

"Stop thinking so loudly."

I start. Does the man have eyes at the back of his head or what?

"Comes with being Fae, and then top it off with my shifter blood, I can promise you that I can track you without looking at you."

And then there's the fledgling mating bond that connects us. The ball of heat twangs against my rib cage. I rub my chest.

Does he have something similar to show at the other end of the connection? Almost as if my thinking of it had activated it, the pulsing warmth extends out.

It zooms up my spine to my crown, then whooshes out of me, and I gasp.

He stiffens, then turns around to stalk over to me. "What did you do?" He comes to a pause on the other side of the table.

I shake my head, not daring to speak.

His eyes glow, blue with tiny golden sparks, his pupils flash verti-cally...*Oh! Wow. When he does that it means...he's turned on, right?*

He leans across the table. I scoot back, but he's too damn tall. Too fast. He lunges forward and grabs the nape of my neck. "Don't go around messing with stuff you don't have any control over."

Right. If only he knew.

I want to follow the fledgling mating bond to find his presence on the other side. I want to understand what it means to be joined to this man in such a unique way.

As a human, I've only heard about what it means to be one half of a mated pair—to find your soul mate in the true sense, where you are connected on the psychic plane, where you are able to tune into the other person's thoughts, can sense them like they are your other half, because that's what they are. Because that's what he is, the other part of me.

The breath rushes out of me.

I stare at him, unable to take my eyes off of him. Unable to fathom exactly what it is that I have stumbled upon. The truth. That's what it is. I am his. His to command, to do with as he wants. I am his submissive. I lower my gaze and nod.

I sense him stiffen. His gaze bores into me, but I don't dare raise my eyes. How can I, after the enormity of what I have just realized? Why have I been fighting the inevitable all along? I was born to be bound to him. It is the logical conclusion of the chemistry that has been building up between us for so long. And I want this. I want him. I want everything he can do to me.

I swallow down the cry that threatens to bubble up.

Tension leaps off of him. His brow furrows.

What is he thinking?

Will he notice how much things have shifted for me? It isn't about him, or his dominance, or how much he wants to control.

This...this is about finding the nurturer in me.

About coming to terms with that part of myself I have run away from for so long, that I have been scared to acknowledge. That I am submissive, but not to anyone else. I only want one Master. Him.

I want him to be my world.

Only to him will I surrender. I want to carry the child that would be the natural conclusion of our union. My womb shudders with the realization. It's all so intrinsically linked. It isn't about giving in, it's about discovering what I truly want. Us.

"You've gone pale, Red."

His voice washes over me. He flattens his palm over the nape of my neck and massages the skin there, brushing his fingers up and under my hair so it grazes my scalp. All of my nerve endings flare at once, and I shiver.

I can't speak, and not only because my alpha asked me to stay quiet. It's because I don't trust myself to make much sense. I tilt my head until my hair comes in contact with his arm and I rub up against it.

Some of the tension drains out of him.

Something in the language of my body must have reassured him, for he pulls his arm away and straightens. Turning, he crosses the floor back to the counter, and I hear the sound of him moving around. I stay where I am, trying to process everything. Why do my shoulders feel lighter? I rub my palms over my face. I seem to be coming out of some kind of hibernation, suddenly realizing my entire life so far has been me fighting against my true nature.

Maybe that's what happens when you are a lone human among Fae; you have nothing to benchmark yourself with except for the bloodthirsty Fae. And all the Fae women I know...they are fighters, physically much stronger than me, and I have been compelled to try to match up to them. All along I have been trying to be something I'm not, when the answer has always been inside of me. *Philosophical much?*

I chuckle, and the sound is soft under my breath. But my alpha hears it.

He brings a plate heaped with sandwiches—there must be at least ten on that plate—and sets it in front of himself. Then lifts my chair, with me still in it, and carries me around to set it down next to him. *Right.* Of course, he's strong, but this...it takes the awareness of his power to new heights. I gulp and keep my gaze on the food. He snatches up one half of a sandwich and holds it to my mouth. I bite into it, and *hmm, it tastes good*. Tart and pungent and sweet all at the same time. I lick my lips and finally raise my eyes to his.

"Good?" He takes a massive bite of the sandwich, then offers me the other half.

I nibble on it. He coaxes me to eat a little more, then polishes off the rest of the food. *Uh, okay,* he has a big frame in which to pack it all away, but still...I seem to have underestimated his appetite and in more ways than one.

He stands, carries the plate to the sink, then returns and lifts me in his arms. Should I protest? *Nah.* It's kinda nice to be carried. His touch is gentle as he cradles me.

He walks out of the kitchen to the bedroom we'd left earlier, crossing to the bed, where he lays me down. "Scoot over, Red."

Huh? I stare. Doesn't he want to, you know, fuck me now?

"You need to get some sleep." He nods toward my face.

I frown.

"You have dark circles under your eyes, and you look ready to keel over."

Well, thank you very much. I huff and move over.

He gets into bed and pulls the covers over both of us. Then he closes the gap between us, scoops me up, and deposits me on his chest. *What the...?* Thud-thud-thud, the beat of his heart fills my ears.

I rub my cheek against the cut planes of his beautiful chest.

The heat of him cocoons me. Tension drains from my shoulders. I've felt his dominance, sensed his perusal as he monitored my response to his ministrations, but this...the way he winds his arms around me and tucks my head under his chin, then runs his wide palm over my back, soothes me.

There's something so incredibly sweet...and sexy to be cradled by this giant of a man. My breathing steadies and darkness pulls me under.

A sound drifts over me. A strangled shout, and the terror in it. The pain cuts through me and my eyes fly open.

It's dark around me; the light coming in through the unshaded windows lights up the room with a dim glow. THUD-THUD-THUD, *is that my heartbeat?* No, not mine…it's his.

I straighten and almost slide off of his chest. I touch his shoulder, and my palm connects with moisture. He's sweating, perspiration running down his throat, his chest. He mumbles under his breath, and I can't understand the words.

"Nyet. Otets. Nyet." *He's speaking in Russian?*

He thrashes his head to the side, his throat cords flex, and his chest heaves. His biceps bulge as he grips the sheets.

"Alpha?" I lean over him, unsure what to do.

"No. Please." He groans, and the sound rips through my heart.

My chest hurts; the ball of heat in it twitches and shudders. Grief comes down the mating bond, barreling into me with such force I gasp. I can sense him…red, white, swirls of gray; all of it melds together and falls apart, then swoops down on me, and I scream out. Sweat slicks my palms, adrenaline laces my blood.

"Don't do this." His biceps strain, his chest heaves.

I touch his cheek. "Doc."

He shakes off my touch.

Another guttural cry leaves his lips, and my heart stutters. I can't just stand by while he's in anguish. There must be something I can do. Something. "Nolan." I touch his shoulder.

His eyes fly open, and I freeze.

Vertical pupils glare at me.

His nostrils flare. He tilts his head, and that's when I notice his ears have extended. He peels back his lips, showing those sharp, pointed teeth, and I gulp. He looks like he is lost in a nightmare, caught up in whatever turmoil haunts him. I pull back my hand, and he snakes out his arm and grabs my wrist.

"Ouch."

I try to yank my hand from his grip, and he snaps his teeth. I flinch. He takes in a breath, and his chest muscles seem to expand. His biceps flex. His eyes are fixed on me. Blue glitters with those strange golden sparks…does that mean he is about to do something I am not going to like?

"N…Nolan?"

He sits up, and at the same time, tugs at my hand. The next moment, I am draped over his lap. He's sitting cross-legged, I realize.

He wrenches my arm behind my back, and I stutter. "Let me go."

He doesn't reply, and somehow his silence is worse than his anger. More lethal than the dominance implied by his sheer presence.

He grabs the waistband of my pants and shoves it down with such force that it rips. Holy hell. Is he that strong?

He scoops up my hips up just enough to shove down my pants until they are looped around my ankles, effectively tying me and holding me in place.

I gulp and try to turn, but he places his other arm on my back and, *damn it,* once more I can't move.

Once again my ass is exposed, and he palms my naked butt cheek.

The width of his hand is hot and hard as he cups my flesh. A squeal bubbles from my lips.

I squeeze my eyes shut and force myself to stay still.

If I struggle, he'll only make it worse.

My belly clenches, my pussy quivers. I am already wet. And waiting… waiting for him to bring his hand down on my butt and spank me. He pulls his palm away, slides down my body. His hot breath sears the curve of my butt.

No, no way. He isn't going to do that.

27

Doc

Her flesh is so soft, so sweet, so juicy, I need to taste it. I need to wash away the bitterness that fills me. The acidic tang of regret that fills my mouth, I need to get rid of it.

I drop my head and bury my fangs in the curve of her butt.

She screams. Her entire body jerks.

Her hips wriggle, and she tries to shove away from me.

"Stay still."

The sound of my voice cuts through the haze of red that fills my gaze. The taste of copper infused with that honey of her arousal sweeps over my palate. She stops struggling. The fact that she obeyed me with no protest...*fuck*. My balls grow heavy. I flick out my tongue and lick the skin I marked. Her hips twitch, and a whimper trembles from her lips.

The sound goes straight to my cock. *Ah fuck.* I can't stop, not now. Not when she's bared for me, in my lap and vulnerable. So beautiful.

I trace the curve of her hips over to the cleft between her ass cheeks, and she groans.

I lick her all the way to the moist core of her pussy. She shudders, and moisture trickles down from between her legs. I lap it up. I am already hard, my dick straining to rub against her core. A ripple runs over her spine. The throbbing in my chest grows. It mirrors the beat at my temple, at the tips of my ears, even in my fucking balls. *The fuck happened to my control?* All thought of holding back leaves my mind.

I lick and suck my way up to her back hole then ease my tongue inside. She writhes under me, and every muscle in her body trembles.

I straighten and place an arm over her back, holding her in place. "Relax, Red."

I bring down my left palm on her butt cheek. *Whack.*

She shudders but doesn't say anything. Doesn't move. I follow it up with another slap to her other ass cheek, *whack-whack-whack.* I stop at ten. She's panting heavily. So am I. Her breasts tremble against my thighs. I slip an arm under her chest and tweak her nipple, pinching it until she groans. Then drag my fingers back up to her shoulder, down her spine, all the way to the apex of her legs. Her pussy is melting.

"So fucking wet." I breathe out the words, and she moans.

Scooping up her cum, I smear it over her back hole. Then I move her to the bed and place her on her knees. Placing my palm flat on her back I urge her down. Once she is balanced on her elbows and knees I stretch over her.

She turns her head, and her gaze finds mine.

"You ready for me, Red?"

Her chin quivers, but she nods.

Her pupils dilate, her irises going that light green until they almost resemble colorless pools of water.

I bend down, then cup the back of her head. Angling her face toward me, I kiss her, nibble on her mouth. She opens her lips, and I swipe my tongue inside.

A groan wheezes out of her, and I swallow it.

I reach between us, and slide one finger inside her back hole. Her lips part, and I absorb the moan. Slipping an arm under her, I pinch her clit, and she shudders. I slide another finger inside her back hole, and stretch her further.

She moans, and her back brushes against my chest.

Her entire body trembles. The vibrations echo the pulse that throbs at my temples, at my wrists, in my balls. I slide my fingers in and out of her then add a third and a fourth.

She jerks and sinks her teeth into my lower lip. The pain lances across my spine, and my dick throbs.

I angle my lips and sweep my tongue inside her mouth, sucking from her, taking in her essence. All the while I increase the speed of my actions, yanking my fingers in and out of her. She wriggles and writhes under me, but I don't let go. The scent of her arousal deepens, and the intensity with which I pump my fingers into her only increases. A trembling grips her body, she is so close to coming. I slide my hand under her and pinch her clit. A strangled whimper leaves her lips, and I absorb it with mine. I kiss her deeply, plunging my tongue inside her in imitation of what I want to do with my dick. The climax races up her legs, her butt, her spine snaps back, and inner muscles clamp down on me, and that's when my dick hardens to the point of pain.

I tear my mouth from hers and survey her flushed face, her fluttering eyelashes. Another shock wave in the aftermath of her climax rolls over her. She moans, then cracks open her eyelids. Her almost colorless irises fix on me, a dazed look in them. Heat pools in my chest.

"I need to be inside you, Red."

I part her ass cheeks then drag my dick across her back opening.

28

Alice

He's going to fuck me in my other virgin hole.

He's not going to stop until he's filled me up completely, taken me everywhere, anchored me with his dick and penetrated me with that thick, big cock. My thighs tense; my stomach flip-flops. His tongue slides over mine, sending little jolts of pleasure down my spine. His shaft stays poised at my back hole—the head is hard and rigid and throbbing, and there's no way I can fit it all in, no way. I shake my head, wanting to speak, wanting to say something, but my throat is too dry.

All the moisture in my body seems to be concentrated in just one place, between my thighs.

I honestly hadn't thought it would be possible to come with him simply shoving his fingers up the one place that I would never have thought would be an erogenous zone...*jeez, I can't even say it to myself.* Another jolt in the aftermath of that climax shudders through me. He lets go of my pussy, and I feel bereft. Goosebumps slither over my skin, and I push out my butt, straining to meet him… I mean, I don't really want his monster cock in my back hole...*do I?*

A whimper escapes me.

If he slides that thing inside of me, in that tiny space…he's going to break me. A gasp catches in my throat.

The hard muscle between his legs slithers in the groove between my ass-cheeks. Every muscle in my body coils, every instinct is focused on that turgid column that throbs against my butt.

Leaning down, he licks my lips. I quake.

"Let me in, Red."

Gah, I want to, I do, but…what if it hurts and I can't bear it? What if…what if I like it? What if he makes me come all over again? I swallow, then jerk when the head of his cock nudges my back hole. My shoulders spasm. My muscles tense up.

"Look at me."

He clicks his tongue, and my gaze swivels to his face. I hold on to those glittering blue eyes. Sparks of gold and flickers of indigo coalesce in those beautiful irises, which snap vertically just for a second. Mesmerizing. Feral. So damned masculine. I can't look away.

"You want this, Red."

Yes.

"You want to find out if you can take this completely new experience."

Kinda…okay, I admit it. I am curious. More than curious. I am greedy for the reactions he can wring from my body. I can't wait for him to show me what I need.

"You'll let me take your virgin ass, and when I'm done, you'll ask for more."

His voice sinks into my blood. Insistent. Confident. The dark edge of its dominance seduces me. Pinpricks of fire flare in my belly.

I open my mouth, and he sweeps his tongue in at the same time he lunges forward and the head of his dick slides in. Too much. Too soon. He's filling me up. Fierce pain cleaves through me, and a scream bubbles up. But he absorbs it. He stays where he is, the hardness of his flesh pulsing, stretching, urging me to take him.

I suck in a deep breath, and the scent of him fills my senses.

His eyes hold mine, and I allow myself to drown in them. The warmth from his body washes over me, and I groan.

The dominance of his personality pins me down, and I... I give in. Something inside me dissolves. A resistance I hadn't been aware I had been holding onto disappears. A warmth creeps over me, and my muscles relax.

He tilts his head, and the tone of his kiss changes...sweet, almost gentle. His nostrils flare, and I am sure he's sensed the change in me, that he is aware I want him, that I trust him, that I am secure in the knowledge that he knows what I want...even if I am not sure...yet.

His grip tightens on my butt, and then he pumps his hips, and his dick lunges forward, filling me, thrumming inside of me. White heat lances my nerves. My brain cells seem to all fire at once. I'm hot and cold at the same time.

The breath catches in my throat.

He tears his mouth from mine, and his chest heaves. Color burns high on his cheeks.

"You're so fucking tight and hot and..." His gaze narrows. He swallows, and his throat moves. "What are you doing to me?"

Hey, that's my question too!

The ball of heat in my chest burns as if in answer. *No, not that.* The mating bond doesn't mean anything, *does it?* Not when he hasn't acknowledged that he's marked me...or that he wants me as his soul mate, that he is mine. *Mine.*

The mating bond twangs, and heat strums down my spine to coil at the base of where my back meets my butt, where he's joined inside of me.

His forehead creases; the skin stretches around his eyes.

Still holding my gaze, he leans back and pulls my hips up, so my butt is up in the air.

I am balanced on the front of my shoulders, and every part of me has been stretched and caressed and spanked and...and loved. *Huh? Is this his way of showing how much he cares for me?*

A nerve throbs at his temple, and he sets his jaw.

Ouch, now what?

"I am going to make you come, Red. I am going to make sure you have the most intense orgasm of your life."

29

Doc

This woman…she gets under my skin, and without saying a word. All she has to do is look at me with those big green eyes, *and fuck me,* but I'd do anything for her. Don't tell her that, okay? Don't hint either about the insanity that grips me, this compulsion to see her come apart under me, to give her so much pleasure that she'll remember me even after I have left her.

The shard of heat embedded against my rib cage throbs.

My dick extends. My groin tightens. I grip her hips and yank her to me and slide all the way in.

She throws back her head; her breasts thrust forward. I let go of her and wrap my palms around each of her breasts. The flesh fills my hands, just right. Soft, and yet her nipples pebble, pushing into my skin. I squeeze her breasts, bringing them together, then drag my fingers up to pinch each of her nipples. At the same time, I pull out of her just enough to cause friction, just enough for each ridge of my hardened dick to scrape against her sensitive walls.

She wraps her fingers over my wrists and presses down with enough force for her fingernails to dig into my flesh.

The white streak of pain travels up my arms and straight to my groin.

With a roar, I thrust forward, and my cock nestles home. She screams and throws her head back so it hits my chest. The vibrations ricochet over my body, straight to my dick. My balls draw up, and I hold on, hold on, waiting for the telltale signs of her climax. For the scent of her arousal to deepen, her body to tremble. Letting go of one of her breasts, I drag my hand down to her pussy and shove three fingers into her cunt. In-out-in, the wet squelching noises as I assault her channel fill the air, fill my senses, drown out all other thought.

"Come for me, Red. Now."

She cries out, and a gush of liquid squirts out from between her legs, overflowing my hand. The walls of her pussy clasp my fingers even as her butt contracts around my throbbing shaft. My vision tunnels, my cock weeps to extend, and I can't. Not yet.

I clamp down on my dick, hold back my shaft from extending all the way so as not to hurt her.

Her little body goes limp, and I wrap my arm around her shoulders, holding her to me as she collapses.

I pull out of her, then turn her over on her back.

Planking over her, I lick the tears that wet her cheek. My balls grow heavy. I can't hold back. *Fuck.* I nudge my thigh between her legs, then ease my dick into her soft pussy. Soft. Wet. Beautiful. My thick flesh slides right in, and I groan.

"I need you, Red."

She whimpers and opens her eyes.

Another tear streaks her cheek, and I lick it up.

I grit my teeth and my biceps spasm with the effort of holding up my weight. I stay where I am. I shouldn't do this, not so quickly after I had taken her, but say that to my dick which strains to be deeper inside of her.

Her breathing grows shallow, then she tilts up her chin. She wriggles her hips just a little, just enough for my cock to sink in deeper.

I groan, and she whimpers.

"Take all of me in Red."

I thrust forward, and my balls slap against her tender flesh. Color rises up her shoulders, flushing her throat, her cheeks. I drag my arm down her hip and loop one leg, then the other, around my waist.

She grips my hips with her thighs and presses up.

The thick, seething muscle that is my shaft extends. My balls harden and swell, my fangs elongate, and the tips of my ears tingle. I lunge forward, knotting her behind her pelvic bone.

A whine spills from her lips, and the sound of it pushes me over the edge.

I close my palm around her throat, squeezing. Her gaze widens, the color fades from her cheeks, but I don't loosen my grip.

She strains against me, her breasts pushing up. She brings her fingers around my arm digging her nails in, tearing at my skin.

I sense her pain, her need, her complete ruin, and I can't stop. Can't let go of her.

Her legs thrash, her spine rises off of the mattress, and her heels press into the backs of my thighs.

I tilt my hips just another millimeter, enough to slide my swollen cock further into her weeping channel. My knot expands, and a shudder grips her body. She opens her mouth but no words emerge.

All of her muscles tense, her pussy clamps around my dick, and my control snaps. My balls draw up and I come, shooting streams of cum into her.

30

Alice

His dick pulses, and the hot jets of cum bathe my womb. The waves of my climax roll over me, once, twice... I lose count. I try to take in a breath and can't. Darkness tugs at the edges of my conscious mind. A cold feeling rolls in my chest. Helplessness grinds down on my shoulders, pinning me to the bed. Terror infiltrates my thoughts. Then his fingers loosen, I gasp out, and draw in a sweet breath, then another. Oxygen rushes down my parched throat, fills my burning lungs, and starbursts of white and blue drum against my closed eyes. The climax roars up and crashes over me. My back jackknifes off of the bed and I crash against the wall of his chest.

The heat of his body holds me immobile just as much as his cock spears me to the mattress. A second climax sweeps over me, leaving a trail of liquid honey in its wake.

The ropy muscles of his back tremble; his glutes flex. He's still knotted inside of me.

A heavy feeling overwhelms me, and it's not just the weight of his presence which throbs around me like a living, breathing thing.

The hot fireball in my chest thumps in sympathy, the beat picked up by the aching flesh between my legs.

The wound where he bit me seethes.

My entire body is one colossal ache, and yet the aftershocks keep pulsing through me. I sense him move, then he licks the claiming mark. The pain instantly drops to a low hum. *What the…?* I crack open my eyes, and the world tilts. I moan and squeeze my eyes shut.

"Stay still, Red."

Yeah, not like I am going anywhere.

Not after the way he'd…he'd ripped into me, torn me apart, made me climax… again and again. I mean, I have lost track of the number of orgasms I have had, can't get over how he fucked me in the ass and then knotted me.

A shudder rolls down my spine. The pressure behind my eyeballs grows, and a trembling grips my arms, my legs. Can't stop the tears that roll down my cheeks. But can you blame me?

My body is not my own anymore. It belongs to him.

He's possessed my soul, my emotions, occupied every part of me. Everything I am is gone, swallowed by the man above me. I'll never be the same again. Never.

A hiccough swells my throat, and I try to swallow it down.

Only I end up making a strangling kind of noise. Now he's going to think I am having a meltdown or a panic attack of some kind—not far from the truth. But I don't want him to know the effect of what he's done to me. I want to keep this last part of me to myself.

My hands drop away to my sides, and I curl my fingers into fists. Another tremor jolts my body, and I grit my teeth, trying to find some balance, some composure. Something that will help me cope with the emotions swirling around in my head.

He licks my throat, tracing what must, no doubt, be the marks of his fingers, and the pain recedes further. He slurps his tongue down to the swell of my breasts. It's strangely intimate. Another hiccough swells up, and I can't stop myself from shuddering.

"Shh, let me take care of you."

He sweeps his tongue down to my breast where he licks a swollen nipple. Oh! That's nice. My muscles unwind and the throbbing in my breasts recedes.

He continues to lap his way down my front, over to my belly, then thrusts his rough tongue into my belly button. I wriggle a little.

"Did that hurt?"

I shake my head.

"You may speak now."

Guess I had been waiting for him to give me permission, and I hadn't even known that, eh?

I sense his gaze on my face; okay, so I still have my eyes closed. I don't want to open them and meet his eyes, and yes, I am embarrassed. And I shouldn't be, considering this man knows my body so intimately. A blush flushes my cheeks.

"Tell me what you are thinking."

His voice lowers, but that pushy tone presses down on my chest, and honestly, I can't stop myself from saying, "That you know better than I do about what brings me pleasure."

He stays quiet. But a slight lightening of the space around confirms what I am sensing—that he...he is pleased with my response. A flush of something like—*wait, what? No way*—like satisfaction fills my chest.

He moves, and his shaft slides out of me with a wet sound. I sense liquid gush out of me, his cum, mine. Goosebumps slide over my skin, then I squeak, for he cups my pussy and smears the liquid over my cunt, rubbing it into my belly over my waist. It's sticky and gooey and so soothing. *Oh!* I sigh.

"That's it. Let go, Red."

Not that I am fighting or anything. A cool sensation seeps into my blood. My arms and legs tremble, then the rough edge of his tongue licks the curve of my belly and I stiffen. He sweeps his lips over the strip of skin just above my pussy.

No, not again.

I cringe a little...not that he hadn't given me pleasure, not that he hadn't sent me flying into that space between pleasure and pain where I don't exist anymore, at least not physically. All that had existed then was my spirit that soared and reached for the edge of white-hot satisfaction that only he could push me toward.

"I am not going to penetrate you again. I just want to soothe the parts I have ravaged."

I gulp. Those words shouldn't have made my pussy quiver, but they do. My sex clenches, and heat flushes my cheeks. Again. What's happening to me that just his words make me want to sit up and beg for him to bring me to climax again? I shake my head to clear it.

"It's okay to be confused; it's worse if you keep all of your thoughts to yourself."

I jerk my chin. *Fine, I get it. Best to talk it out, but I can't. Not yet.*

He pauses a beat, then I sense him lower his head again. "The dragon blood in me allows me to secrete an anti-swelling agent in my saliva which will help me soothe your aches. As does rubbing my cum into you."

Oh, okay.

"I already told you, you may speak, Red."

I nod. "Th… thank you."

"You're welcome." There's a slight almost-smile in his tone.

I open my eyes just as he lowers his head and licks my pussy. *Oh. Oh. That's so good.* Whatever he's doing, he can continue with it. I stay silent, not daring to even breathe.

It's a testament to how far gone I am in this world of his that I don't see anything strange in what he told me. That it is more animalistic than human. He caused me pain so it makes sense that he can soothe me, right?

He licks over the folds of my pussy, down to the opening of my channel, where he curls his tongue inside. *Ah!* The soreness subsides. A warmth tingles over my legs. One more swipe, all the way up to the nub of my clit, and a hum rolls up my throat.

He chuckles.

"Don't stop…" I breathe. "I mean, please don't stop."

"You bet."

He parts my legs then scoops up my hips.

"Wha?"

My eyelids flutter open in time to see him drop his head, and he licks my back hole, sliding his tongue inside, and the burning softens away.

A pleasant tingling sensation sweeps up to my core.

He pulls out his tongue then eases it in again, and again.

A melting sensation fills my belly. Oh, wow, it's the singular most amazing thing my body feels, outside of those orgasms he gave me, of course. A whimper escapes me. "You…what are you doing?"

"Lie back and enjoy it, Red."

His voice rumbles over me, and all of my muscles go slack. I can't protest any more or pull myself away, because truth be told, him lapping me all over with that magical tongue of his…he's covering me in his essence and I've never felt closer to him. Cherished. Seduced. My insides melt into a gooey mess that mirrors the stickiness coating my skin.

He swipes his tongue up from my back hole, up to the opening of my channel, then all the way up to nub of my clit. My entire body hums. My sex spasms, and liquid pools between my legs. He licks it up, and I groan.

He goes at it licking, sucking, curling his tongue over my clit, down inside my slit, then sliding it into my back hole, and the climax creeps up over me. Warmth, heat, lust, all of it closes over me, tugs at the edges of my subconscious mind. I am dimly aware of him rising above me, then he kisses me. And it's different, sweet, tender, and the taste of him and me floods my senses and pulls me under.

I struggle against the sleep that tugs around at the edges of my mind. "The pants I wore, who did they belong to?"

"If that's an oblique way of asking me if I've brought any other women here, then the answer is no. I've never felt the way I do about you with anyone else."

Oh. Hadn't expected that. I yawn and my limbs grow heavy. I am too relaxed to stay awake.

"Get some rest."

The next time I open my eyes, I am alone.

31

Doc

I stand on the decking outside the kitchen and cup my hands around the mug of coffee I brewed.

I had left her asleep, her skin flushed, her hair tousled.

She'd barely moved, tired out from my handling of her body.

Her breasts had risen and fallen, the sheets almost slipping off to reveal the valley between her breasts, and I hadn't been able to tear my gaze away from it. I had almost stayed back. Wanted to run my fingers over the curve of her jaw, down the soft skin of her throat to where her breasts rose. I had wanted to tweak her nipple, trail my fingers down to the indentation of her waist, to where the glistening lips of her pussy waited, and that's when I had torn myself away from her.

I take a sip of the coffee. It's scalding hot, burning my tongue. I wince. I deserve the pain. After everything I've done to her…I hadn't been able to hold back, I had not only knotted her again, I had claimed her a second time.

I had woken up from that nightmare at my lowest. I hadn't dreamt about my father in years, but the images had transported me straight back to the hell of my growing years. I had come out of it hurting and angry and needing to hurt... and she'd been there.

My very own redeeming angel.

Soft hair, curvy hips, melting cunt that had called to me to bury myself inside and forget the world. I couldn't resist palming that beautiful backside, shoving myself into her virgin back-hole and making sure no part of her had been untouched. And then I had choked her. My fingers squeeze around the cup and some of the coffee sloshes over the side. I had cut off her breath, without any care for her needs. I had stayed true to my nature. I had taken. And she had opened herself up to me completely.

I had made her come, but at what cost?

A few seconds more and I might have...I squeeze my eyes shut.

Deep down I'd known it would come to this. That it was only a matter of time before I lost myself so completely that I'd betray her trust. My being at my lowest, and not quite in my head was no excuse.

I had successfully put her life at risk and there was no way I would let that happen again. I was wrong for her, the proof was irrefutable. It's not just that I am afraid of opening up to her. When I am with her I am afraid of losing control and hurting her.

I need to get her out of here and back to Singapore. It was a mistake to bring her here.

I drop into myself and tug on the telekinetic energy. A whisper of the blue-green force inside of me rises to greet me, then dissolves. I am heal-ing, but not fast enough. And that's a surprise. I have never been incapaci-tated for so long. If someone were to attack her now, I wouldn't be able to protect her either. My belly tightens. I have been selfish keeping her here.

There's a sound behind me, and I stiffen. The scent of jasmine floods the air. I turn to find her standing at the entrance to the decking by the large double sliding doors. "You're awake?"

I take another sip from the coffee.

"You left me."

I tilt my head. "I didn't want to disturb you."

I turn to walk past her, but she doesn't step aside.

"What's wrong?" She frowns up at me.

Everything. I can't afford to feel for you. I need to save you...from the biggest threat to your wellbeing... me.

I set my jaw. "Let me through."

She shakes her head.

"Don't challenge me, Red."

She bites her lips, "Talk to me, Doc. Tell me what you are thinking."

If only it were that easy.

"You don't want to know."

"Try me." She swallows.

And I am tempted, so tempted to tell her everything I am feeling right now. How I am falling for her, and then...then what? What have I got to offer her but this twisted mind? This body that needs perversions to survive? My emotions that need her pain to get off? My soul that wants to hear her scream and choke? To take her captive and hide her away from the world until I have filled her belly with my spawn? *No.* My breath catches. *What am I thinking? Letting the beast inside me come to the fore?*

"Step aside, Alice." My voice is rough, and I infuse a thread of dominance through it.

She winces; her shoulders tremble. The shirt she's wearing, my shirt, slips off of her shoulder, baring the pale skin of the curve of her arm. It's right that she wears my clothes, my scent, that she comes for me again and again. I take a step forward, closing the distance between us. She tilts her head all the way back to look at me. Her green eyes shine with adoration... *love?* She's falling for me, too... *Damn.* I can't allow it. Will not let her do this to herself.

"Last warning, Red."

"I don't understand why you are so angry. I did everything you wanted, didn't I?"

I hesitate, choosing my words carefully. "You were too pliant."

She frowns. "I don't understand."

"I get off on the resistance of my victim."

"But...but...I thought you wanted me to submit."

"The more you defy me, the greater my enjoyment." My gaze skitters away. "You are too weak."

She gasps and my chest hurts.

"You gave in too easily, Red." I raise my head and survey her pale features. "Who'd have thought under that human façade you are no better than the pain-whores who hang around the Fae."

She sways, and I want to reach out to hold her close, to comfort her and tell her I am only doing it to hurt her. I don't mean any of it. That she is beautiful, the only woman I have ever wanted to take for my own. That I never want to let her go.

"Nolan..." She presses her knuckles to her cheek.

I stiffen. My name from her lips sends a rush of desire swirling down my spine and I shove it away. "Don't call me that."

Her voice quavers. "I don't believe you."

"I never say what I don't mean." *And the lies keep piling up.*

She swallows, and a pulse beats at her throat. She throws her arms around herself. "I don't understand why you are doing this, but you are wrong. Whatever is between us—"

"—should never have started. I should never have touched you."

"Don't say that." She wrinkles her brows.

"Oh, I am just getting started." I peel back my lips, making sure to show her my canines. She doesn't even blink.

"You don't scare me."

"You don't"—I bend my knees so I can peer into her eyes—"do anything to me."

32

Alice

I rub my damp hands over the shirt I had pulled on and which comes all the way down to my knees.

Nolan...no Doc's shirt.

I should have showered when I woke up, but hadn't wanted to wash away the scent of our mating. The chord in my chest tightens; the wound at the curve of my shoulder itches. I refuse to show how much discomfort I am in. I swallow and my throat hurts, though that pain is fading quicker than expected too.

Truthfully, it isn't as bad as I had expected. That tonguing thing he'd done to me all over my body—my cheeks grow hot as I think of it—had rejuvenated me.

I had woken up filled with hope, feeling more rested than in a long time...except for the flickering heat tucked against my rib cage. The one I am not going to tell him about. The one that twangs whenever I am near him or think of him. Or when he is in a heightened state of emotion as he is now.

"Why are you pushing me away?"

His lip curls. "We were never close enough for that."

He turns and prowls toward the sink.

He's dressed in fresh combat pants and a black T-shirt that clings to the breadth of his shoulders. His hips undulate with that slow, sliding walk that I equate with him. What is it about these Fae men that makes them so macho and stubborn? The most alpha-hole, the most perverted of them all is him.

"Doc."

He doesn't respond, just rinses off his mug, then proceeds to place it on the drying board.

Such a homey task. So not what I would equate with him.

But then, I wouldn't have thought that Doc's tastes would run to such sadistic tendencies either. Oh, I had guessed he was kinky, given I'd seen him leaving the club famed for sadomasochism in the city, but the extent to which he needed it, and not just on a sexual level...had taken me by surprise. He requires that intensity of pain to feel anything.

Only he won't admit it aloud.

It should frighten me, or at the very least disgust me.

My pussy clenches, and my thighs squeeze together.

Fact is, that edge of harshness to his every move, that danger that clings to his shoulders, the sensation of that rough, callused palm connecting with my ass arouses me. And when he'd choked me, I'd been afraid...and I'd also felt closer to him. Is that strange? He had saved my life and if I were to die, there is no other way I'd rather go than knotted to him. That is the ultimate submission I could give him, and I want more of it.

More of what he could do to me.

I want everything he can give me.

I want it enough to goad him. What would happen if I disobey him? A shiver of anticipation tugs at my nerves.

I twist my fingers together, then walk into the kitchen. *Can I do it? Can I?* I gulp, then bite the inside of my cheek. One chance, that's all I have. Before this day runs out, he takes me back, or we go our separate ways.

He straightens, and the sheer size of his physique, the dominance of his presence, just how powerful he is, how dangerous he can be, all of it hits me.

He's already shown me what he can do to my body…how much I turn him on at the physical level. Can I push him over the edge, so he cracks enough to reveal what I do to his soul?

I cross the floor, my bare feet making no noise on the floorboards. Reaching the table, I slide up on it, then draw my legs up. Reaching down, I pull off the shirt. He stiffens.

I'm sure he's scented my nearness.

My stomach flip-flops; my heart hammers. *Am I really going to do this?* I draw in a breath, then part my legs and begin to play with my pussy. I run my fingers through my folds, then insert a finger into my channel. A shudder runs down my spine. I am still sore, and the skin is so sensitive that a lick of pain flares up my belly. I slide my fingers in and out, and a moan wells up my lips.

He swivels around so fast I gasp.

My fingers tremble, but I don't stop myself. In-out-in, I continue to fuck myself with my fingers. His gaze drops to the triangle between my legs. His nostrils flare. A fine sheen of sweat glistens on his upper lip. His chest rises and falls, and he takes a step forward.

I keep shoving my fingers in and out of myself. *Keep going, don't stop.* I press my tongue into my cheek.

He cants his head, and his ears flick back. The tips elongate, and *why is it that I find that so sexual?* I rake my gaze over his chest to his crotch, and *hello!* His monster dick strains his pants.

"What. Are. You. Doing?" His voice is soft, so controlled.

I frown. That's not right. He's turned on, all the signs clearly point to that, so why is he acting like he doesn't see it? Like he doesn't want to acknowledge what I am doing to him, how much he wants me? Well, too late to stop now.

I drag my fingers up my clit, over my belly, no doubt trailing cum all the way up to the valley between my breasts.

Goose bumps flare over my skin; my insides quiver. I raise my fingers to my mouth and suck on them.

He leans forward on the balls of his feet, his gaze fastened to my lips. "Stop."

"Don't you like it?"

"You forget you are not in control, I am."

"Whatcha gonna do about it…Nolan?" I twist my lips.

His mouth firms, his gaze narrows, and my breath catches in my throat. He takes a step forward, and another, until he's standing in front of me. Another step, and he'll be between my legs and that hard shaft of his will brush my core and… Liquid pools between my thighs, and I fight the urge to squeeze them together.

No, this is about teasing him, seducing him, making him see how much he already misses me, reminding him how much he wants to be inside of me, right?

His hands curl at his sides, his shoulders go rigid, the cords of his throat stand out, and I almost lose it then. *No, not yet. Stay where you are, stay.*

"Tell me, Doc." I jut out my chin.

He moves so fast he blurs.

He grabs my thighs, pries them apart, then shoves four fingers into my pussy and I scream. The makings of an orgasm radiate out from my core. He plunges in and out, in and out. The climax surges up my legs, and I gasp and pant, my vision going narrow. *What's he doing to me?*

I can't come that quickly, can I?

He tears his fingers from my pussy, and the orgasm recedes. *What the—* a whine spills from my lips.

One side of his lips curls in a smirk. "Nothing. I am going to do nothing about that, Red." He walks around me and heads to the door. "Get dressed, we're going home."

I blink, then swing around so my legs dangle over the table toward the side facing the door. "But…but you can't do that."

He pauses at the exit and shoots me a look over his shoulder.

Right. I bring my knees up.

"You can't teleport."

His features harden.

"I put in a call to the Fae Corps." His gaze wavers. "They'll be on their way to get us out of here."

My chest squeezes. "You said…we have another day together?"

"Changed my mind." He squares his shoulders.

"I don't want to leave." I hug my knees close to my chest. I sound whiny, and very needy... but...desperate times and all that.

"You broke my rules. You took the lead, you initiated." He drops his gaze to my pussy. "A very bad seduction scene, I may add. Guess what happens to little girls who break my rules?"

"Wh...what?"

"No orgasms for you. You don't get to feel my hands on you, you don't get to have my dick throbbing inside of you. You don't get to kiss me. You don't get to come."

"No." I breathe out. "You can't do that." I squeeze my thighs together. The very cells of my body seem to ache with the distance he's put between us.

"I am...doing it." He taps his fingers on his chest, his tone already bored. His gaze grows distant. "Cover yourself before the rest arrive." He stalks out.

Hold on just a damn moment. Did he just walk away from me? Did he just deny me an orgasm?

I had...had let him spank me, and take me in my ass...and uh, fine, fine, I had enjoyed it, but I need more, ya know?

The ball of fire in my chest stutters.

I had gotten more.

I had received his claiming mark, twice. He had taken me and knotted me as a Fae would only to his mate...but it doesn't mean anything to him.

I reach for his shirt and shrug it on.

The stroke of the cloth over my sensitive breasts, chafing my still sore ass, all of it sends a wave of heat straight to my pussy.

Well, if he doesn't want me anymore, he won't miss me if I leave, right? I slide down to standing, then walk toward the sliding doors. Pushing them open, I step onto the decking. I don't have shoes...this is going to hurt.

I can withstand more abuse than I thought.

Nolan has taught me that much. I can't stop the smile that curls my lips. We'll see what he has to say about this.

When...if he finds out I am missing and comes after me.

I swing my leg over the parapet and drop to the ground.

33

Doc

The fuck was I thinking? I wasn't. Not at all. That's the problem.

I stride away from the kitchen and curse myself.

I had gone there with the intention of feeding her, taking care of her. Trying, for once, to have a normal conversation. 'Trying' being the operative word, for a glimpse of her sprawled on the table with her thighs open, breasts heaving, pussy lips glistening at me…I had almost pushed her back and taken her right there.

Just the sight of that succulent flesh between her legs had me extending in my pants…*fuck.*

Her presence crawls in my blood, her essence fills my chest, the mating bond a sliver of connection between us. Translucent in places, it's just a thread that binds us, but it's enough for me to reach out and sense her presence. Anger and need pulse down it.

Lust crawls down the shared connection, and a throbbing yearning incinerates toward me, burning a path in its wake. I slap down a barrier on the psychic plane to prevent it from reaching me. She's aching for me. She needs me, and I... I cannot, will not go to her.

I hurry my steps and walk to the study. Going to the table at the far end, I snap my fingers, and a hologram appears. I need to talk to someone, but Tristan is away on another of his jaunts with Jess and her younger daughter. Which leaves...not Dante, who's also mated.

Hawke's hologram appears. "Don't make this a habit bitch." He rakes his fingers through his already disheveled hair. "You've disturbed me twice in one night. That's got to be a record, considering you normally refuse any offer of help."

"Shut up, wanker, and get your ass down here."

"Huh?" He frowns. "Thought you wanted us to stay away for another day and give you ah...what was it you said? Some time to figure out what to do with the problem that has arisen? Assuming you have come to some conclusion then?"

"Yeah, I need you to get her to safety."

"Let me get this straight." He stares, "You are asking me to come get you and Alice back to Singapore?'

How dare he say her name, how dare he even think about her? I set my jaw. "Yes."

Hawke laughs. The bastard throws his head back and cackles so hard his entire body shakes.

"The fuck is so funny, asshole?"

"You, dickwad. You."

The blood thuds at my temples. I am going to kick his sorry ass when I see him next. "Shut the fuck up. Just because I can't teleport temporarily—"

"—is all the more reason for you to stay where you are with her and figure out what the hell it is you are going to do with whatever it is between the two of you."

"There's nothing between us." I roll my shoulders.

He shakes his head, "Good luck trying to convince yourself about that load of shit."

"What-fucking-ever," I hold my elbows wide from my body. "And I am taking relationship advice from you? The man who has it bad for a seventeen-year-old?"

"Eighteen…she's going to be eighteen in a month, and I have kept away from her. I am going to make sure I stay the fuck away from her." He sets his jaw.

"Ha, famous last words."

The man has it in bad for Charley, Jess' older daughter, and that is a problem. When a Fae males gets this fixated on a woman, there is only one way for it to end. Badly. As in, he's gotta take her for his mate or else… make himself scarce and never see her face again…and *the fuck am I empathizing with him when I am in the same position?*

Worse… I did the one thing I shouldn't have. I had claimed her and knotted her repeatedly.

"Hold on." Hawke raises his hands, palms face up. "I am not the one who needs kinky shit to get me off."

I grit my teeth and glare at him.

"You tell her yet?"

I curl my fingers at my side.

"Right, so you have…and?"

"I can't believe I am standing here talking to a fucking hologram and laying out this emo stuff."

"For a doctor, you sure are stupid. Did you even study to do what you do? Did you have the IQ to pass your exams and put in the hours to learn surgery…or…?"

"Shut up."

"Right. So no talking about your profession, or about your woman or—"

"Not my woman." I grumble.

"Fine, about the human you rescued. Where did you find her?"

"It was Boris who took her."

"Motherfucker." Hawke stiffens and his gaze sharpens. "And you are telling me this *now?*"

I rub the back of my neck.

He's right. I neglected my duties. I should have called in to them the moment I reached the safe house, should have told them what Boris intended to do. "He was trying to sell her at the auction."

"The global auction for virgins that takes place every month in St. Petersburg?"

"Yeah." I drum my fingers on my chest. "You're right, I should have updated you'll earlier. Should have called it in to Dante, who—"

"—is gonna be so pissed, man, you are so screwed."

I wince and shift my weight. "Yeah…well. I am calling you now, aren't I?"

Twenty-four hours too late, but still…I came to my senses. That has to count for something, right?

"What were you doing all this time?" He scratches his chin, "We lost track of you after you reached St. Petersburg, and before our scouts on the ground could report back, you had surfaced…in the safe house in Belgrade."

"Ah." I thrust my chest forward. "None of your business what happened here."

"Not that I can't guess." He angles his head.

I resist the urge to shuffle my feet. This entire line of questioning is not what I had expected when I'd called into Hawke.

"It's not a secret, that you are one sick mofo and that you have it bad for Alice."

"You done yet?" The beginning of a headache claws at my temples.

"Don't go getting your panties in a twist. Not that I am getting any sleep here, I'll just have to alert Dante and—"

"—don't tell him."

"He needs to be informed of the developments."

"We are safe…for now. But my telekinetic energy is not yet fully functional. I need your help to get us back, then we can tell him together."

"You live too dangerously, Doc."

And that's an under-fucking-statement. I rub the back of my neck.

"You sure you guys will be safe there?"

"There's a screen around the safe house. As long as we don't step out of it, no way can Boris find us…"

The ringing of a siren blares through the house.

"The fuck?" I stiffen.

Alice, it has to be her.

I drop the barrier on the psychic plane, and instantly, fear and pain crashes into my chest.

I gasp and bend over, massaging the skin over my heart.

"What have you done?" Hawke's voice slashes through my head.

"Alice," I gasp out. "She's in danger. She stepped out of the safety net."

"And you can sense her *how*? Did you mate her, motherfucker?"

Yes. The bite of her panic screams through me. My ears pop, my heart hammers, and adrenaline spikes my blood. "I need to go…" I stagger back from the hologram.

"I am on my way, Doc."

Hawke's voice follows me as I stumble out of the study.

Pain whines over my nerves…and for the first time, it's not the kind that makes my blood sing.

It's a different kind of hurt, one that squeezes my heart, makes my chest ache.

All the pores on my skin pop.

A surge of fear races through the bond and bursts over me. It swells my throat and slams into the backs of my eyeballs, almost blinding me.

The world darkens, my head spins, and my legs threaten to give way from under me. Bile lurches up my throat and I swallow it down.

I can't let the fear get to me.

Alice. I flail with my arms, and my hands connect with the frame of the door. I hook my fingernails onto it and right myself. Take a deep breath, and another.

My heartbeat lowers, my pulse rights. I reach out through the bond for her. Her fear leaps forward and nearly suffocates me. I draw in a breath and my lungs burn. The metallic tang of blood fills my mouth, and only then do I realize I am biting my tongue.

I force myself to loosen my jaw.

Draw on that small thread of telekinetic energy inside of me that's beginning to regenerate. Locking in on Alice's location, I pull the energy over me. My muscles tremble. The world tilts around me, and I teleport.

34

Alice

I race through the greenery surrounding the house.

It's strange that we've been here for more than a day and I haven't even bothered to look outside and check our surroundings.

Probably because the alpha-hole had kept me in a sex-hazed state. And no, I can't put all the blame on him either; I had been a willing participant to everything he'd done to me. To how he'd thrust into my pussy and slapped my ass, and to how I'd kissed him back. I lick my lips and the salty dark taste of him fills my mouth.

I can almost imagine the touch of his fingers on my skin, ravaging me, bringing me to climax again and again, and yet he'd turned me down and walked away from me.

He'd cheapened what had been between us to little more than lust, and maybe that's all it had been on his side. *Not. No, it wasn't.* It couldn't have been. It was more, so much more. If only Doc would stop being stubborn and acknowledge it. The thrum of heat in my ribcage reminds me that I had pushed him enough to do that...briefly.

I had made him give in to at least one basic urge: to mate me. And I had wanted it, damn it. I hiccough. Tears fill my eyes, almost blinding me.

I had wanted him to take me and bind me to him so there was no way for him to escape. No…so there was no way for him to let go of me, or so I had foolishly thought. Stupid, stupid woman. He had let go of me all the same, and now… I was spoilt for anything. There was no way I would ever sleep with anyone else. Never allow anyone else to fuck me or spank me or expose my soul in such a vulnerable fashion. I had trusted him. *Bastard.* I had given myself up to him willingly, and he…he had broken my heart.

A sob rips out of me, a trembling grips my muscles, and I stumble and fall, then go rolling down the slope. Over bushes, rocks, thorns that stick into my side. *Ouch.* I bounce off a boulder then another bush and come to a stop with my leg bent under me. A piercing pain sweeps up my ankle, and I groan.

I take in a breath, and dust fills my nostrils. I cough, then shove myself to turn over on my back.

A shadow falls over me. "Well, what have we here?"

The scent of something rotting assails me and I gag. *No, not him. It can't be him.* Boris can't come onto the grounds, can he? Doc had told me that there was a security net all around the safe house…but maybe I broke through it when I fell down the slope?

I keep my eyes shut. It's cowardly of me, but *damn it,* I am not ready to face any other challenge. Not when every part of me aches…for him. For Doc. That jerk who turned his back on me.

"You going to get up, or should I help you, and believe me, I'd love to have my hands all over you."

My eyes pop open.

The sight of Boris' hateful face sends a surge of fear pouring into my chest. I try to breathe, but my throat is too dry. My rib cage compresses, and I am sure I am going to come apart right then. I bite down on the inside of my mouth and taste blood.

"What do you want?" I swallow the urge to scream.

I will not show this man how nervous I am.

He holds out a hand. "Let me help you up."

I scoot away from him, and his gaze widens.

He pulls back his lips, and the gaps in his front teeth are a horrifying sight. A jolt of fear races down my spine. My heartbeat ratchets up.

Calm down. Don't give in to the fear.

I hoist myself to my feet, and my injured leg protests. Red-white sparks flash behind my eyes. I swallow my groan, then thrust out my chin. "I am…up."

"You haven't lost your spine. That's good." His gaze darts past me to the house. "Tell me why he brought you here. What is he to you?"

Everything. I almost say that aloud. *No. Don't tell him anything.*

My instincts scream to hide the truth from him. To not give him a clue as to what had just happened.

"Nothing." I firm my lips.

"Is that right?" He rocks forward on the balls of his feet and the scent of rotting flesh deepens.

I skitter away, but he grabs my arm, *ugh!* My skin shrivels. I raise my shoulder and try to break his grasp, but his hold tightens. I put weight on my hurt ankle , and a fresh burst of pain drums at my temples. I almost sob out.

"So why do you smell of him?"

"I… It's because he brought me here, so obviously some of his scent is going to rub off on me." Please let him buy the story. Please.

"Hmph." He purses his lips. "Maybe you are telling the truth…"

The breath wheezes from my throat.

"Maybe not."

I stiffen.

His gaze drops to my neck. "So how do you explain that?"

Ah, hell. The claiming mark. *Damnit.* Couldn't Doc have held back? *You hadn't wanted him to hold back, remember?* So I can't blame him completely for the mess I am in, except he had pissed me off, and I had walked away and I…I shouldn't have. Why are mistakes so easy to spot in hindsight?

His gaze narrows and I firm my shoulders.

"I hurt myself when I slipped and fell earlier." I raise my chin.

"Don't believe you." He clicks his tongue. "Not that it matters. I am going to kill him and take you." He begins to drag me up the incline.

I struggle, and he yanks me along, and I almost fall.

"No, wait. Don't hurt him. Please.'

"'Don't hurt him, please, spare him.'" He raises his voice to a high-pitched tone, "Isn't that what you mean to say?"

In that moment, I have never hated anyone more than this man. To think, at one point he was the leader of the Fae Corps…I can't imagine Doc ever toeing the line to his leadership.

Doc… I can't let him get to Doc, not in the wounded state he is in. So what if has a swollen head, and other parts of him are rather large and big in size, too…and *hold on just a second, why are my thoughts heading right back to the source of all that pleasure he had given me?*

I can't let this man get to Nolan. Period. I need to distract him, buy enough time for Doc to get help or at least rejuvenate his powers. "I'll come with you."

He doesn't slow down.

"I'll do anything."

He laughs. The air wheezes between his front teeth, and the sound is horrible. A drop of sweat trails down my spine.

"I'll…I'll let you sell me off."

"Not interested" He tosses his head. "You're not a virgin, ergo, you lost your value. You don't mean anything, your death even less."

My stupid, stupid plan backfired. No, I don't regret Nolan taking my virginity. It's just, I need something more to bargain with, I do, but what? "I'll serve you."

His steps slow.

"You can fuck me." *No. No. What am I saying?* I'd rather kill myself first. "I'll be your slave."

He turns to me. "You may have something there…Red?"

I stiffen.

"Isn't that what your Fae Corps soldier likes to call you?"

"How…how do you know that?" A cold sensation coils in my chest.

"I was just in time to witness that very tender scene between the two of you in the kitchen."

"You spied on us?" My skin crawls.

"What do you think? He laughs, making that strange rattling sound. Is it the air escaping between his teeth?

The skin across his face stretches. Clearly, the muscles of his face are paralyzed…or he's had reconstructive surgery done. A whole lot of it.

Enough to leach all evidence of emotion. I'd only heard of how the Fae Corps had hurt him, all but burned him alive. Yet here he stands, fully recovered, thanks to his Fae regenerative powers and of course the surgery; which begs the question, why had he decided to leave the gaps in his teeth?

Is it to add to the overall creepiness of his profile? If so, he is succeeding.

"How did you find us?" I frown.

"I followed the trail. You were bait, and so was he."

"What do you mean?" My stomach churns.

"I kidnapped you to bring the Fae Corps men into my territory where—"

"They are most vulnerable?" My vision wavers and I shake my head to clear it. *Focus, focus on his words.*

"And then all I had to do was wait for one of them to rescue you, and you played your part beautifully in that, my compliments to you."

"So you…you let us leave?" No, it can't be. He'd hurt Doc…hurt but not killed when he could easily have done so.

He tilts his head.

"You allowed him to escape his bonds?"

Boris claps his hands. "Knew you'd figure it out. My aim is never wrong." He points from his eyes to mine. "Knew you'd come through for me."

"So you let us go, then gave us time for what…to alert the others to come?" My heart begins to thud.

"I'll take down half the Fae Corps in one swoop, kill you, then him, then all I have to do is wait for the others to arrive."

"I won't let you harm him." The thought of him getting his hands on Doc while he is still vulnerable sends adrenaline pumping through my blood.

"You and which army?" He tilts his head.

"Someone mention me?"

35

Doc

"Move, Alice."

Even before the words are out of my mouth, she drops to the floor, and I draw on the last remaining source of telekinetic energy inside me.

Wrong, so wrong. If I do it, I am going to combust. I'll go into a negative spiral from which recovery will be much longer. I should protect what little of that source still sparks inside of me. But seeing her with him, seeing the man who had kidnapped her, risked her life, not to mention had tried to kill two of my closest friends, sends rage curling over my skin.

My shoulders bunch and my biceps broaden. I pull on the thin stream of telekinetic energy so it sparks my fingertips, drawing it into a ball, and aim it at Boris.

It hits him square in the chest, then dissipates.

The fuck?

He bares his teeth, and his canines grow. He raises his arms, and tendrils of energy curl over his skin, down to his fingertips which glow.

He raises his palms, and a ball of energy forms and rotates. He throws it at me. It slams into my chest, and the vibrations ricochet down my body. My back slams into the ground, and I gasp.

"Nolan."

I hear her voice from far away. *Alice*. She's in danger, and I can't let him get to her. It's my fault. I put her in danger. I had turned my back on her, I had all but thrown her out of the house, told her to leave, and she had. And now she is going to die... *No. Not as long as I am alive.*

Not as long as there is a single breath left in my body.

I am going to kill him first. I stagger to my feet. My muscles protest, my shoulder screams, and my chest aches like its center has been gouged out with a flaming, serrated dagger. "You have to get past me first."

"Gladly." Boris widens his stance, then raises his arms, and I rush him.

Muscles straining, adrenaline pumping, I cover the distance so fast that my feet barely touch the ground.

I fling my entire body weight at him...clumsy, clumsy, but whatever. If I have to protect her with every last breath in my body, I will. I crash into him.

The impact careens us down the slope, across the bushes, and over boulders that tear at my back. We hit the bottom and jolt to a stop.

I try to rise and find my body doesn't cooperate. When I crack open my eyes, the world spins.

Darkness rushes up to greet me. I push it away and look up to find Boris standing over me.

"You are going to die knowing I am going to take her sweet cunt. I am going to fuck her again and again, and when I am done with her, I am going to kill her."

"No." I rasp and shove my elbows into the mud for leverage. I manage to lift my shoulders off of the ground.

He smashes his foot down on my rib cage. White-hot agony spears through my chest and the mating bond screams in pain. *No.*

"Alice." I form her name on my lips, but no words come out.

I grab hold of his ankle and shove. My muscles flex, my biceps bunch, but he doesn't move. *No, no, no.* I growl, and the bastard smiles.

"Sweet. The Fae have defeated me twice. This time I will have my revenge."

He steps up, putting the entire weight of his body on my chest, and I can't breathe. Can't do anything but shudder as I feel the blood drain out. My life. My heart. Her. I can't save her. I will never forgive myself.

"Alice." Her name rips from my throat.

Boris' lips twists. He brings down his other foot, and the world goes dark.

When I come to, the first thing I feel is…nothing. I am a disembodied spirit floating, untethered. It's like I am staring down at my body, watching Boris turn away and stride to Alice and grab her. She struggles, and he slaps her. Her body shakes, and the impact almost floors her. *No, I can't let him hurt her.*

I press up with my arms, only to fall back. Sweat pours down my back. My legs tremble.

"Alice." I say her name on a breath, but she doesn't hear it.

She kicks out, and manages to catch Boris in the groin.

Boris' shoulders bunch. He snarls, then grabs her neck and lifts her off of the ground.

Her legs flail, she grabs his arm, and he shakes her.

Her entire body shudders. He brings her close, then licks her cheek. Anger sweeps over me. My muscles coil, my breathing grows harsh. Blood pumps at my temples, and I straighten to a sitting position. But Boris doesn't notice.

"I am going to fuck you, little human, and then I am going to kill you."

The air around me thins, all of the oxygen seems to be sucked out, and the energy flows up his body, swooping over both of them as he teleports.

Rising to my feet, I lurch forward. If I can make it to the teleportation channel, I can follow them. I must. I reach for them and grab at empty air.

"Fuck. Fuck. Fuck." The scream rips out of me, my legs tremble, and I fall to my knees. Liquid flows down my cheeks. I touch my face and find it is wet. Tears? How strange. I've never cried before.

Not when I'd heard my father's confession, and not when I had killed him. Faced with the consequences of my actions, knowing I may have lost her forever, a burning heat floods my chest.

Bloody hell, so pain does serve a different purpose than to forget. It helps to focus. It fuels the need to crush another, blow him to pieces and save her. Get to her.

The burning sensation in my ribcage gushes out, overflowing my cells, my mind. Darkness screams over me, and I reach for it. I couldn't save her; I deserve to die.

"Doc."

A touch on my shoulder makes me shudder.

"What happened here, Doc?

I lift my gaze, and Hawke's worried features fill my sight.

"Alice." I grip his proffered arm. "He took her, and it's my fault."

36

Alice

Taken. Again? Can you believe my sodden luck?

The geometrical designs soar over us, my guts churn, my head spins, then the vortex spits us out. The back of my head hits the hard ground; the dust rears up and slaps my face. I roll over and over, my shoulders hitting the ground, my knees knocking together until I slam into a wall. I lie there, chest heaving, my breathing coming in pants.

"Nolan." The sound of my own voice jolts through my head, shoving all other thoughts away.

I use the hard stone barrier to struggle upright. My head spins, and my guts heave. The scent of rotting flesh floods over me and I look up to find Boris towering over me.

"What are you going to do to me?"

Wrong question, not one that I should have asked.

It's only going to help him lay out his intentions. Not that I have been in a situation like this before, but when you are fighting for your life and you see your man…your mate…brought down by this monster, trust me, you don't care anymore. Not for your own life. Not for anything. Nothing except this burning need to get back to him. I bare my teeth at Boris.

He chuckles. "I can't sell you, so I am just going to keep you here, until the Fae Corps comes for you."

"They'll never let you live after this."

His face darkens, and anger spools off him in dense, grimy waves. "They tried to kill me twice and failed. The Fae Corps is responsible for what I have become, and I won't stop until they are dead."

My stomach twists; my chest hurts. The mating bond... I reach down into myself and find...nothing. "What did you do to him?"

Terror grips me, making it difficult to breathe. I spring up and dive toward him. The next moment, I am hurtling back through the air.

My body bends, my neck twists, and then my head connects with the hard stone wall. Pain lances through my skull, down my side. Blackness claws at the edge of my vision; my throat closes. *No, I can't die.*

I need to find Nolan. I slump down to the ground and lie there gasping. The tightness in my chest closes in on me, pushing down. My head spins. *No. I am not going to give in.* I crack my eyes open to find Boris walking away.

"I am tired of being made into a prisoner, you know?" I wheeze.

He doesn't answer, just pulls open a door.

Another man steps through. He's tall, almost seven feet. Almost as tall as Doc.

Broad shoulders fill the doorway.

He wears a suit. *A suit?* White shirt, black jacket, pants that cling to his powerful legs. His face... I gasp in a breath. Strong, square jawline, high cheekbones, pale green eyes that seem familiar. Goosebumps pop on my skin. *I know him, but from where?*

He saunters over to me, stopping more than five feet away. His gaze rakes over me, but he remains expressionless. His forehead is smooth, yet the muscles of his body are coiled and ready to strike at the first sign of threat. A chill rolls over my skin and I draw in a shaky breath.

This man will not hesitate to kill.

He will not indulge in the kind of histrionics that Boris does. He will simply focus on what needs to be done and not be deterred from his goal.

"So this is her?"

His harsh gravelly voice screams danger. Lethal. I shrink away from him, then almost groan as every muscle in my body protests.

"She's no longer a virgin." Boris steps forward.

I glare at him. *Yeah, that's right, asshole, I gave away the most important part of me to the only man who was worth it.*

"This is the human who the Fae Corps will come for." Boris shuffles his feet. "I have no use for her now, so if you want her —"

The man angles a look over his shoulder.

Boris gulps. His cheeks pale. *The hell?* What kind of hold does this new arrival have over him?

The new arrival squats in front of me, blocking out the sight of Boris.

The stranger drops his gaze and when he meets my eyes something rolls over his face. A low hum swells from his lips, so fine that I almost miss the notes. The sound ebbs and flows, curves and narrows, and wraps around me in a distant memory of home.

The fine hairs on my nape rise.

A memory tugs at my subconscious mind. He can't be my half-brother can he? The boy I'd known had been thin and lanky, he'd had overgrown hair that brushed his shoulders. He'd had kind eyes. The same color as this man's, but there had been so much love, so much life in them. Nothing like the darkness that lurks in the depths of this stranger's eyes. And yet, that subvocal hum, it's how my half-sibling had calmed me and put me to sleep on so many nights, while my mother had been away earning a living.

My heart begins to race.

I open my mouth to ask and he shakes his head.

I bite my lips. I am not sure what his game is but it's clear he's trying to reassure me. I am not sure why but I'll take every break I get.

I force myself to meet his gaze, then lower my head in a nod.

He straightens, then turns and walks toward Boris, his gait casual, steps evenly paced. "She'll do, to set the plan in motion."

Plan? What plan?

I gnaw on the inside of my cheek. Best to stay quiet and see how this plays out. Besides, the more intelligence I gather, especially on this stranger, the more I can share with Doc. I rub my chest. He has to live. He will live. Haven't I heard that amongst mated Fae pairs, if one dies the other dies too? And Doc had definitely mated me. He had. The mating cord that had imprinted into my chest was not a lie. Even if I can't feel it right now, I am alive. So he must be.

I cower against the wall, fold into myself, and try to take up as little space as possible.

"That was not our deal." Boris whines, "I've already risked my life twice in trying to lure in the Fae Corps. It's getting dangerous for me and—"

The stranger moves so fast that, before I can blink, he's shot out an arm and grabbed Boris by his neck. He lifts Boris off of his feet...and I gasp.

Boris is no light weight, and the stranger did not even pause mid action. He's as strong as the Fae Corps men.

"You will do as I ask." His voice lowers, so cold, so menacing. Goose-bumps dot my skin.

My heart beats faster, and my mouth goes dry. How did he get so strong? Clearly he's stronger than Fae. My brother had been as human as me. But this guy, he's much more than that. He's stronger than anything or anyone I have seen or heard of. Who or what is he? And if he is my brother, how did he get this way? A slave trader? No, that's not possible.

Boris' arms and legs twitch, and his eyes bulge.

"Do you understand?"

Boris makes a strangling sound.

"Is that a yes?"

Boris jerks his chin.

The stranger who could be my half-brother drops him, and Boris crumples to his knees.

The man brushes his palm against the material of his pants. "Get her cleaned up."

"But..." Boris gasps. "She's not a virgin."

"The clients won't know better."

"And when they find out?" He keeps his gaze lowered.

"I'll kill them before that happens." He leans forward on the balls of his feet, and Boris winces. His throat moves as he swallows, the stink of ammonia fills the air. *The hell? Did Boris piss his pants?*

What hold does my half-brother have on him?

"This time we'll go according to my plan, and no slip-ups." The stranger fixes his gaze on Boris. "You have one chance left."

He swivels around and walks toward the exit.

"Gabriel," Boris calls after him.

My heart lurches. My half-brother's name had been Gabriel. It is him. It has to be.

"What if it doesn't work?" Boris shifts his weight from foot to foot.

The larger man pauses, then turns to rake his gaze over me before glancing at Boris. "Then you die with her."

Doc

"I need to go to her." The words echo around in my head.

Rage tears at my composure, pressing down on my shoulders.

I strike out, but my movements are sluggish. Something...someone is holding me back.

"Let me go." Fear rips through me; sweat pools in my armpits. I gasp out a breath, and my throat burns. My thigh muscles spasm, and I kick out with a leg and connect with something.

"The fuck, Doc?" A growl rolls through the air.

Despite the anger that laces the tone, I recognize it. My shoulders slump. "Hawke?" I force my eyes open.

Sure enough, the other man cradles his arm and glowers at me.

"Sorry, man, I thought... I thought..." That it was her and he was taking her away...Boris, our asshole former General had kidnapped her again, and I had let it happen.

I rear up from the bed, and my head spins.

My chest ignites with pain; red and white sparks flash behind my eyes. My entire body trembles, and sweat beads at my temples. I collapse against the pillow. "Fuck, fuck, fuck."

I am as weak as a newborn.

At this rate I will never get to her, not until it's too late. I groan and fist my fingers into the mattress, and even that hurts. A ball of emotion clogs my throat.

"The fuck am I going to do, Hawke?" I wheeze.

"You are going to get better, that's what you are going to do. You are no use to her dead."

"I am no use to her...period."

"Pull yourself together, brother."

I shake my head. "She was there with me. All I had to do was keep her inside the safe zone and send for you all, and I failed. Both. Because of my ego. Because I wanted time with her. Because I didn't want anyone else to have her. Because...I..."

"Love her?"

My eyes snap open. "What? No."

Hawke rakes his hand through his hair. "Considering the state you are in over her loss, at how you went after her without a thought for your own safety, it's logical to conclude that you are drawn to her."

"Lust." I grit my teeth. "That's all it is." *Not. Bloody-fucking-hell, now I am arguing with myself?*

"Hmm." Hawke scratches his chin. "That's what I meant, obviously, and the fact that you mated her."

"The fuck you talking about?"

"You going to deny it, asshole?"

"No." My breath stutters. "But how did you...?"

"Let's see." He pretends to count on his fingers, "One. You are falling apart at the thought of her in danger. Two, you are wound up so fucking tightly I am sure you are going to explode. Three, you delayed calling us by an entire motherfucking twenty-four hours..."

"Yeah, there is that." I drag my fingers through my hair.

What had I been thinking? Not much.

That's the answer.

My head and my cock had had only one agenda after I'd managed to get her away from the slavers. To mate her and bind her to me so no one else could have her.

Oh, and she had pushed me, too.

She had all but begged me to take her virginity—and *you could have refused, bastard.*

But I hadn't.

I had ignored all of the warning signs, forgotten every single lesson the Fae Corps had ever taught me, and I had claimed her.

"I failed her. Fuck." I snarl and push up from the bed, and my entire body protests.

My shoulder screams, my chest feels like someone stabbed me with a burning sword, and it's not just because Boris had struck me there twice with his weird-shit energy bolts.

"The fuck you doing?" Hawke grabs my shoulders, and I shake him off.

I swing my legs over and try to stand, and almost topple over.

Hawke rights me. "You are too weak to do anything but lie back and be pathetic, you piece of trash."

"Am not."

"What?"

"Not weak." I gasp as I struggle to stay conscious.

"You are a piece of shit and you sure are pathetic...and newsflash, you are too bloody obstinate to back down when you should."

"What-fucking-ever."

He lets go of me.

I almost fall, then straighten my spine. "You need to let me out of here." I take a step forward, and sweat erupts on my forehead. My heart gallops against my rib cage. *Holy fucking hell.*

"You are in such bad shape, man, that if you walk to the door, it will be a miracle."

I take another step forward, and the world spins. I press my feet into the floor for purchase.

"You are better off trying to recover first. Not doing her any favors, my man, by trying to hurt yourself this way."

A-n-d something inside of me snaps.

I turn on him, struggling to remain upright. "And if someone were to take Charley away and leave you behind wounded, would you try to get to her at the first possible opportunity or would you just cry and cower under the sheets?"

He frowns. "It's not the same thing."

"Oh, wait," I snarl. "I forgot that you are a coward. That's why you prefer doing everything the right way, and waiting until you are stronger when your woman has been hurt."

"Shut the fuck up." He cracks his fist forward. I manage to weave, and the breeze from his move wafts by me, and I sway –I fucking *sway*—from that near hit.

"Oh wait." He snaps his finger. "I forgot that you are so weak that all I have to do is this."

He taps my forehead, and I collapse on the bed.

"The fuck you doing, Hawke?" I huff out, then grab at my chest. The bloody thing hurts, and it shouldn't.

Not more than the pain that swells my jaw. For she's not my mate. *Not. My. Mate. Not yet.* Not until I find her and make love to her and knot her again and…

Hang on a fucking second. Love? You are talking about love? You, the perverted alpha-hole Fae, the one who needs pain to get off, is going to ask her to love you? You are going to ask her to give up her innocence completely and stay with you?

"Doc."

Hawke's voice reaches me, and I shove it aside.

My head spins, and I grip the sheets in my fists so tightly that my fingers protest.

"Focus, soldier." A slap to my face has me rearing back.

"What. The. Fuck?" I roar, and the next moment I am on my feet and my fingers are squeezing Hawke's collar.

He raises an eyebrow. "That's what I thought."

"What?"

"If you have enough fight left in you, maybe there's one thing that can help."

"Oh yeah? And is it going to restore me back to my feet?"

"Maybe."

"Huh?"

"You remember the test drug that you were going to wait to try out on a subject?

I stare. *Fuck me. How did I forget?* "I can try it out on myself." I lurch to my feet and stagger forward, another step, and I almost keel over.

But Hawke, the bastard, the motherfucker, my friend is here. He lifts my arm, slinging it over his shoulder. "Easy, Doc."

I don't want to take his help, I don't.

But hell, I owe him one for reminding me of the antidote. The one that will help accelerate recovery from a complete burnout, the kind that I am suffering from now.

"It's okay to lean on me."

"That's what Alice said, too," I mutter.

"She's sensible and kind and gorgeous."

I shoot him a sideways glance.

"And entirely too good for you."

I snarl.

"Not that I noticed or anything."

"No, you are already pussywhipped by a girl half your age." I smirk.

"Fifteen years."

"What?"

"I am fifteen years older than her." He firms his lips.

"You trying to convince me or yourself?"

He tosses his head. "We weren't talking about me."

"Yeah, the antidote." I snicker. "And by the way, thanks for helping me here."

"I'll extract my due from you, dickwad. There's just one thing, though."

"What?" I frown as he comes to a stop outside the exit.

"Wish you'd cover your ass before flashing the rest of the world."

Cold air rushes over my butt. I look down and realize I am wearing a hospital gown gaping at the back. Just my fucked-up luck.

I step away from Hawke and hold on to the doorframe for support. "I'll get the antidote. You grab me some clothes. Meet me back at the lab."

37

Alice

"You should let me go; I am no good to you."

I look at the stage. I am standing in the wings, my knees all but trembling, and isn't this a familiar nightmare?

Me, surrounded by the upturned faces of men all out for just one thing. To pillage. To take.

Only difference is that I have been showered and forced to wear a sheath that clings to every part of my body as I walk. I may as well be naked for all the protection the cloth provides. But it is meant to reveal more than hide.

Waves of lust roll at me from the audience, and I flinch. I turn to Boris, wondering why the hell I am even bothering to point out the obvious. "Why am I still here? I am damaged goods after all."

His jaw hardens. "Shut up."

"They are going to find out the truth eventually." I jerk my chin toward the audience.

"By then it will be too late; you'll have played your role."

"Role? What role?" I swallow.

He rocks back on his heels. "Nothing that is of consequence to you."

I move in closer. "Tell me."

The smell of rotting flesh deepens, and my stomach lurches. I can't be sick, not now. I swallow down the greasy taste in my mouth.

"Who was that man?"

Boris shifts his weight from foot to foot.

"Are you working for him?"

His features darken. "I work for no one."

He snakes out his fist and catches me in my stomach. I double over, gasping, tears filling my eyes, and I blink them away. *Bastard.*

I straighten and almost moan as the pain radiates out from my stomach. Bile sloshes up my throat and I swallow it back. "You heard Gabriel, he wants me untouched."

Boris thrusts his face into mine. "I don't listen to everything Gabriel says."

The rotting breath of his overwhelms me. I clamp down on the need to turn and scamper away. "Why are you so afraid of him?"

Whatever my half-brother has become, those eyes of his belong to the boy I knew.

"You are beginning to piss me off, human."

Boris raises his hand and his fingers glow, he points them at me and fear grips my heart.

Coldness coils in my chest.

"If you kill me, Gabriel won't let you live either." Actually I am not sure about that, but if...if he is my blood then he won't let me die.

Boris' jaw tightens; he hesitates. *Gotcha again.* I peer up at him from under my eyelashes, "You can't ignore that."

He drops his arms; the glow fades. The breath I had been unaware of holding rushes out. Then he grabs me by the long strands of my hair and yanks me to my feet. A cry catches in my throat. My vision falters, my heart hammers so fast I can hear the blood pounding in my ears. He's going to kill me. He is. *Where are you, Doc?* I reach inside and the mating bond in my chest is still silent. He's still hurt, and perhaps he's hiding from me; that's the only reason I can't sense his presence.

Boris' lips curl.. "Slut." He snarls. "All you women are the same. You are gagging for it, aren't you? You want to be fucked, don't you?"

Only by Doc.

"Do you want my cock, human?"

No.

"Suck my dick and I won't kill you." Boris presses me down and I drop to my knees.

Let me go. Get your hands off me. I scream the words in my head.

My stomach clenches. My breath comes in pants. I can't lie to save myself.

I'll never let another touch me again, no one but Doc. I belong to him, only him.

I squeeze my eyes shut, and every part of me freezes. My heart rate ratchets up; my throat closes. *Coward.* That's what I am. Not able to face up to this monster. I have to do something. Anything. His hold on my neck tightens, and the oxygen to my lungs cuts off. I struggle and try to break free, and he chuckles.

Another man stomps by, dragging a woman along with him, "You're up next." He jostles my legs as he passes.

"Saved by the bell and all that." Boris chuckles. He hauls me up to my feet, up the steps. I stumble and he yanks me up, then shoves me onto the platform.

I lurch forward, and the sheath that I am clad in clings to my legs outlining my every move.

A spotlight falls on me, blinding my eyes. A roar sounds from the crowd.

"I bid ten thousand."

Huh? Ten thousand what? I fling my arms around my waist, and my shoulders hunch. I want to run away and hide, but where…a whip slaps over my front, and pain licks over my skin. I straighten and snarl. Boris' lips twist, and he raises his hand again, and I flinch, waiting for the slap to land on me. When Doc had spanked me, I'd loved it. I'd wanted more. It had turned me on, that edge of pleasure-pain rousing me to climax.

But from anyone else, the pain only hurts. There is no pleasure in being touched by another, other than Doc.

There is a difference between being hurt for pleasure and being hurt with malicious intent.

Boris hurts to flaunt his power, to seem superior when really, he is the weak one. There is a gurgling sound, and I look up and...blink. *What the...?* My mouth opens and closes.

It's Gabriel. He's grabbed the whip, its lash looped around Boris hand, and he yanks at it. Boris goes stumbling and falls in front of me. The crowd screams.

Yeah, that's what they want. They have come to bid on a virgin, but hell, they'll take anything, anyone's blood, even of the man who's been supplying them with victims.

Gabriel lets go of the whip, and Boris springs up to his feet. "What the hell?"

"Don't tarnish the merchandise." Gabriel jerks his chin in my direction, not bothering to even look at me.

My throat closes. Had I misjudged him? Does he not care for who I am? I could have sworn I'd seen a flicker of recognition in his eyes, but maybe I was wrong. I tuck my arms into my sides trying to make myself as small as possible.

Boris pauses and Gabriel angles his head, "Well, what are you waiting for? Continue with the auction."

Boris waves his hand, and another voice from the audience screams, "Twenty thousand for the bitch."

I snarl. I am not a bitch or a whore or a cunt. Just a human here, people. A very angry one, and one who isn't for sale either. I need to do something, say something. *What?*

Gabriel stalks off the stage, and my muscles tense. Maybe he is my half-sibling, but right now, he's not acting very brotherly, is he?

Okay so maybe he has a plan or something, but he could have shared that with me, eh? I toss back my hair. I am tired of waiting for someone to rescue me...Face it, I am on my own, and about to be auctioned off, and damn if I am going to take this lying down.

I step up and around Boris. Walking to the front of the stage, I raise my palm and the crowd quietens. Sweat beads my brow. *I can do this. Do this.* I draw in a breath then hold up my head. "I am not a virgin."

38

Doc

The fuck is she doing? I rush up the aisle that cuts between the audience that has fallen silent. Does she have a death wish?

I had managed to get to the antidote and injected myself with a double dose—*yeah, okay, not advisable. But what-fucking-ever.* Desperate times and all that.

I'd teleported out without waiting for Hawke. No way was I going to endanger the life of my best friend. He is going to be pissed, but I'll cross that bridge when I get to it. I couldn't put him in danger too.

Besides, my life doesn't matter.

I don't care what harm the extra shot of concoction does to me. Within seconds, the fast-acting drug had pumped through my system and restored my energy levels.

The antidote had amped up my recovery. My cells had seemed to rejuvenate, and my Fae healing powers had surged to seal up every last scratch on my body...everything except that hollowness in my chest where the fledgling mating bond had begun to form—something I didn't want to examine too closely.

The fiery ball of heat throbbed, reassuring me that she was alive, and that was all that mattered. I had to keep the connection steady just until I got to her and rescued her.

I had gotten her into this mess, and I would not stop until she was safe. *I only have to get her out and back home safely, and then I can walk away. Yes, that's what I intend to do.*

The crowd around me clatters to its feet, and I look ahead and almost stumble. She stands there with the light flowing over her, bathing her in its glow. The white sheath—*What is she wearing?*—is almost transparent.

The glow illuminates her curves. The jut of her breast, the flare of her hips, the hollow between her legs…she has nothing on under that.

The bastards put her in that outfit knowing full well that it would reveal her assets, show her in the best possible way. Not that the crowd needs any goading.

They surge to their feet and move forward. Someone tackles me from behind, and I fling off the man only for another body to hit me, and then another and…

"What…the fuck?" I fling away the intruders, but more keep coming.

There is a pounding of footsteps, then a throng of people running toward us…not us…her. I swivel around to face the stage where she stands hands out, almost angelic in the way the light halos her head.

A man dressed in pants and button down shirt steps up to her.

"Boris," I race forward. My heart hammers, adrenaline spikes my blood.

"You want this?" Boris howls at the crowds. The motherfucker walks behind her, grabs the collar of her sheath, and tears it off. "Come and get it then. She's spoiled goods; she belongs to whoever gets to her first."

A wave of heat…sheer avarice ripples through the audience.

Then a burst of noise lashes further as all those sitting spring to their feet. They want her. They will tear into her, and not leave anything left of her…"NO." I howl.

Something inside tears at me, wanting out, wanting to release… My chest expands, my biceps bulge, and the tips of my ears tingle.

·   ·   ·

Something coiled inside of me expands.

Heat surges up my chest and ripples up my throat. I open my mouth, and the flames pour out.

The fire burns clean through the men clogging the path. Some scream, their clothes and their hair on fire, and roll off. The aroma of burning flesh fills the air.

The crowd falls back and I race toward the stage.

The telekinetic energy inside me rumbles. I draw up the bluish flame with the green sparks then hurl it toward the two figures on stage. The fire streams a trail of light behind and encloses her. I reach the stage and open my arms as her burning body collapses.

She falls off the stage and I catch her. The fire blinks out, and she shudders. I cradle her close. "I've got you, Red. I've got you."

She screams and cowers.

"Open your eyes."

"N-no," she stutters. "The fire —"

"Couldn't hurt you, Red."

"What?"

"Not a hair on your head is singed."

She cracks her eyes open, and those green eyes blaze. "How…?"

"You're my mate." *There, I said it. Funny thing? I mean it, too.* "My dragon's fire can't harm you."

She reaches up a finger and scoops up the liquid on my cheek, then brings it to her lips and sucks.

My groin hardens. My balls fucking tingle. We are surrounded by hordes who press up against me, who threaten to rip her away from me, and all I can think is how much I want to throw her down and mount her in front of the entire audience and show them she belongs to me. *Mine. She is mine.*

The crowd closes in on me, and I plant my feet into the ground and stay where I am, holding them off.

She looks up and past me, and her eyes widen.

The hair on the nape of my neck rises. I glance up in time to see the fire blink off. Boris stands there, unhurt.

"The fuck?" I bare my teeth, and my canines drop. I hold her close and hunch my body over her.

"How touching. An alpha-hole Fae laid low by the cunt of a human female."

"Shut the fuck up." Adrenaline spikes my blood.

He raises his arms, and his fingertips glow blue. A ball of heat churns to life between his palms. He raises his arms and flings it at me. I swerve, and it hits two of the men from the crowd who scream in pain. The sound cuts off, and their bodies disintegrate. The fuck?

Boris is canny but he's not the strongest when it comes to amplifying his telekinetic energy, which begs the question, who the hell is he working with to get access to that kind of power?

He drops his chin, raises both of his arms, biceps bulging, fingertips sparking. The oxygen in the space thins and fuck it, I'll come back to resolve that puzzle later. Time is running out. I have to hold back this motherfucker.

I fall into myself and draw on the telekinetic energy, and *whoa*, it gushes up to meet me. Gray-blue and spiked with yellow...my dragon energy melds into it. The combined fire-telekinetic power swirls up and boils at my pores. Every part of me braces, and I yank on the energy, letting it flood out of me, covering her, forming an arrowhead of pure light that surges forward and into his chest. His body arches back, and he goes flying through the air and hits the stage.

"Hold tight, Red." I bend my knees, then spring up and onto the stage, still holding her. *My mate. Mine.* Warmth pools in my chest. The ball of heat trembles then unfolds, and a swell of light streams into my blood.

I bite off a profanity, block out the sight of the crowds.

I can't afford to let her get hurt. I am already stretching my power to the full extent, but there's one thing, just one thing left to do. I prowl forward to where Boris stirs.

He sits up and shakes his head.

His gaze widens as, still holding her close, I draw upon the combined Fae-Dragon shifter energy, let it boil right up, collecting every last bit of my anger, my hate, my love for her...*yeah, I fucking love her!* All those emotions flood into my blood and mix with my power. It flows up my chest, my throat, and stops. *The fuck?*

39

Alice

Doc starts above me. His shoulders flex, the tendons of his throat move and every muscle in his body goes rigid. He shakes his head, then I sense his eyes snap into focus. He seems to be struggling with something...trying to get in touch with that energy inside that I had sensed, the part that made him so Doc. So unique. Fae and Dragon. Animal and human. A confluence of my worst nightmares and every wet dream come true.

The cords of his neck twang. "I can't... I can't focus my energy long enough to teleport."

"You're burning up." I huddle closer and place a palm over his chest.

I sense his heart thudding so fast, hammering against his rib cage. The planes of his chest clench; the tendons of his throat strain. The mating bond coiled in my rib cage throbs in response.

I reach out to him through the bond, searching for that connection that had always been implied, just there, just out of reach. I had been afraid to reach for it and show him just how close we truly are.

"Fuck." His gaze darts forward, and his shoulders tense.

"I am going to kill the both of you."

Boris' voice slithers over us.

"Getting tired of that dialogue, asshole," Doc's breathing is labored, "you need a new fucking threat."

The stench of rotting flesh creeps over me, and I push it away. *No, I cannot let this happen.* We've faced too much, come too far, and I cannot, will not allow Doc to give up. Not now. Not when everything I have always wanted is so close to me. There is only one thing I want in this world. Him.

"Let me help you, Doc."

I sense him start.

He doesn't take his gaze off Boris. "I can't endanger you, Red."

"Just once can you listen to me, you stubborn, obstinate alpha-hole?"

"You turn me on when you are bossy." One side of his lips twists. "Not that I'll ever let you be in control."

The fetor of rotting flesh intensifies.

Boris has moved in closer. The heat in the space rolls over me, all the oxygen seems to be sucked up, creating a void around us.

There's a hush in the air.

Something is coming, a storm that is going to wipe us away, push us to the end, make us do something we are going to regret. The thoughts bounce around in my head. "Don't, Doc... Nolan...don't do it."

I follow his gaze. Boris' gaze narrows, his lips draw back, and his canines drop. The tips glow with an eerie white spark. His ears extend, and he pulls them back. He swings his arm, and energy crackles from his fingertips. He rolls his telekinetic power into a ball of lethal energy that glows between his palms.

"I am not going to let you hurt her." Doc swings around, turning his back on Boris. He hunches over me, pulling me close to his body, so close that my nose is buried in his chest, my arms curled around his massive torso. He's all around me, enfolding me, shielding me. Then, the energy sweeps over us.

Red and white. Hot and cold at the same time. It's Boris, he's hit us with everything he's got, and Doc is shielding me with his own body.

"No." I strain in his hold but his arms don't give. His body doesn't move.

I look up, and all I can see is the curve of his chin, the fold of his body that shields me from the worst of Boris' assault.

The energy dissipates, only he doesn't move. He stays where he is.

"Doc."

His heartbeat ratchets up, pounding against my skin.

He doesn't reply. I peer up and find his jaw tense. A pulse beats at the base of his throat. He's holding himself so tightly, so silently. *Is he hurt?* Sweat pours down his shoulders, drenching me, enfolding me in that essence of his that is so Doc. His body quivers, once. He is in more pain than he is letting on.

"Let me help, Doc."

"No." He coughs, then shakes his head. "Can't let you risk yourself for me." His voice is harsh.

"So you'll kill yourself?"

"If that's what it takes."

I set my jaw. Stubborn macho man. "If you die, I die, too. You realize that?"

"Huh?" He swallows and glances down at me, and I gasp. His irises snap vertically, the blue in them coiling into pools of hope and pain. And something else. A fierce need to protect.

The air around us thins, and Doc tenses. His shoulders draw up. "What do you mean by that?"

"You mated me, Doc."

"The bond is not consolidated."

"You fucked me....a lot." A chuckle spills from my lips. "I'd say that was enough to strengthen whatever is between us."

"There's time. You can go on without me, find someone more worthy." He draws in a breath.

I reach up and grab his chin, and he lets me coax his head down. "I want only you. If you die, I am going to kill myself, too.'

"You won't." His gaze grows fierce." You'll live…"

"Not."

"What am I going to do with you?" One side of his lips curves.

"You can let me help you."

His jaw firms, and he pulls me even closer. A roar rends the air; all of the oxygen is sucked up. I try to breathe, and my lungs burn. He's going to hit us. Boris won't stop, not until he's decimated Doc, and I will not let that happen.

"Please?" I cup his cheek.

He grits his teeth, and another ball of fire crashes into him from behind. "No, Red. And that's final."

His big body goes rock-hard, then sways.

He drops to his knees, taking me down with him, still hunched over me, sheltering me. My heartbeat mirrors his. My throat goes dry. Goosebumps crawl over my skin. It's now or never. I drop into myself, reaching for the ball of fire in my chest. I follow the trail of blue light leading to Doc, flooding the bond with everything I want for him, for us.

Let me in, Doc.

I pulse the thought at him, then chuckle.

He'd said the same thing to me once. When he'd tried to fuck me in places I'd never been taken before. When he'd trod virgin ground—literally. I snicker under my breath. He had been hellbent on filling me up, on causing me the kind of pain that pushed me over the edge into a whole new kind of pleasure, and now...this...will he let me in?

Please. My heart races. *Let me help you, Doc. Let me help us. It's okay to lean on someone else on occasion. It's fine to allow your mate to share the pain.*

He groans and his eyelids crack open to fix on mine. "What are you doing to me, Red?"

"Just showing you how it can be between us. Will you let me do that much? Just this once? Will you trust me as much as I do you?"

40

Doc

Her question hits me with the force of a storm.

Can I trust her?

Do I allow her to look into the shadow of my mind where I have never dared venture myself?

I am so afraid of what she'll find there, of what *I'd* find there.

The edge of my perversions. The reason for what makes me what I am. The fact that it's more than the brave façade that I put up. I don't make excuses for how I turned out. I am a result of the choices I made. But hell no one wants to be deviant. No one wants to spend their life in pursuit of pain. That's all it had been…a way to forget…until her. And now she's asking me the one question that lays me bare. That exposes the kind of weakling I am. It's now or never.

Can I finally give in to that last barrier between us?

The one that had insisted I let go of her? Can I give her what she wants? Yes. *Yes*. I can't deny her. Even if it means stripping myself completely so she can see exactly what I am.

I bow my head. My shoulders bunch.

I lower the barriers between us, and the mating bond expands.

The blue-green energy swoops down on me, spinning through the parts of me inside that I have never wanted to face, lighting up the dark corners of my mind. My heart. My soul.

I allow her energy to sweep through me, sink into my blood, flow down my spine then whoosh back up.

It surges forward to twine with the ball of energy in my heart. My heart stutters. My breath comes in gasps. I draw upon our combined energies.

It swells my chest, my throat. I raise my chin, open my mouth, and the energy spirals forward. I rise up, widening my stance as I lock my muscles to hold myself in place; then propel the energy the rest of the way toward Boris.

The vortex spins over Boris, whirling faster and faster; then it blows out. The blue-green energy swoops up. Sparks of gold fountain from it, lighting up the entire stage, almost blinding me; then it winks out. A few dust motes flutter in the air, then those too drift away. He's dead, and this time the motherfucker is gonna stay that way.

I stand there, legs trembling, my thighs refusing to support me anymore.

"We did it." Her voice flows over me.

I look down at her. "You did it. You made me see how wrong I was."

She frowns. "About what?"

"Everything."

"You are scaring me, Doc."

"You showed me the error of my ways. That everything I had thought was right so far is not. That what I have become is a mistake. What I subjected you to is wrong, so wrong."

"It wasn't." She shakes her head, raises her palm, and places it on my face.

Her touch is so gentle, so soft, I wince. "I don't deserve your love."

Did I just say that?

Me, confessing to not being good enough? And last I checked, I still have my balls. I toss my head. *Why am I having these thoughts in the middle of dangerous terri-*

tory and surrounded by a crowd of marauding men, all of whom have their eyes set on her?

"Let's get out of here."

A scream lashes through the space, and I look back over my shoulder. The crowd flows forward, people pressed into the stage. Two men clamber onto the platform and come toward us. Followed by another and another.

I turn around to face them, then take a step back, and another. The energy inside me sparks, then fizzles out.

I need time to recharge.

I just depleted a big burst of my power to get rid of that bastard Boris. I need to recuperate for a few seconds before I am ready to teleport.

The crowd closes in on us. She trembles in my arms, and I hold her closer.

"I won't let anything happen to you." I don't take my eyes off of the stranger who approaches us.

"I know." She loops her arm around my waist. Her hair falls over her shoulders.

The new arrival's gaze swivels to her.

His gaze rakes over her body, and I snarl.

"Back the fuck off."

He takes another step forward, his gaze sliding back to my woman. *Fuck, fuck, fuck.* A few more seconds, that's all I need for my energy to rekindle. Even alpha Fae warriors who are highly trained soldiers have their limitations when it comes to teleoperations. A shudder grips my body. *Damn,* the antidote's effect is fading away.

My knees buckle.

"Doc, you okay?" Her worried voice cuts through the thoughts crowding in my head.

"Fine."

Another man jumps onto the stage, and a third and a fourth. *Motherfucker.* The crowd is closing in on us. The stench of their unwashed bodies presses down, along with the intent to harm, to do much worse to her. I bare my lips, and my canines drop.

Sweat slides down my temples. I cannot fail her. I will keep her safe at any cost. I bring her close. She shudders and presses her face into my chest.

"They have to get through me to get to you." I am saying it aloud more to calm her, to keep her from realizing the hopelessness of our situation — the fact that we are cornered, cut off, and facing a pack of feral men who wouldn't hesitate to rip us apart.

She leans up and places her lips near my ears. "I trust you."

Three simple words.

They shouldn't mean so much. They shouldn't lay me low. But they do. My heart squeezes, and a pressure pushes down on the backs of my eyes.

The throng on stage sidles in slowly, slowly. Their gaze fixed on the woman in my arms.

Alice chokes and burrows in further. Her shoulders shudder and I tighten my hold on her.

"They are going to kill us." Her voice trembles.

I hate the fear I hear in her tone, the fact that her body is shaking, that I scent her nervousness.

And I am helpless, fucking helpless to do anything.

I hunch over her, making sure to keep as much of her covered as I can.

My back grazes the wall at the back of the platform. Only then do I realize that I have backed up all the way to the far end.

White pain screeches over my nerve endings, reminding me that I am hurt.

The telekinetic energy inside me rolls. I am so close to being restored.

Just a few more seconds, that's all I need.

I'll do anything to get that time.

To turn back the clock to when I was with her in the safe house. I had a chance to love her the way she deserved, and I failed. If I get out of here… I will put her needs before mine. I will care for her, cherish her, tell her that…"I love you."

She trembles, then turns to me. She flings her arms around my neck, literally climbs up my body and presses her lips into my cheek. "I love you Nolan."

The words flow over my skin, and a calmness enfolds me. If I die now…it will have been worth it.

She makes everything right.

Why didn't I see that before? Why had I turned her away? Never again. I wrap my arms around her, trying to cover as much of her body as I can with my own.

Silence sweeps over the space. The crowd breathes as one, then they break rank and hurtle at us.

Fuck this. It's now or never. I draw on the telekinetic power inside of me. It sparks then falls back. I draw on it again, and this time it ignites.

All of the faces of the throng meld into one.

I brace myself for impact, don't take my gaze off of them. I will not cower, not even in the face of death. The telekinetic power inside of me flickers to life. I draw up the thin tendril, shove it over her, loop it around her body.

Her muscles tense, and I know the exact moment she realizes my intention for she screams, "No!"

"You have to get out of here."

"Not without you." She reaches out to me through the mating bond, and her emerald-green energy latches on to mine, twines with mine.

"Let go," I growl.

Fear pulses in my veins. I don't have enough energy to teleport both of us, and no way will I risk her life. I am going to get her out of here if it's the last thing I do.

She doesn't reply. Another beam of energy reaches out to me on the psychic plane, a ray of green, another and another, all of it hooks onto me, fusing with mine, until there is a thick, blue-green mass connecting us, enveloping the both of us.

The first man reaches us only to be yanked back.

"The fuck?" I stare.

I can't take my gaze off of him as his body is twirled around and around.

The man screeches and wriggles, and just as suddenly, he's let go.

He flies through the air, arcing over the stage many rows into the audience, and crashes down.

There are screams from the audience, and the impact ripples through the ground. People fall over, scatter away, the stage trembles, and the people on the platform stumble.

The men in the row closest to me fall to their knees in front of a new arrival standing with his back to me. He's wearing a white shirt, black jacket formal pants, all tailormade for his build. I shake my head to clear it. *Who is this guy?*

He raises his hand, the tips glowing.

Sparks of light shoot from them as he drags his hand over the ground, creating a margin that separates us from the crowd. The row in front pulls back; some of them jump off of the stage.

I growl and the suit clad man shoots me a look over his shoulder. "Leave."

"Who the fuck are you?"

41

Alice

I sense the energy ripple over Doc. The telekinetic energy vibrates up his chest, seeping out of his pores, cocooning me and pulling me close. It pulses over me, and the oxygen in the space thins. He's trying to teleport me out, and no way am I going without him.

"Get out of here." Gabriel snarls.

Danger rolls off of him in waves.

Doc stiffens above me; he growls and moves forward. I pat his arm and he stops. His muscles vibrate with unleashed energy, but at least he's not snarling anymore. I narrow my gaze on Gabriel, who stands unmoving.

Those green eyes, bore into me. In their depths something flashes: pain, fear, a plea to get the hell out of here? He jerks his chin and I nod.

I turn to Doc, rise up to tip-toe, then pinch his chin, forcing him to look down at me.

"I will not leave without you."

I drop my head and bury my teeth into the curve where his neck meets his shoulder.

The taste of blood fills my mouth; the scent of him fills my senses. His energy screeches through the mating bond and infuses me with his essence. Blue, gray, white—the colors surge over me. My breath catches. My chest squeezes. Then, a wave of green and purple rises from me to meet the bond. The connection snaps into place. The bond barrels down my rib cage to embed in my womb, and I scream.

The pain…oh, the pain…it sweeps through me.

White and red and so hot. Sweat slides down my back; my entire body shakes.

"Alice, what have you done? You sealed the mating bond?" Doc's voice is anguished.

My head falls back; I don't think I can hold myself up. My body crumples, and my forehead hits his shoulder. "I need you, Doc."

A shudder grips his big body, rumbling up his chest, spilling over me. The air in the space thins.

The fine hair on my neck rises. Geometric designs blur past, and we teleport. The psychic breeze buffets my face, my skin, tugs at my hair, and I huddle close to him. His big body shields me, his heat cocoons me, and his scent envelops me. If I were to die now, I'd be happy. I close my eyes and let the darkness pull me under.

When I open my eyes, all I see is white.

White walls, white floor, white light that shines through the window and into my eyes. I move my lips but my throat is so dry. No words emerge. I cough and my lungs burn.

"You're back?"

A figure moves into my line of sight, blocking out the light. I can't see his features, but those shoulders, that voice—harsh and soft, smooth and grating over my nerves. My body begins to tremble. "Nolan." My voice emerges on a croak.

"I'm here Red."

I raise my hand and he grips it. His palm is big, warm; it dwarfs mine. My fingers tremble and he leans in closer. There are dark circles around his eyes. He seems to have lost weight; his build is leaner. His hair stands on end as if he's been running his fingers through it? "You're alive." I gasp out on a breath, then cough again.

"Let me get you some water." He starts to tug his hand from my grasp and I cling to it. Hating my weakness, hating that I can't let go of him again. Hating that I feel so vulnerable right now. And a part of me doesn't care anymore. Maybe being near death does that to you? Makes you want to throw everything you knew to the winds and race for the one thing you want. The only thing that makes my life worth living—him. "I love you Doc." I wheeze out on my next breath.

His fingers still over mine. His muscles tense. Anger vibrates off of him and my gaze darts to his face. Those blue eyes burn at me, flecks of gold in them hinting at the turmoil inside.

He loves me too. I heard him say so earlier. So why doesn't he say it now that we are back home and safe?

I wriggle around, trying to make myself more comfortable.

His grip tightens and a pulse of pain darts up my arm.

I wince and his gaze falls to our joined hands. I look down and find the skin stretched white over his knuckles. *Huh?* Who'd have thought. He's as nervous as me? Or angry? Or both.

He lets go of my hand and I lower it to the bed, then tuck it under the cover. Stupid tears burn my eyes.

"How long have I been out?"

"You've been asleep for three days." He rubs his chin and the rasping sound of his fingernails raking over his rough whiskers shivers over me. My nerve-endings spark and a burst of heat flares low in my belly.

That entire unshaved and hollow-eyed look only adds to his potent sex appeal. My sex quivers. *Nope. Not going there. Not now.*

"You didn't change?" I jerk my chin toward his torn clothes.

"Nah." He rubs the back of his neck.

"You didn't leave my side all this time?"

He doesn't reply. Just leans back and his massive frame dwarfs the chair.

"You brought me here to the infirmary and stayed with me?" I know it, but I want him to confirm it to me. Just blame it on my insecurities okay? I want to know that this man wants to be near me as much as I crave his proximity.

"Mmm hmm." He dangles his hands loosely between his legs.

My gaze drops to his crotch and the bulge that tents his pants. I've seen him aroused, felt the beauty of his cock throb in my palm, shared his pain when he was hurt in a fight, sensed how much he cares for me, seen him put his life on the line to protect me...so why is he still holding back?

Damn the stubborn man, he knows more about me than any living person. He's the only person I have been this intimate with, and I don't plan on having this...this feeling with anyone else.

He shifts again, then winces.

"Are you hurt?"

"It's nothing." He leans over to reach for the jug of water, and I gasp. "Your poor back." I can't take my gaze off the tattered remains of his shirt. Pale pink flesh peers through it. Fae's heal quickly, so whatever Boris had hit him with again, must have burned through all of the layers of skin.

"I'll survive," he holds out the glass, "thanks to you."

I try to sit up but my entire body protests. My breath catches in my chest and I fall back against the sheets. "What do you mean?"

"How do you feel?" The heavy ridge of his eyebrows flexes. He answers my question with one of his own.

Typical Doc. He can rip me of all my barriers and expose me until I am physically and emotionally naked but god forbid if he were to share any of his true feelings.

"I feel..." I examine the different parts of my body—my shoulders, arms, legs—all of it seems whole. My limbs feel a little heavy, my muscles a little sore but other than that I feel, "fine."

He tilts his head and I square my shoulders, "Honestly, my muscles are sore but other than that, I am fine."

He nods.

"Shouldn't I take longer to recover?" I frown.

He hesitates, something coils in the depths of his eyes and I watch, riveted. *What is he thinking?* "You are more resilient that you realize. Besides your body is changing." He firms his lips.

"What do you mean?" A ripple of apprehension skates over my skin.

He fixes me with a penetrating stare. *Okay not reassuring at all, that look.*

"Are you thirsty?"

Hmm, and he's changing the subject. My lips throb, and my throat feels too tight and I let the thought escape. "Water would be nice."

He picks up the glass of water on the side table, then slides his arm under my neck and props me up. He holds the glass to my lips and I drink from it. Some of the water slides down my chin and he wipes it off with his fingers. His touch raises goosebumps on my skin.

Even in this recovering state, I am so damn aware of him. I look at the jug and he fills up the glass again, then holds it up to my mouth. I drink it, the water sliding down my throat. He lifts the glass from my lips, "Enough, or you'll be sick."

The whiff of dominance in his tone ripples over my skin. The fine hair on the nape of my neck rises. Only when I catch myself nodding, do I realize what I've done. I've obeyed him without hesitation. When he's around, the force of his personality seduces me, giving him the leeway to have his way with me. "You can't help it, can you?"

He frowns.

I raise my chin, "This entire telling me what to do thing, it's just in you. You can't stop yourself from being dominant anymore than—"

"Your wanting to submit completely and yet denying yourself?" His voice is hard. His gaze narrows and a tinge of dragon smoke seeps into the air. *Why does that turn me on?*

Goosebumps pop on my skin.

I wrap my arms around my waist, then look down to find I am wearing a hospital gown. The material is rough and gray in color. Awesome. It couldn't be any uglier, eh? If only I was on a stronger footing, in a space where I could hold my own with a dominant alpha Fae. All I have are my words. "So you know better than me what I want?"

He smirks.

Damn. I gave him an opening.

"You said it Red," He leans forward until his eyes are on level with mine, "*Only* I know what you want. Only I can give you what you need. Only I can sink my dick into your pussy and strum your cunt and drive you to madness...again and again."

I have felt the edge of his palm, felt his thick fingers in my cunt. Been helpless to stop my pussy from clamping down around his throbbing dick but...hearing him elaborate it all out in that harsh voice of his adds an edge of darkness to it all.

He tilts his head and I gulp.

His gaze holds mine. His presence anchors me. Every cell of my body is captive to him. All he needs to do is flick his gaze to me and I'll do anything he wants. No words. No need to tell me. I know what he needs. Me.

His lips thin. "Do you understand?"

"Yes, Alpha." I lick my lips.

"Good girl."

The blood roars at my temples. Heat stabs between my legs. His approval sets my skin on fire.

"There's just one thing." His jaw firms and my pulse begins to race.

A sense of foreboding tugs at my subconscious mind. Whatever he's going to say next, I am not sure I want to hear it.

Don't say it. Don't say it. I tilt my head, "Wh...what?"

"You made a mistake."

42

Doc

She worries her lower lip with her teeth, and I can't tear my gaze from her mouth. I should have brought her here and left. Should have left her to my team and gone straight to Dante and debriefed him on what I had seen and heard, but one look at her helpless, unconscious, and no way could I have torn myself from her side.

I feather my knuckles over the wound at the curve of where my neck meets my shoulders. "You shouldn't have done it, Red."

Her gaze widens and she swallows. She knows exactly what it means.

"You took control." I purse my lips.

"I was trying to save your life."

"You went against everything I have tried to teach you, you bit me and claimed me. You took the initiative and completed the mating bond."

"You bit me first." She squeezes her fingers together, "You initiated the bond."

"Exactly. I started it; it was mine to complete."

"I only did what anyone else would have in my place."

"Is that right?" Anger laces my blood. The pulse thuds at my temples, at the base of my throat, at my wrists. *Fuck*, every part of me seems to be coming alive, stirring, stretching, yearning for her. The ball of fire in my chest flares to life and I gasp.

Her gaze lowers to my chest and I realize that I am massaging the skin over my heart.

"You feel it too, don't you?" She raises her chin. "You can sense the intensity of whatever it is that stretches between us."

"You completed the bond, so yeah, no surprise there." I raise my eyebrows in an expression that's meant to be casual. The exact opposite of everything I am feeling inside.

She sits up and the cover dips. *Don't look down, don't.* My gaze drops to her chest. To the beautiful curves of her breasts outlined by the fabric.

My throat closes. I only have to close the distance between us, shove down the covers and all that trembling flesh will be bared to my gaze.

It was a bad idea to have stayed on. My dick twitches, insisting otherwise. My fingertips tingle to reach out and cup her swollen flesh. To drag my tongue around her pebbled nipples and take them in my mouth and suck on them.

"You want me Doc."

Her voice is breathless and her chest heaves.

"You can't always get what you want."

"This...this you can." She brings her hands up to cup her breasts, then squeezes them. "All this is yours." She moans and blood rushes to my groin.

Fuck me. I had barely managed to get her out of there with both of our lives, but a few seconds in her presence, and all I can think of is turning her over on my lap and teaching her a lesson for having taken matters into her own hands. "It wasn't your place to lead and complete what I started."

I fold my palms over my chest. Best to keep them in front of me where I can have control over my arms. Because when it comes to Red, my body has a mind of its own.

The scent of her teases my nostrils and my pulse begins to thud.

The intensity of those green eyes that bore into my soul, the heavy bond that throbs between us... all of it crowds in on my mind. I surge to my feet and she cowers back against the bed. My shoulders jerk. I raise my hands, "I am not going to hurt you, Red."

"I know." She wets her lips. "But I am still not used to how big you are."

"Oh?" A smirk tugs at my lips.

She pouts, "That's not what I mean."

I angle my head.

"I wasn't implying the size of your...ah, cock." Her cheeks redden.

"Love it when you talk dirty, Red."

She grips her hair and pulls at it, "You're so annoying." She huffs.

"And you are still not recovered from our earlier interlude." I half angle my body away. Get out of here while you can. Give yourself some space. Some time to work this out.

I move toward the door and the bond twinges in my chest. Her uncertainty shudders down our shared connection. I curl my fingers into fists and keep going.

"I can't do this without you Doc."

I almost come to a stop, then force myself to take one step. Then another. "You are better off without me."

"That's not true." I turn to find her swinging her legs over the side of the bed.

"Stop." My words ring out in the space between us.

She pauses. Her head lowers, that thick hair of hers flowing down over her chest to cover the sight of her breasts.

I want to go back and close the distance between us and shove it aside.

She peers up at me from under her eyelashes, "Why are you doing this?"

"I can't accept what you gave me. I can't take you for my mate. I am all wrong for you Alice. If you are with me, I'll only hurt you, and you deserve better."

"But you love me." She wrings her fingers together in front of her.

I draw myself up to my full height. "Do I look like I am capable of love?"

"Yes." She takes a step forward and I stiffen.

If she comes closer, if she touches me, I won't be able to stop myself from taking her.

She's right, I do love her.

But I can't give her what she wants.

It's because I love her that I cannot give in completely to the animal inside of me. I'd almost choked her the last time. What if I can't stop myself from going further?

What if the combination of my newly awakened dragon blood combined with the Fae in me pushes me over completely?

Her sealing the mating bond had forced me to acknowledge the last missing pieces of me. The next time I make love to her, I won't be able to stop in time.

What if I endanger her life because of it? I couldn't bear that.

That's why I am going to put distance between us. I can't kill myself, for that will hurt her, but if I am gone long enough, maybe she'll forget me. Maybe she'll find someone else who can protect her and give her everything I can't. The band around my chest tightens. *What the fuck? Not the time for emotions now, asshole. Turn around and leave now.*

I set my jaw. "Get back into bed."

She juts out her lower lip, and I am sure she is going to protest and then...I am not sure what I'll do. March across and tie her to the bed? Probably. I just want her to give me a reason to do so. So I can have her restrained and at my disposal. Mine to command, to do with as I want. *Sick fuck that I am. She's better off without me.* I ball my fists at my side, "I won't repeat myself."

She pales. Then she scoots back and slides under the covers.

Thank fuck.

"You will stay in bed and concentrate on healing. You will cooperate with the doctor I am going to send to take care of you."

I infuse enough dominance in my voice that the color fades from her cheeks. She has no choice but to obey me.

"What about you?" Her voice rises in tone. "I want you to take care of me Doc."

"Not possible."

"But—"

"I need to focus on healing myself." I shift my weight from foot to foot. *Nice one, play on her guilt.* "Besides, I need to get to this briefing with Dante."

Yeah, I am not above using her emotions to turn the conversation in my favor. I am not playing fair again, but fuck that.

She swallows, then folds her arms over her chest. "You'll be back to see me?"

"Maybe."

She opens her mouth and I hold up a palm.

She bites her lip, looks like she is going to keep talking, then subsides.

Whew! Dodged that one again. I drum my fingers on my thigh. One chance. Give me one chance to follow through on my threats. *One chance to spank your butt, to squeeze your flesh and mark it and suck it—Fuck. I gotta get out of here,* "Stay." I stab a finger at her.

Swiveling on my feet, I all but race out the door, and come face to face with Gabriel.

43

Alice

"The fuck you doing here?"

Doc's voice rumbles across the space. My scalp tingles and I shiver. *Why does he have this effect on me?*

I just have to hear him or scent him and my insides twist, my emotions buzz around in my head, jolting up and down my spine, and I miss the other man's reply. Or perhaps all I have is eyes for the massive alpha male whose back is now turned on me. His very big, very broad shoulders fill the doorway, blocking off the sight of whoever stands outside.

"I saved your life, or have you forgotten that already?"

The other man's voice is pitched low.

I stiffen. *It can't be, can it?* "Gabriel?"

I breathe out and Doc's shoulders go solid. He slaps his arm across the doorway cutting off the other man's entry,

Damn, that's not good, is it? I swing my legs over the bed and he snarls, "Don't move Red."

I pause, then place my toes on the floor.

"Get back into bed." There's an edge to his tone that threatens to rip through all of my defenses. I shiver. My nerve-endings fire. Why the hell does his protectiveness turn me on so?

I fold my arms over my chest, "The man saved our lives so can you at least let him speak."

He goes still. He's going to refuse me. He's probably going to challenge Gabriel to some half assed fight just to prove that he can protect what's his, yet when it comes to accepting I am his, the hard-nosed man simply refuses to accept it. A low growl tears out of my throat.

Doc shoots me a look over his shoulder. "Hmm."

"What?" I throw up my arms.

His gaze rakes over me, then he nods toward the bed. "Under the covers."

I frown.

"If you think I am letting him enter when you are all but naked —"

"I am wearing a hospital gown." I huff out a breath.

"As I said, you are half dressed." His features close. Bet he wouldn't hesitate to stand there blocking the entrance all day. Obstinate alphahole.

So why am I picking this fight when the chances of my winning it are minimal? Sometimes you have to give in to get ahead... ya' know. I pull my legs under the sheets.

He jerks his chin and I stare. "Now what?"

He angles his head and I pull the covers up to my chin, "Happy?"

He merely swivels around to face the other man. "How did you get in here?"

"Security here isn't the best." Gabriel drawls. "Best you do something about it."

"Motherfucker." Doc clenches his fists at his side. "What did you do to the guards outside the building? If you've killed them —"

"Relax, I came to meet Dante. The guards were instructed to let me in." Gabe sounds like he's taking a stroll in the park.

How does he manage to sound so casual, especially when faced with the nearly seven foot powerhouse of cut muscle that is Doc.

Doc's shoulders bunch; he widens his stance.

"If I'd wanted to kill you I'd have done that at the auction." Gabe lowers his tone. "I held the crowd back and gave you a chance to escape."

"Which makes me distrust you even more." Doc thrusts his head forward, putting him right in Gabriel's face, and I wince. "No one does anything without wanting something in return."

"You're right." Gabriel's voice sounds reasonable. "Ten minutes with both of you, that's all I ask."

Doc cracks his knuckles, "You have five minutes and you say what you have from here."

"Really? —" I huff out a breath.

At the same time, Gabriel holds up his hand, "That's all I need."

Doc's jaw firms. A pulse flares to life at his temple. *Why does he look so angry, like he's going to strangle someone?*

Most likely Gabriel, who steps past him, Doc at his shoulder.

"That's enough." Doc stalks up and angles his bulk between us.

I huff. "You may as well pee a line around me to mark your territory."

Doc's head comes up, and there's a gleam in his eyes.

"Wait, I was joking."

"I am not." Doc folds his arms over his chest.

"You may have something there." Gabriel peers up at me from under hooded eyes.

Is that a smile playing around his thin lips?

"Never thought the day would come when my half-brother and my mate would unite on some stupid ass suggestion of mine —" *Oh!*

I swivel my gaze to Doc's face to find...no surprise on his features. "You knew who he was?" I stab a finger at him.

"I guessed."

"So why couldn't you let him into the room so we could have a conversation?"

Doc glares at me. "Half sibling or not, I am not letting a stranger in the same room with you." His features soften, "Your safety is my priority. I'll not compromise that."

"Yeah." My shoulders slump.

I mean how can I be angry with him when he only wants to protect me?

"And you," Doc stabs a finger at Gabriel's suit-clad chest, "You haven't answered the question as to what you are doing here." His voice lowers and the hint of danger rolls through the room.

I shiver. Doc all alpha and protective is so hot. Just something about this sexy man who is my mate. *My mate.* On cue the ball of heat in my chest stutters.

Doc's shoulders bunch.

Did he sense that?

Nah, I mean I did consolidate the bond between us. Doc claimed so, at least, but I don't feel any different. Not unless you count the fact that I can sense his every breath, the way the muscles of his shoulders ripple and the planes of his back flex under the remnants of the shirt. A tingling feeling fills my chest. It didn't mean anything. Didn't.

"I met Dante about a possible treaty." Gabriel runs his fingers through his hair. He's not as composed as the front he is projecting.

"A treaty?"

"I need his help in taking on the Berserkers."

I sit up in bed. "They attacked our city. Killed our mother."

"They took me." Gabriel says it in a cold voice bereft of any feeling. He's lived with this...his reality. So different from mine.

"You saved me." It comes to me in a rush. "You hid me in the cellar, so they couldn't find me."

"It worked." His lips twist in a smile that lights up his eyes. For the first time I see a glimmer of something... life? Hope in them. "It was that thought that kept me going all these years. That you survived."

"My adoptive Fae mother found me crying next to our mother's broken body." I swallow. "She took me in, gave me a home, a family."

"You are happy?" His gaze narrows.

I shoot Doc a glance.

"I am."

"He good to you?" Gabriel aims his thumb at Doc.

"Umm." I run a finger under my collar. "I am trying to decide that."

A low rumble rises from Doc's throat. It rolls over my skin and I shiver.

"And you?" I twist my fingers around the cover. "What were you doing at the auction, Gabe?"

"I am a trader."

"You buy and sell women?" Doc snarls and Gabriel holds up a hand. "It's a front."

Doc's arm shoots out and he grabs Gabriel's collar. "The fuck you talking about?"

Gabriel doesn't react.

Not a flicker of change in expression. If I hadn't recognized the likeness in our features I'd have never recognized him as my half-brother. The boy who had wiped away my tears and bathed my knees when I had fallen down and skinned them is lost somewhere in the hard muscles that wrap around his arms, the corded chest, the leanly roped shoulders which are not as massive as Doc's but just as coiled with power.

"The Berserkers took me to their stronghold." Gabriel's gaze holds mine. "They passed me around, used my body, kept me as their slave."

"Oh, Gabriel." I swallow and tears surge into my eyes.

Doc drops his arm but doesn't move away from his position at the door.

"Then I discovered our mother had been keeping a secret from me." Gabe's features twist.

"What do you mean?"

"I turned eighteen and transformed."

"What are you?" I angle my head.

His lips thin. "I am Fae but also exhibit vampire traits."

Doc snarls. "Hate those bloodsuckers." The scent of dragon smoke bleeds into the air, revealing just how close to losing his temper he is.

Gabe's jaw tightens, "It's served its purpose. Turned out I was the perfect weapon to slaughter those who'd kept me and my fellow prisoners captive."

"So you freed yourself and now what?" Doc props his big arms on his hips, "You took on your captor's roles?"

"Only because I mean to infiltrate the highest ranks of slave traders, those who organize the monthly virgin auctions. I mean to hunt them down and kill them all one by one." His voice grows hoarse.

"So what are you doing here then?"

"I need the Faes to help me in that."

Doc's jaw clenches. "That's why you met with Dante?"

"Yep, he is considering my proposal. Meanwhile I thought I'd visit with my half-sister." He angles his head at me.

"You are her half-brother; there's enough resemblance there for me to believe it. But I don't trust your suited ass."

Doc thrusts his face in Gabriel's and I wince.

The two of them going toe to toe is an awesome sight. Doc with that raw power, and ridiculously sculpted body that would shield me from anything, and Gabe with that leashed anger that crackles off of him and which he wouldn't hesitate to use to cleave through any resistance. Including Doc. "Stop."

Neither man takes notice of me.

"You may be her mate but you let her get into trouble. You allowed Boris to kidnap her and take her to the auction."

Doc's fingers clench at his sides.

What the—? Why is my half-brother inciting Doc?

"Clearly you failed to protect her." Gabriel's lips flatten. "You are not fit to be her mate."

Doc moves with that lithe speed that belies his massive bulk. He lifts Gabe up to the balls of his feet. Gabe's forearms tense, his muscles bunch, and I have had enough.

I lurch up onto the bed with the stupid hospital gown flaring around me, put my fingers to my mouth and whistle. A piercing sound slashes through the room.

Both men turn to look at me.

Doc glares; his nostrils flare. Gabe merely looks amused. One eyebrow rises. His unspoken words imply, *"Couldn't think of anything else, sis?"*

And something slots into space. He really is my half-brother. I mean, not that I'd questioned it. Yeah, okay I knew it, but I hadn't accepted it. He just looks so very different from the image of the half-brother in my head. But that slightly sarcastic, all kidding expression of his is so familiar. It leaves no doubt as to who he is.

"Will the two of you ease up already?" I grab my hair and pull at it.

"You don't tell me what to do, or have you forgotten, Red?" Doc frowns, then jerks his head at the bed, "And you are tiring yourself out by throwing a tantrum."

"I am throwing a tantrum?" I raise my head heavenwards. "Of all the idiotic things to say—" My knees buckle under me, but I refuse to let on just how weak I still am.

Doc leans forward on the balls of his feet. "Sit down before you collapse, Alice."

I set my jaw, "No."

A vein bulges at his temple and I am sure he is about to close the distance between us and put me over his knee, regardless of the fact that that my half-brother is watching us, when a new voice pipes up. "I have an idea."

Gabriel tenses. He lifts his head and sniffs the air. Then he swivels around to stalk the girl who's just slipped in. "Who're you?"

His voice is harsh, nowhere as controlled as it has been for the limited time that I have reacquainted myself with him.

"Hey y'all, I'm Lily." The girl takes a step forward.

Her blond hair hangs in straight thick clouds to her waist. She's skinny, and her skirt trails behind her. Her white cotton blouse brushes her waistband and falls loosely over her shoulders. Her ribs are visible in the V of her clavicle.

"You're Charley's friend?" I recognize her from having seen her with Jess' sister. Also, Lily is human. So of course, I had stayed away from her. I'd wanted to blend in with the Fae. Go figure. I'd gone about this all wrong.

Lily nods, her gaze connecting with mine and holding.

"Gia sent me to ask if you needed anything." She swallows, but her voice doesn't waver. She has some spine holding her own in a room with two alpha males. Takes more than an overdose of testosterone to scare this one. *Hmm.*

"I am here to make sure Alice is taken care of." Doc's tone brooks no argument.

Gabe twists his shoulders and releases himself from Doc's grip, only to angle his body between them, half blocking Lily from Doc's gaze.

"What were you going to say?" He fixes all of his attention on her.

Whoa. What? My head spins. Partly it's the adrenaline fading and the relief that I am no longer the cynosure of the attention of two angry dominants, but also because the chemistry between Gabe and Lily is like off. The. Charts. It reminds me of how it was when I first saw Doc.

"She could do with feminine company about now." Lily tilts her head at Doc and a smile lights up her features.

Gabe stiffens and takes a step forward.

Lily turns her wide-eyed gaze on him. "I propose that you settle your differences with a Dare."

"Predictable but effective." Gabe props his hands on his hips. "What's in it for you little girl?" He frowns.

"A chance to watch two alpha Fae males clash. Hey, how could I pass up that opportunity?" She props a hand on her hip. "Besides Doc's gonna whip your ass." She shoots Doc a smile, "Right, Doc?"

Doc bares his teeth at Gabe. "Can't. Wait."

Gabe stalks toward Lily.

She gulps, and her chest rises and falls.

He pauses in front of her and color sweeps her cheeks.

Lowering his knees he peers into her eyes, "Challenge accepted."

The hell? Is he talking to her or to Doc?

He snaps his teeth and she squeaks, then presses a hand to her chest.

Gabe chuckles and the sound is so cruel, that if he was not my half-brother, honestly I'd have scuttled for cover behind Doc's protective presence. The signals these two are sending each other is like whoa! Just insane.

Gabe straightens to his full height—which makes him tower over her—then shoots a glance over his shoulder at Doc, "I'll meet you out there."

He swerves around her and strides to the exit.

Lily's shoulders tremble and she draws in a breath. When she turns her eyes on me, her pupils are dilated. Yeah, I understand how she feels to be overwhelmed by the sheer dominance of a larger-than-life male, but honestly, I could have done without seeing how my half-brother eyeballed her. A half-brother who I don't know at all.

Doc turns on me, "You." He fixes me with that glaring blue gaze. "You stay here and recover."

"Of course." I plop back on the mattress and crawl under the cover.

Doc rubs the back of his neck, "Why don't I trust this sudden attack of your being docile?"

44

Alice

I hate bossy alpha-holes. I hate dominant Fae males. I hate my mate...okay, not completely. Not always. But just at this instance, I'd give anything to scream in his face.

He'd pointed his finger at me and told me to stay, then commanded Lily to stay with me and this despite the fact that Lily had wanted to watch them fight. Did I mention the man was bossy?

Then he'd swiveled around and stalked over to Gabriel. He'd jerked his chin at the other man, and something had passed between them. One of those very male gestures where there is an unspoken alpha to alpha signal sent and received.

They had marched out together, shoulder to shoulder, and he'd locked the door behind him.

I had staggered to the door and pushed at it, and of course, it hadn't budged.

My legs had shaken with the effort, and I knew it wasn't like I could have exactly torn out of there and followed him. Not when I didn't have any clothes to do so... not when my body still hurt like I had been trod upon and pulled apart. So I had stayed there curled against the door, then realized the stupidity of it all. I had almost given in to my fate, decided I had to simply take what he sent my way... not.

I had come this far.

I had survived the spankings, taken the edge of pain that he had subjected me too. I had enjoyed it. I gulp.

I had learned so much about myself.

Learned that I could withstand more than I had thought possible. I hadn't cracked under his ministrations.

I hadn't allowed any of them at the auction to break my spirit. I had survived this far. And damn if I was going to stay back here and wait for my fate to seal itself. If I let him go...I'll never get him back. He'll find a way to reason out of whatever is between us. He'll deny that I am his mate. He'll find a way to break the mating bond. I don't think it's actually possible to do so, but Doc's stubborn enough to find a way. Something inside me shrivels. I sit up with my back flat against the door.

Taking a deep breath, I steady myself.

I have to find a way out of here. Using the door to support myself, I stagger to my feet, then bang on the door. "Let me out."

"What are you doing?"

I glance over my shoulder to where Lily lolls in the chair next to the bed. "What does it look like?" I blow the hair out of my face. "I am trying to get out of here."

I hammer again. And again. The door doesn't even tremble. Damn it.

"Maybe if you put more weight behind it?"

"Maybe if you come here and help me?" I glower at her.

"Oh, right." She slips off of the chair and ambles over to stand next to me.

"On the count of three. One, two..."

She puts her shoulder to the door at the same time that I shove with all of my strength. My muscles strain, sweat pops on my brow. Nope. Nothing. The door stays firm.

Why is it that to be human means that you cannot physically push your way into anything, that you often feel helpless and always needing someone else? *Just for once, can't I save myself?* I drop into myself, to where the mating bond thrums against my chest. It flares up and I gasp.

Gray-blue sparks laced with of amber and green.

The flames rise up my chest, flood my blood, pulse through my veins. My vision narrows, the tips of my ears tingle. I peel back my lips then fold my fingers into fist and slam it against the door. It cracks. Just a little. Just enough for me to see through the gap. To put my mouth against the space and yell, "Get me out of here!"

Footsteps pound up the corridor and I stiffen. They race toward me, coming to a stop in front of my room. "Alice...are... you, are you okay?" A thin voice sounds through the door.

"Charley?" Lily hammers on the door.

"Lily?" Charley's voice rises in excitement. "What are you doing in there?"

"I came to see if Alice needed anything, only to meet this man..."

"Gabriel." I snap, "he's my half-brother."

"He is?" She turns to me, her gaze wide. Color smears her cheeks.

"Yeah." *Thought so.* "And the answer is no," I firm my lips.

"You have no idea what I was going to ask." Lily pouts.

"You wanted to ask me about him. You're interested in him, that's obvious. You should keep away from him. He's dangerous Lily, and totally out of your league." And that was the wrong thing to say. I huff out a breath. If I had been on the receiving end of that tirade I'd have redoubled my efforts to go after whoever I had been warned to stay clear of.

"Right." Lily says in a tone that implies, you've gotta be kidding me.

"Look, Gabriel's an asshole." I wince. "He's cruel and vicious and won't hesitate to hurt you." That's my half-brother I am talking about, but I feel protective about this girl, maybe because she's human and because I understand how it is to be trapped in the spell of a dominant man. I am not sure she can stand up to Gabriel. She's too delicate.

"You don't want him, Lily."

She juts out her chin.

"He'll break you. Dominate you. Consume you completely. Make you wish you'd never met him."

Her eyes gleam.

Oh hell, what have I done?

"Hey, hold the gossip you guys," The sound of the door being unlocked reaches me.

Charley opens the door and Lily throws herself at the other girl with a squeal. The two hug each other. You'd think they hadn't seen each other in years instead of hours. Teenagers. I roll back my shoulders, "How old are you Lily?"

"Just turned eighteen."

"Well, small mercies," I mutter.

"I'll be eighteen next month." Charley's gaze bounces between Lily and me. "You sound... edgy Alice." Charley frowns at me. "Your color is high. Are you sure you should be on your feet?"

"Don't you dare nag me." I stab my finger at her, "I have had enough with that alpha-hole Fae."

"Your mate?" Lily pipes up.

"Thank you" I raise my eyes heavenward. "Even little girls get it, but tell that to that too-full-of-himself man who knows it, but for some reason still refuses to accept it. And after everything we'd been through."

"Told ya, we're not little. Hell, you are only a few years older than us, Alice." Lily sets her jaw.

And isn't that the truth?

Only I feel so much wiser. Enough to be aware that imparted wisdom is never gladly received. You have to experience the consequences of your choices first hand, to learn from it.

"You're right."

I look down at myself and then at Charley. She's taller than me. Lily is closer to my size. I narrow my gaze on her, "I need your clothes."

"I don't think Doc will be happy if you leave the room." Lily chews on her lower lip.

"And I thought you were all grown up, hmm?"

Lily flushes.

Gotcha. "You are not going to allow some macho male to tell you what to do, are you?"

Silence.

I can almost hear her think, and a part of me feels sorry that I am manipulating her. But if there's one thing I have learnt from Doc, it's that anything is justified.

When you want something, you have to go after it. And right now, I have to get to him. He'd walked off in a rage, and I am sure he and Gabe are going to hurt each other. I don't want that. I can stop the fight before it gets too vicious. Oh, he is strong and can take care of himself, no doubt, but everything inside of me insists that I should go to him. Now. The heat in my chest flares up, sparks of blue and gold spurt through my nerves, and my ears tingle again. The wound at the curve of my neck throbs. It's Doc. He needs me. Pain slams into my chest and I groan. My vision wavers and my breath comes in pants.

"Help me Lily." I move forward and grasp her shoulder. "If you were in my place, and it was your mate rushing into something that might hurt him, then you'd go against his wishes too."

She winds a strand of hair around her fingers, then pulls it to her mouth and chews on it before letting it go. Gross habit.

"I know what you are doing." Her lips curve.

"Oh, yeah?"

"You're trying to emotionally manipulate me."

"Maybe you can face up to Gabe, after all." I chuckle, then square my shoulders. "Well what's it gonna be, Lily?"

"Yeah, I'll help you."

Charley holds up her hand and Lily high fives her. "I'd have done the same for Hawke, ah!" She licks her lips and darts a look at me.

"Not a secret." I jerk my chin at Charley. "His gaze eats you up when you don't notice it."

"He's in denial." She shifts her weight, "He thinks the age gap is an issue."

"Isn't it?"

"Nope." Both girls chorus.

My head spins. They have no idea what's in store for them. It would be a tough journey for both to claim their men. But they've gotta figure this out for themselves. I mean I am not giving up on Doc and me... yet. And I'll bet these girls are smart enough to hold their own against their alpha males

"Jeez. Look at the us." Charley drags her fingers through her hair. "I mean, are men even worth the effort?"

"Yep." This from me and Lily.

She smiles at me; her face lights up. She senses the kinship between us.

I look from Charley's angry face to Lily's thoughtful one. "You'll work it out you guys, I promise." *Yeah, look at me talking as if I have all the answers,* I chuckle to myself. "At least you two have each other to lean on."

They look at each other and something passes between them. "Okay then." Lily shrugs out of her shirt and hands it to me. "You go to Doc, we'll be right behind as soon as I grab a new set of clothes for myself."

I look at her sneakers. "I need those too, by the way."

45

Doc

I face off with the man who'd saved my life once already. My mate's half-brother.

My mate, I roll the words around in my head. *Why do I insist on calling her that? I mean she is, but... I can't possibly be considering owning the relationship that she had bonded with me? Not when I am all wrong for her.*

I need to find a way to break the connection...just as soon as I show this motherfucker who is more powerful here.

The beach is empty when we step onto it.

It's still early evening, the time when kids are back from school, and mothers are cooking evening supper. Not that I'd know. I never did have a normal life growing up, but it's what I have heard from the newly mated members of the Fae Corps. Both Dante and Tristan—the latter having gotten a fully-fledged family with Jess' sisters—have changed around the timing of the Fae Corps recons to accommodate the schedules of their mates and families...*Would I be doing the same once I took Alice home and recognized her for what she truly is? My heart? My soul? Why the hell are these thoughts racing around in my head now, when I need all my focus?* Focus. On defeating this mofo.

I shake my head to clear it.

Ahead, Gabriel loosens the buttons on the cuffs of his shirt. He rolls up his sleeves, and takes his stance.

I hold up my fists, then watch him as he takes a step to the side, then another. I mirror his moves in a counterclockwise direction. The fucker has something coming if he thinks I am going to be that easy to defeat. Footsteps sound and Hawke jogs up to stand outside the makeshift ring. "Well, that didn't take too long did it?" He takes a step forward into the margin of the circle in which we pace around.

"Stay the fuck out of this." I growl, not taking my gaze off of my opponent.

"You owe me." Hawke calls out to Dante, who prowls up to stand on the other side.

"You guys laid bets?" I bounce on my heels.

"Hawke thought you might last a week without picking a fight. Somehow, I thought otherwise." Dante drawls.

Gabriel doesn't show any reaction. No change in expression on his face. He may not have noticed Hawke's arrival at all. I could pretend to believe that, but I am not fooled.

"The man's not to be underestimated."

I shoot Dante a sideways glance. "You doubting my ability to hold my own in a fight?'

Dante raises his hands, "I just don't trust the motherfucker."

"You and me both." I swivel around to face my opponent.

Gabe bares his teeth, continues to circle. Sweat shines on his forehead. *What is he playing at?*

More steps sound and a group of girls come racing up. They mill around at a safe distance. Another family ambles up, then another to the other side.

I continue to pace around the wide circle, mirroring his motions. I am not going to be the first to charge. I am not going to give away any advantage I have here. He widens his stance and bends low. A chorus of gasps echo from the women.

Gabriel rights himself and, takes another stance.

"Go stranger!" One of the women screams. A smile flashes across his face, then it's gone. *Fucker's preening to the crowd. What the hell does he want?*

"I trust you to come out of this in one piece, you hear?" Dante mutters.

"You're insulting me." I crack my knuckles.

"Just looking out for your hide. Given you are recently mated." He leans forward on the balls of his feet.

"Not." I grit my teeth.

"All the evidence points to the contrary." Dante's voice is mild. "But if you want to deny it, be my guest."

"Shut the fuck up." I bite down on the anger that rages inside. "Sir."

"Good to see you're as respectful as ever."

"If you don't mind, I'd like to focus on whipping his ass."

"I wouldn't expect anything less." Dante backs away from the perimeter.

"Guess Alice has the backbone to stand up to you after all, huh?" Gabe grins at me.

"The fuck you talking about?" I shake out my arms, then roll my shoulders.

"You ready to lose this fight before your girl?"

Her scent reaches me first and I swivel around to watch her approach.

She's wearing a skirt that wings behind her, a T-shirt that clings to her curves as the wind flings it back against her body. It leaves not much to the imagination, showing off her figure, the way her nipples stand out against the fabric, and the skirt dips into the hollow between her legs. Her steps falter as she notices my attention on her.

Then she raises her chin and increases her speed and comes to a halt on my side of the ring. Her gaze flows over me and relief floods her features.

Warmth pools in my chest and I shove it away. I can't become weak, not now. I chose my path, to stay away from her. And I owe it to her to at least see it through. Just as soon as I kick the ass of this man who dared try to get past me to talk to her.

"Leave Alice." I growl, then wince. *Didn't mean for it to come out that way, all imposing, but hell. What is she doing out of bed, when she should be recuperating?*

Her head comes up. Her eyes flash. The sass in her. It fucking turns me on. No one has challenged me the way she has. No one means more to me than her.

"When I finish here, I am going to whip your ass, Red."

"Promise?"

The fuck did she say? My vision tunnels, and it is at that moment that I sense the shift in the air.

All of my instincts go on alert.

The hair on the nape of my neck rises.

I turn around just as Gabriel barrels into me. He tackles me around the waist. The world tilts. I crash into the ground and the impact sweeps through me. All of my bones seem to shake.

Dark spots flash in front of my eyes.

My body hits the sand and Gabriel buries his knees in my ribcage.

I try to take in a wheezing breath, only he leans forward. His weight pins me down. I try to breathe and my lungs burn. My ribcage screams in protest. He plows his fist into the side of my face and my head snaps to the side.

Red and white flash through my head. Before I can recover, he lands another hit to my shoulder, then back to my face. Pain whips over my side and my body shudders. Sweat slicks down my spine. Blackness licks the edges of my vision. I need to get the motherfucker off of me.

I scissor my legs up and bring my knees up into his back. The bastard doesn't stop. He continues to paint my body with a flurry of punches and jabs; he moves so fast he blurs.

Guess I underestimated him. Typical. He comes across as a suave, sophisticated man, but he's learned the same techniques I have, and he has the advantage of not being distracted. Less than a minute, that's all it had taken to lay me low. Am I going to let him get the better of me? Nope. *Nyet.*

I lock my fingers together, then strike out. My fists connect with his chin and his body snaps back and off of me. He rolls aside and I spring up to my feet. Raising a leg I bring it down on his chest. Only he grabs my foot and heaves.

For the second time I arc through the air and crash into the sand. *Fuck.* The jolt shudders down my spine, displacing the sand around me, which flies over me, covering my face and my chest. I rear up to my feet and race forward, and we clash chest to chest. The muffled thump echoes through the space. Fucker is strong, I'll give him that.

I reel back, then dive forward.

He raises his arm, the tips of his fingers spark. A bolt of white flashes across the space and slams into my chest.

The energy overpowers my cells. My nerve endings flood, my brain cells spark. White noise envelops me and I can't see, can't hear. When the static dissipates I crack my eyes open. I am on my back, the blue sky above me, white clouds in the distance. The sound of screams, voices yelling, reaches me.

I try to get up, but pain lances down my side, a burning heat lodges in my chest. I gasp and I'm gripped by a sudden, unfamiliar fear. My vision begins to fade. I grit my teeth. *I can't give in. I can't.*

"Nolan."

I am sure I am dreaming. *I can't hear her voice in my head, can I?*

The scent of jasmine teases my nostrils. It's as if she's reaching out to me through the bond. The heat in my chest intensifies and I cough.

"Let me help you, Nolan."

I groan and crack open my eyelids. My blood thuds in my ears. My heart begins to race so fast I am sure it's going to burst out of my rib cage.

Once again, I failed you, Red."

I pulse the thought at her, knowing she'll read it. I had denied her everything. Refused to acknowledge who she is to me. Now here I am, unable to protect my mate.

It's not over, Doc.

I chuckle. *You are an optimist Red, but you have to admit, me on the ground is a sign that I am not as strong as I thought I was.*

You're right.

Huh?

You're not the man I thought you were.

I pause, then pulse back, *Using reverse psychology, Red?*

Is it working?

Her voice lightens, and I swear the little minx is laughing at me. Heat pulses down the bond, and mixed with it is love and laughter... All the dreams, everything I had wanted is there within reach. All I have to do is reach out and take it. *Can I? Will I?*

I squeeze my fingers into the sand. The pressure hums down on my chest, behind my eyes, pulsing through every part of me. *Do it. Do it. Let her help you.* It's not a conscious decision. It's as if the barriers dissolve. That last remaining hitch around the mating bond bleeds away.

Sparks of heat and light, so much light, whooshes through the bond. Green like her, it's her spirit that floods my chest, my blood, my heart. I drop into myself and pull on my telekinetic energy. The blue and gold inside of me explodes, racing out to meet and entwine with the green. It slices through me, clearing my head. My eyes snap open.

Adrenaline laces my blood.

I spring up to my feet and I feel...fine. Ready. Strong. I raise my hands, palms parallel, and a ball of light appears. I swirl it and it grows more intense, the pulsing of it reflecting over my face, catching the glow from the surrounding space, drawing in every last bit of radiance. I thrust out my hands and fling it at him.

The ball of energy catches him in the middle of the chest, shoving him away. His body arcs back through the air and he falls on his back. Only to spring up again.

Motherfucker.

I am going to kill him.

I fall into the energy inside of myself, then pull it up, shooting it up over my chest, up my throat. It races to the edges of my fingertips. I raise my palms parallel to each other and another ball of energy flashes to life. I roll the energy together, then raise my arms to fling it at him when she screams, "Nolan, don't hurt him. He's my family."

46

Alice

"The fuck?" Doc freezes mid-motion. The energy between his palms ebbs and flows. He angles his body to shoot me a glance over his shoulder. Anger thrums from him in a dense cloud and I swallow.

He's every inch the alpha male Fae I fell for, my mate.

I take a step forward and another. The tips of my ears tingle, my scalp itches, my skin tightens.

What is happening to me? I push aside all thoughts and focus on the seething male in front of me.

The planes of his back flex.

More tension spools off of him. The strength of his dominance is so thick, it's an almost visible force, layering a cocoon around me. He wants to hide me from the world. And his possessiveness should anger me, but it doesn't. It's his way of protecting me and keeping me safe.

Warmth flushes my chest.

The ball of energy between his palms glows, and the gold of his eyes picks up the glint. His biceps bulge.

Reaching him, I touch his shoulder and he blinks.

I reach for him through the mating bond, *Please?*

His muscles go rigid, his triceps ripple. I can sense the struggle inside of him. I drag my fingers down his arm to circle his wrist. His pulse thuds against my fingers, so fast, so hard. My heartbeat picks it up and thuds along. Mirroring him. Needing him. Wanting him. The glow of energy switches off.

He lowers his arms to his side.

"For you, Red." He swivels around and I gasp. Those eyes snap vertically, his ears pull back, he peels back his lips and snarls.

I heave out a breath and the orb of heat in my chest throbs.

A burst of need surges down the bond and my ribcage constricts. I shudder, then step closer, until my breasts brush his chest.

He swallows and his gaze holds mine. His breathing calms, his iris' revert to their human shape. He wheezes out a breath.

"Seems you needed a little push there to accept her as your own."

Doc stiffens.

I peer around his massive body to frown at Gabe, "You baited him into this fight?"

Gabriel props his hands on his hips, "You are too good for him, but clearly you have your heart set on him. He makes you happy, Alice." One side of his lips curves, "He knew you were the one for him, he just needed a nudge to accept what was staring him in the face."

The tension in the air ratchets up.

The planes of Doc's chest twitch; I sense the anger drum in his veins as surely as it is my own. We are joined. We are one. *Can he sense just how connected we are?*

Rising up on my toes, I brush his lips. He stays unresponsive, his mouth hard. My throat closes.

I made a mistake.

*He's mad at me for leaving the room, he's angry with me for stepping in and asking him to stop before he hurt Gabriel. I hurt his ego, he'll never forgive me, I—*he closes his big palm around my nape and hauls me close enough my breasts flatten against his chest.

He tilts his lips, thrusts his tongue into my mouth and he takes.

My gums tingle, my canines ache.

He closes his mouth over mine and sucks from my essence. The mating bond twangs, and heat floods my chest.

He swipes his tongue over my teeth, and a hum rolls up my throat.

His breath scorches my cheek. "You've been a bad girl, Red."

I gulp.

He glares at me and my pussy clenches.

"You disobeyed me by coming here." He whispers in that hushed voice that sends goosebumps crawling over my skin. "You saved my life again. Showed me that my energy is incomplete without you. I need your essence in me, pulsing through my blood, I need your spirit to fill in the missing pieces of my body so I can fight again. I am nothing without you, nothing."

I hold his gaze and his intensity sears me.

His big palm squeezes my nape and pinpricks of lust sizzle down my spine.

"I love you, I can't live without you, but I still have to punish you."

His lips thin.

Omigod, this man, he can reduce my insides to mush with that cruel demeanor.

I nod. Not daring to trust myself to speak. How can I tell him that I can't wait for whatever he has in store for me. His touch. His bites. The rugged calloused skin of his fingers dragging over the sensitive skin of my butt. Emotions coil in my chest, my heart begins to pound. Sweat beads my forehead and my vision wavers.

"What's wrong?" He frowns.

"N....nothing." My ribcage seems to tighten. The tips of my ears tingle and my gums stretch. "There's nothing wrong with me." My toenails prick against my skin.

His gaze roams over my features and he starts, "Your ears."

He raises his arm and traces the tips of my earlobes. Sparks of feeling pierce my skin and I gasp.

"So fucking beautiful." He licks his lips and another tingling sensation runs down my spine.

He lets go of my nape and cups my cheek. "It's the effect of the mating bond. You're transforming, Red."

My teeth chatter and his eyebrows knit.

"You're cold?" His arms come around me, and he holds me closer. Heat from his chest rolls over me and I sigh.

"I am fine now." My knees give way and he swoops down and hauls me up into his arms.

"You should have told me. I knew this would happen. I knew mating you was—"

"The only thing I have ever wanted."

"I knew your body couldn't take the strain."

"You're mistaken." I cuddle closer. "I am not going anywhere, Doc. I trust you to keep me safe."

"I don't deserve you, Alice, after everything I did to you."

"I wanted it too, Doc. You taught me how to live, to feel. You showed me I wasn't just another weak human."

"You're the strongest person I know." His eyes glitter and a teardrop runs down his cheek. I raise my finger to scoop it up and lick it, then frown. "Your tears...they are.."

"Sweet?" A smile curves his lips.

"How?" I raise my gaze to his.

"I have enough dragon shifter blood in me to exhibit characteristics of mated shifter pairs."

"I want to experience it all, Doc." Pain squeezes my chest and I gasp.

"What's wrong Alice?"

His face ebbs and flows, a coldness grips me. "I am scared, Doc."

"Don't be. I'll be your strength. Lean on me Alice."

I sense his muscles shift, hear the sounds of people talking, and realize he is striding away from the beach.

"Gabe," I cough, try to turn my head to look in my half-brother's direction.

"He's not leaving." Doc shoots a glance over my head signaling to someone. Dante probably. "Gabe will wait until we are ready to speak with him."

"Don't let them hurt him."

His jaw tics and he continues stalking forward.

"Promise me, Doc. You can't refuse me this." *Drama much?* But I am not above using emotional coercion. I learned from Doc, after all, how to manipulate someone into giving you what you want.

"I am not going to let you die." His bites out the words. His features are hard but a nerve throbs at his temple giving away just how scared he is.

"I know." I chuckle and the sound comes out broken. "And I am still waiting for your promise."

"Stubborn woman." He glances down at me, and there's a softness in his gaze.

Something I hadn't seen before.

It's as if in the last few seconds he's dropped all pretense. No more barriers. No more walls between us. The ball of heat in my chest surges, and waves of blue and gray sweep over me. He's sharing his energy with me. A warm pink laces it all. *Am I imagining it?*

"That's why you love me."

His throat moves as he swallows. "I do. I have loved you from the moment I set eyes on you."

The warmth grows and envelops me, folding me in a caress that is so sweet. So soft. I want to roll around in it and never let go. I want that and so much more. Darkness tugs at the edge of my consciousness. I try to push it away, but it's too strong. Too overwhelming. It swoops up and over me and my eyes flutter close. "I need you, Doc."

47

Doc

Her body goes still and my heart fucking stops. I yank her close to me and break into a sprint. I am not going to let her die, no way. Hawke falls into a jog next to me, "What's wrong with her?"

"Nothing." *Everything.* It's my mistake that she is unconscious and struggling for her life. My mistake that she not only consolidated the bond, but also reached out to me through the mating bond and shared her energy with me.

She reactivated my telekinetic energy so I could draw on it and hold my own against Gabriel.

She used up the last remaining strength she had for that, even as her body was transforming. She was becoming Fae right in front of my eyes and I hadn't even noticed. That's how caught up I had been in my own head. I had wanted to protect her. I had thought I'd done my bit by getting her back to Singapore. I had been so intent on walking away from her that I hadn't noticed that the damage had already been done.

"Talk to me Doc." Hawke's voice follows me.

I increase my speed and the fucker simply keeps pace.

"She's not well."

"I can see that."

"She's transforming."

"You mated her. You're Fae. She's human. What else did you expect?"

I'm gripped by cold; sweat breaks out on my brow, "Her body is not taking it and she's fucking dying." *And it's my fault. If something happens to her I'll never forgive myself. Never.*

Silence follows. We jog side by side for a few minutes. We reach the turn off for the infirmary and I go the other way.

It takes him a few seconds to realize that he's going in the other direction. I hear him turn around and charge back at me.

"You are going the wrong way." He mutters, then turns around to catch up with me.

I am going in the right direction, but I am not going to tell him that. I am not answerable to anyone.

Least of all him.

I increase the pace of my steps, breaking into a sprint as we approach the row of bungalows within the compound where Fae, shifters and humans live.

When Dante had mated Gia, he'd picked up a bungalow in the Compound built in the heart of the city and along the beach. Each of the eight Fae Corps members had been allocated a place. I've never used my place, preferring to stay in the barracks. But it feels right to bring Alice here.

"Not speaking are we?" Hawke growls.

I come to a halt in front of my bungalow, then turn to face him. "I mated her. Only I can save her." I meet his gaze.

His forehead is furrowed, the wrinkles between his eyebrows show he is worried about me. "What are you going to do?"

I draw in a breath then my gaze drops to the woman in my arms, "Whatever it takes." I shoulder the door open and he calls after me.

"There's only one thing you need to do to make sure she survives, and I am not sure if you have the guts for it."

I shoot him a glance over my shoulder, "Don't second guess me."

"You think she deserves better than you, and you're right."

"Fuck off."

"Either accept the mating bond and everything that comes with it or let her go."

I cradle her closer and shake my head. My heart begins to thud harder.

"All you have to do is break the bond and release her."

Anger builds behind my eyes and the blood pounds at my temples. Funny, he's echoing my words, but hearing it from him brings home the fact that I can't let her go, *I can't.*

"Hanging in between the two decisions, you see what happens." He nods toward her. "You will only end up hurting her."

I snap my head forward and catch him in the chin. The bastard stumbles back. "Good to see you have some balls left."

"Get the hell off my property."

"Gladly." He chuckles then raises his hands as he backs off.

The door shuts in his face.

Bastard's right, though. Can't blame him for laying out what I knew all along. I need to own up to my responsibility. Face this and do what is best... for her. Her body quivers and I race up the stairs, down the corridor, past the two empty bedrooms to the one at the end. *My room. My bed. My mate.* A fierce possessiveness grips me and I lay her down on the bed. Her eyelids flutter open. "Nolan?"

48

Alice

"I am sorry for everything I put you through, Red."

He drops to his knees next to the bed, then takes my hand.

His touch sends shivers of longing shooting over my skin. It shouldn't be possible for him to arouse me with just a touch, but where he is concerned, all rational thought goes out of the window.

His blue eyes are stormy, and in their depths, I see an emotion I can't quite understand... Regret? Does he regret everything that happened between us? Is he not happy that I disobeyed his orders and came to him? Once more I had reached out to him through the bond and..."I couldn't stay away. I had to come to you."

He swallows and his eyes blaze, "I know."

"I didn't mean to go against you, but you shouldn't have left me locked up in the infirmary."

"You're right." His shoulder muscles tense.

I wriggle under his scrutiny. His gaze sears my features, touches on my breasts, before lowering to my waist. Every square inch of my skin prickles with awareness. He doesn't need to touch me. I can sense him, know when he is angry, upset... when he is sad. "I am gonna be fine, Doc."

His lips curve, creases fan out from the edges of his eyes.

I search his features but there is no anger. *Huh?* I totally expected him to be furious with me, to make me pay, by spanking me... then fucking me, and maybe I secretly hoped for it. I reach out my other arm hand, fully expecting him to grab my wrist and tell me not to take the lead, but he simply leans forward and allows me to run my fingers over his jaw line.

His whiskers scratch at my skin, sending pulse-points of heat flaring in my belly. My nipples tighten.

His nostrils flare, but he doesn't comment.

"You need to rest, Red." He leans forward and places a finger on my lips.

He rises to his feet and turns to leave. "Where are you going, Doc?"

"Giving you time to recover, something I should have done earlier, rather than getting all in your face." He shoots me a smile over his shoulder and my heart skitters.

I want to believe him, I do.

That he is a doting boyfriend or a mate who is devoted to me. And he is both, in a way.

He'll take care of me, protect me, even subdue me to his needs.

He'll make me weep, make my body his...but he'll never agree to everything I say. He'd never just go along with my suggestions without trying to get his way unless..."You are going to walk away from me?" I breathe out the words. "After everything that happened, knowing I am transformed, that I am becoming Fae, sensing the intensity of my emotions for you, you are still going to leave?"

He halts. "I am going to ensure that you never lack for anything. That I'll always be there to watch over you and be your friend when you need someone. But I can't...put you through what happened. I can't risk your life again. And if I sleep with you, if I make you subjugate yourself to me, I risk hurting you to the point of no return. Don't you see I can't let that happen."

"Wait." My throat is dry and I swallow, then pull myself up to sitting.

"So you are suggesting that we stay mated but that you will not fuck me again. You will not be my master and I am not your slave?"

"You are free of that relationship, you can choose another."

"You don't mean it."

He stiffens, then draws himself up to his full height. "Don't doubt my words."

"I bloody well will." I draw my legs up. "If you absolve me of the relationship, it means I can question you."

His nostrils flare.

"It means I can sleep with another."

His jaw tics. A vein throbs at his temple.

"It means I can take another master."

He moves so fast that he blurs. The next second he's hunched over me and his palm is over my lips. "Don't you dare."

A breath rushes out of me. I don't speak, just look at him, trying to understand what's running through that complex brain of his. He straightens and drops his hand to his side then begins to pace.

"I tried, I fucking tried, but it's difficult. It's going to kill me." He walks to the window and grabs the sill. The skin across his knuckles is white.

"What are you afraid of?"

"Myself. I am afraid of losing control and going too far. When I saw your body slump out there... I thought... I thought I'd lost you all over again." He lowers his forehead to the window pane. "I need pain to feel anything. What if I forget myself, what if I push it too far, and not only mark you but do something irreversible?"

"Not possible." My belly constricts and I push myself up to stand on my feet. My shoulders scream, my muscles ache, but already, my flesh is knitting back together. The heat in my chest throbs and begins to spread out to my extremities. My fingers tingle. My toes flatten. I move around the bed and approach him.

"You are forgetting something, are you not?"

His shoulders bunch but he doesn't look around. "Every time I am with you, I forget who I am and want to simply rut you." He chuckles and the rough sound curls around my waist.

"Look at me, Nolan."

He jerks. "Don't come close, Red. I am trying to do the right thing here."

"You mean you are trying to assuage your conscience?"

His head jerks up, but he still doesn't turn. "The fuck you mean by that?"

"Clearly, you are being selfish. You are only thinking of yourself. Making sure that you don't have to take responsibility for what happens next. Not caring that you have already changed me. Not only have you left me with a hankering for the slap of your hand on my flesh— His shoulder blades draw back. "—but you've also changed the very anatomy of my existence. Thanks to the mating bond, I am as much Fae as human, I can withstand anything you can do to me, and more."

His shoulders go solid. He grips the sill with such force that cracks form across the wall.

"Fine, if you don't want me then there will be any number of Faes or Shifters or hell... even those at the auction who will be more than happy to—"

He swivels around and a gasp spills from my lips.

"Stay quiet." His eyes flash vertically. *Oh, hell, did I push him over the edge?* He peels back his lips and his canines drop. My pussy clenches.

I want to feel those teeth sink into the delicate flesh between my legs. I squeeze my thighs shut and his gaze drops down to my trembling core.

"You have no idea what you are doing." He shakes his head as if to clear it.

"Don't I?'

I should turn and run.

This is my chance to leave. Finally, I am turning into one of the species I have admired. Now, I can fit in with my family, with this city... but the only thing I want is the angry male standing in front of me, eating me up with his eyes. He won't be gentle. He'll be a lot harsher than before. That final shield between us holding him back is gone. If my being human had stopped him from going that extra mile...now there's nothing to prevent him from showing me his worst. Goose bumps flare on my skin. *Why the hell does that thought turn me on?*

"N...Nolan?" He doesn't answer. His gaze sweeps up to my chest, pausing for a second, then up to my mouth.

He flicks back his ears and I swear they have extended further than before.

He rolls his shoulders and his biceps seem to swell further. He's much taller than me but I am positive he's never seemed so huge, so much larger than life.

"You're scaring me." My voice comes out all breathless and I curse myself.

"Good." He takes a step forward and I sidle back.

He holds his hands away from his sides and claws slide out from his fingers. *What—?* That's never happened before. Those look lethal, the veins of his forearms seem to pop, and honest, that is the last straw. A squeak trembles past my lips. Then I turn and race around the bed and for the door. I reach it just as a bolt slides home on the other side with a loud bang.

I come to a halt with my heart pounding, the blood thudding in my ears.

The air in the space thins, then rights. He used his telekinetic energy to hold me here.

"What are you doing?"

"Making sure you can't escape." His voice sounds strained as if the last piece of humanity in him has shredded.

My heart begins to thunder. I did that. I tore away that final barrier of his control and exposed him for what he is, an animal. Like me.

I turn around and meet his gaze.

One side of his mouth curls. I flick my tongue out to lick my dry lips and his gaze drops to my mouth.

"What's the matter, Red? You too scared to deal with the repercussions of your actions?"

Yes.

Yes.

"Of course not." I fold my arms over my chest.

"That's good to hear." He bares his teeth and I gulp.

He takes a step forward, his pace slow, measured, and my shoulders tremble. My gaze skitters to the door.

"It's too late to escape." He flicks back his ears and the tips lengthen.

My throat closes. My breathing quickens.

"This room is soundproof."

"What?" I blink. "Why?"

"So you can scream as loudly as you want when I fuck you and no one will hear you."

49

Doc

Her pupils dilate. The black bleeds out until only a ring of green can be seen around the edges. The sweet scent of her arousal tinges the air. *Fuck me, but she's aroused.*

My cock twitches and begins to extend and I clamp down on my desire. *Not yet.* Not until I have my way with her. Not until I have shown her that she must obey me. That she can't go against me and risk her life again. I had planned to walk away from her, but the thought of her seeing anyone else, being with anyone else, no way could I survive that. I had been wrong to think that I could let her leave. Or that I could leave her. We are bound together—in heart, in body, and in soul—and it's time I make her mine completely. Time I become hers forever. "Turn around."

She swivels around to face the door, and that little gesture of acquiescence sends a thrill racing over my skin. My groin tightens, my dick hardens, every part of me goes on alert.

"Part your legs."

Her shoulders tremble, and she moans. She fucking makes that tiny noise at the back of her throat that simply makes me want to throw her down and rip into her. I squeeze my fingers at my side.

"I won't ask again, Red."

Her butt muscles flex, her waist twitches and I can't take it anymore. I shove my thigh between hers and kick her legs apart.

The breath wheezes out of her, "Please." She stutters.

"Do you want me to gag you, Red?"

She shakes her head.

"Then stay quiet, and do not move."

I swipe out with my finger and hook my nail in the collar of her T-shirt. "What the hell are you wearing anyway?"

"They belong to Lily."

I click my tongue, "I was testing you. Remember what I told you, Red. You don't speak, you don't see, you don't breathe without my permission, which you may for the moment."

She nods then subsides; her breathing goes ragged. I draw the tip of my nail over her skin. Goosebumps flare on the nape of her neck. *Hmm. Nice.* But not enough. I tug my finger and the T-shirt rips.

She cries out, but I don't stop.

I drag my nail down the cloth all the to the edge of where her T-shirt hits the waistband of her skirt. Sliding my nail between the waistband and her skin I tug and rip through that too.

Another moan bleeds from her and she stands there naked.

"You didn't wear underwear," I growl, "how convenient."

A shiver trembles down her spine and she wriggles her butt. Her thighs grip mine and I click my tongue. "Didn't give you permission to try to relieve the pressure in your pussy...yet."

She takes in a breath and raps her forehead against the door.

"You feeling a little frustrated, Red?"

She nods.

"Then do everything I say and if...I am feeling generous, I may even allow you to touch yourself."

Her shoulder blades wing back, her spine curves and she rubs her breasts against the door. She literally begins to push her flesh into the wood, fucking it.

It's hot. Insane. The sexiest thing I have ever seen. Warmth trickles against my pants and the wet fabric sticks to my thigh muscle, she's dripping, wet and ready and I can't stop myself. I drop down and thrust my face between her legs.

She moans, then shudders.

I tilt my face up and drag my tongue up her clit, then all the way up to her puckered back hole.

Her entire body goes rigid, then she shudders and her fingernails skitter against the door. A whine wheezes out of her. I thrust my tongue into her back hole and her muscles flex.

I shove my tongue in-out-in curling it in her puckered hole, then slide it back to the folds of her pussy.

Sweet, hot, the taste of her is honey spiced with nutmeg. It coats my tongue and my dick throbs.

I grab her thighs and shove them even further apart, then plunge my tongue inside of her wet channel. Again. And again. Her back arches, her butt goes rigid and her pussy clamps around my tongue. More moisture leaks out of her and I swallow it up, every bit. I sense her tense, feel the heat shudder down her pussy. Her breathing grows shallow.

She's so close... my balls grow hard. *No, not yet.* I will not let myself come. Will not allow her to come either. I pull out my tongue and rise. A whine slips from her lips, and she turns around, her eyes flashing, "Don't you dare leave me this way." Color flares on her cheeks and her hair ripples around her face. She's so beautiful, my Red. Wild. Spirited and all mine to break.

I bare my teeth and her gaze falls to my canines. She flinches, then straightens, and sets her jaw.

"Bad girl. You disobeyed me."

She pouts, and her gaze darts to the side.

"Do you know what I do to those who don't do as I ask?"

She doesn't answer.

"Look at me, Red."

Her eyes land on my face.

"I asked you a question. Nod if you understand."

She jerks her chin.

"You broke a rule; now you must pay the consequences."

She swallows, and her face pales.

"You get me?"

She nods, a quick movement.

"You ready to take your punishment?"

A bead of sweat trickles down her temple. The sweet scent of her arousal bleeds into the air. I drag my finger over her clit and find she is even more wet, if that is possible. "I do believe I have my answer."

I swoop down and grab her waist and turn her around to face me completely. Her gaze widens, her mouth falls open, but I don't stop. Bending my knees I heave her and throw her over my shoulder.

50

Alice

He stalks to the bed and my heartbeat begins to race. Should I protest? Should I tell him not to do this?

Should I try to break away from him? *No. No.* I can, but I won't. I don't want to run away and that's the truth. I want every fucked up thing he can do to me. I want him to bind me and gag me and take me. I want him to tell me how to move my body to satisfy him, and the thought sends a tendril of heat racing down my spine.

The world tilts and he throws me down. I bounce on the mattress, once, twice, then come to a stop with the hair flowing over my face. I lean up to push it away. "Don't." His voice stops me.

I let my hand fall to the side. He shoves away the hair from my eyes and I raise my gaze to his.

Blue, burning with intent. He straightens then walks around to stand at the foot of the bed.

"You do as I tell you to and not a breath more or less, get me?"

I nod.

A pulse flares to life at his jaw. He looks feral, and I can't wait for his next command. His lips flatten, "Spread your legs."

I part my thighs and only then realize I've done so without any conscious thought. That's how it is, when he assumes that role of a master, I am helpless to obey.

His gaze drops to the flesh between my legs. "Now, squeeze your pussy lips and part them for me."

Umm... Okay. Isn't that something he's supposed to do? Didn't he say that he wouldn't let me even touch myself, then what is this about—?

"I'm waiting."

I reach down between my legs, and slide my fingers between my lower lips, then I pull them apart. The cool air flows over my clit, and the bud of my pussy hardens. Blood rushes to my core and my thighs tremble.

"Close your eyes, Red."

No.

No.

I snap my eyelids shut.

"Don't open them, not until I tell you to."

I swallow. *Damn him.* He may as well have blindfolded me and gagged me and tied me back. Somehow, the very fact that he asks me to exercise my powers of self-restraint without restraining me is an all new level of fucked-upness on his part. One I hadn't expected.

The keening edge of anticipation knives over my skin.

My nerve endings crackle. My scalp tingles. My fingers tremble and I almost lose hold of myself. *Help me, but what am I doing here, legs spread apart? On my back, waiting for my master to do what, exactly, to me?*

"Beautiful, Red. If you could see yourself as I do now."

I can imagine, okay?

I am sure he can scent the moisture that trickles down between my legs, see the pink bud of my clit bared to him, watch as my channel seeps and aches for him.

I sense him move and then his heated breath sears the tender flesh of my inner thighs. A moan slips up my throat and slips from my mouth. I bite down on my lower lip to contain it. I will not give him the satisfaction of seeing just how much his games turn me on. If he knew, there would be no stopping him again. Not that I want to stop him. Not that he's going to listen to anything I have to say anyway. So why am I resisting him? Why am I holding onto that last measure of sanity that lurks inside?

The rough edge of his tongue curls around the bud of my clit and goosebumps flare over my skin. The tips of my ears tingle and I sense my teeth ache and strain against my gums. *What's happening to me?* My very insides are being torn apart. The band of heat in my chest tightens and I gasp. Sweat breaks out on my brow. He shoves his tongue inside my pussy and I groan.

My fingers tingle and I want to tear them away from my cunt, dig my fingernails into his shoulders and pierce his skin, and draw blood... *Whoa! Where did that thought come from?* I wriggle my hips and he leans the weight of his shoulders on my thighs, holding me down. "Don't move."

His gravelly voice tugs at my skin and I gulp.

The heat from him enfolds me, pushing me down, holding me down. I couldn't move even if I tried. A chuckle tears from my lips. The next moment his mouth latches onto my cunt, his sharp teeth bite into my tender flesh, and I scream. I thrash my head from side to side; my toes curl into the bed... I want to, need to, touch him. Have to. I dig my fingers into his shoulders. My nails dig into his flesh, and the scent of copper rends the air.

So he'll punish me later, but I don't care. I simply need to be closer to him. I tilt my hips up and he chuckles.

He grabs my thighs and lifts up my legs until they are around his neck, "Mine. This is my pussy, you hear me, Red?"

Yes.

Yes.

The visceral need in him reaches through the mating bond and my chest seems to light up. Pain. Need. The sheer primal instinct to have him inside of me tears through me.

I grip my thighs around his head and push up into his face. His tongue plunges into me, again and again. The climax tears up from my toes, up my legs and he presses his hands into my legs and pulls me away from him. The waves recede and I cry out.

No, not again. Pressure builds at my temples, pressing down against the back of my eyes. *He can't do this.* I snap my eyes open and meet his gaze.

"I can and I will." He bares his teeth, the canines white against his dark skin with little droplets of scarlet clinging to their tips.

Blood. *My blood?* A shudder grips my skin. It should disgust me, surely? Then why does the saliva pool in my mouth. *Why does liquid sweep into my core?*

I peel back my lips and mirror his grimace. My gums tingle, then I feel my canines drop, mirroring his. "Holy hell?" I stare. "This is really happening, I am transforming into my Fae form."

"You accelerated the change when you shared your energy in that last fight."

My chest twangs and I bring up my hand to rub at the place over my heart.

"I am sorry I went against your word."

He blinks, then his features lighten and those beautiful lips curve into a smile, "I didn't anticipate otherwise."

"I am obviously also no good at obeying you." I drop my chin towards my chest."

He leans down and peers into my eyes, "Never apologize, Red. If you gave in too easily, where would the satisfaction be in that?"

Huh? I blink.

"It's because the pain still scares you that it turns you on. It's because you are still so surprised that it can feel so good that the pleasure pushes you over the edge."

"You still confuse me."

"Just follow your instincts, Red. There is no right or wrong here. There's only me and you and the chemistry between us that changes every time we are together."

"And that's a good thing?" I frown.

"Very."

"So you forgive me for speaking when you told me not to, for holding you when you told me to stay back?" I draw my fingers over his shoulders and down his chest, leaving tracks of blood in my wake.

His blue eyes burn, "Never."

O-k-a-y.

He flicks back his ears and my gaze flows over his face, down his chest to where the evidence of his arousal thickens and hardens. His angry cock throbs, rises up, the head purple and weeping precum and I gulp. He's as aroused as me, so why can't he simply just bury it in me and put us both out of our misery? My heart begins to pump harder and I lick my lips.

He sits back on his haunches, then grabs my waist and turns me around so I am perched on my hands and knees. His strength still surprises me. The ease with which he is able to maneuver my body is so fucking hot. My belly squeezes, my sex aches. Damn if that doesn't turn me on even more.

The sound of his palm connecting with the flesh of my butt reaches me first, before the white pain crashes through my consciousness. *Ow*, I bite my lips. He could have warned me. He hits my other butt cheek. *Ow. Ow.* That hurt more. Back to the first, then the other, he alternates between the two, so fast, that I lose count. All of my attention is focused on my butt.

My pussy clenches, moisture sweeps into my core, and my entire behind is one swelling mass of pain. Red flares behind my eyes. The blue-green energy in my chest sparks to life. He still doesn't stop. He shoves his thigh between my knees, shoving them apart, then slaps my pussy. I scream. Slap. Slap. Slurp. The edge of his palm connects with my swollen cunt and a burst of heat ignites at the base of my skull, sizzling down my spine. He alternates between hitting the two butt cheeks and my pussy again and again.

It hurts. It hurts. A wave of molten lava swells up from my toes and climbs up my calves. My entire body shudders, my back curves, and I raise my head and howl. The sound echoes around the room and I can't believe that's me. "Don't you dare come, Red, not until I give you permission."

I hate him.

I hate him.

I pant. My vision narrows. Sweat drips down my temple. Tears overflow my eyes. My pussy weeps. My channel aches. I am empty, so empty. I just need him inside of me.

He falls to his back next to me, then lifts me over him so I am straddling him. The head of his rigid dick nudges against my cunt. He grasps my waist and holds me there, suspended over him, and he isn't even breathing hard.

"You want me, Red?"

What do you think?

I have a good mind to say no.

I nod my head and he lowers me down so his shaft pierces my pussy. My inner muscles clamp down on him and I am so moist that he plunges all the way through until he hits my cervix. Little shivers of pleasure dart up my spine and I grit my teeth.

"So fucking wet and moist and open."

I raise my gaze to meet his burning one. He flicks back his ears and I feel the tips of my own tingle. My vision narrows on him—his face, his lips. I lean down and close my lips over his and he lets me kiss him. He lets me scoot my tongue inside and over those sharp canines of his. His chest shudders, then he angles his hips and thrusts upwards and slams all the way through.

I feel him extend, feel his knot harden and flex inside of me, and then he locks it in behind my pelvic bone and I gasp.

He drags his palms up and over my spine to the nape of my neck. Grabbing it, he yanks me back, exposing my neck. "You are mine. Never forget that, Red."

Then he rears up and sinks his teeth into my neck.

The pain sweeps over me—hot, biting. It screeches over my nerves and slams into my chest.

Something inside me jolts opens.

Sparks of blue and green explode and I rear back. My back is on fire and streaks of white pain roll down my spine. I open my mouth and scream, then snap back my head. The orgasm rolls up from my groin, radiating outwards screeching toward my extremities.

Gusts of psychic breeze buffet me. I squeeze my eyes shut and the waves overtake me. My hair snaps back and I am sure I am flying in real time.

"Alice."

His voice is filled with wonder, surprise, and something else. Awe?

Huh? I crack my eyelids open.

A shudder ripples down my spine and I gasp.

51

Doc

With the sound of flesh ripping from bone, the wings unfold from her back.

"Beautiful."

The trembling feathers snap out behind her—painted in hues of green and blue and delicate enough for the light to filter through. Sparks of gold dot the flesh between the feathers.

"What...what is it?" She gulps.

"You. You are the most gorgeous creature I have ever seen."

Her pussy clamps around my throbbing dick. My balls draw up and I can't stop the orgasm that crashes over me. Her body arches back, her head thrown back to expose the curve of her throat. Drops of blood stream down her neck.

Her wings snap back and her feathers light up, her body tenses, every muscle coiled, and the orgasm breaks over her.

A moan spills from her lips and she grips my arms, clamps her pussy around my dick, and I let her ride me. Her wings flap again and she rises up in the air, taking me with her. For a second, we stay suspended above the bed.

Another tremor races up her body; her wings snap back, the sparks flare up, lighting up the space, then subside.

Her body shudders and she falls over.

Her wings pull back into the notches on her back. She slumps against my chest and I hold her as I hit the bed with a light thump.

My throat is tight, a tear rolls down my cheek. *Fuck me, am I crying?* Truth be told, that was the most beautiful sight I have ever seen.

She transformed completely, and just at the moment of our union. Warmth fills my chest and I squeeze my arms around her. The ridges on her back bump against my hand and I run my fingers lightly over the grooves. She moans and cuddles closer.

"Did that hurt, Red?"

"Not exactly...I think I dropped into myself fully, for the first time."

"Mating you began the change, and now, when I claimed you again, it completed the transformation."

"What does it mean?" She peers up at me with those big green eyes.

"It means you are both Fae and human with a tinge of dragon." I grip her curvy hips and squeeze. "Enough to give you a pair of very special wings." I hum my approval.

She blushes, her pussy clenches and *uh*... that's an interesting reaction.

"Your wings are the lightest, most exquisite I have ever seen." I growl, and this time moisture trickles down from between her legs. So I wasn't mistaken. Red's even more responsive to me than before. I. *Am. Fucked, is what I am.*

"Do you think it will happen every time we... ah...?"

"Fuck?"

"Yeah," She pushes herself up to rest her chin on her arms, then flutters her eyelashes. "You know what they say? Once you go Fae, you never stray."

"So you like it when I knot you?" I can't stop the smirk from tugging at my lips.

"Um... yeah." She frowns.

"You enjoy it when I fuck you?" I ask only because I want to hear her say it.

"Let me think..." She tilts her head and I thrust my hips just a little. My still erect dick throbs inside of her. She gasps.

"That's a yes, I take it?"

She nods.

"You love it when I..." I bring her down for a kiss and her wings flutter. It's a physical manifestation of her desire, not that she was able to hide her reaction to me earlier, but clearly the wings are a dead giveaway. Poor Red, she has no idea how difficult it is going to be for her to hide anything from me.

I trail my fingertips over her back, over the ridges of her newly transformed wings and she shivers.

"So sensitive." I whisper against her lips.

Her muscles twitch. Her pussy clenches and my knot throbs again.

"You want more when I spank you?"

She hums and this time I don't need to ask her if that's a yes.

I drag my fingers over her shoulder then wrap my fingers around her throat. "And when I choke you...?"

She gulps, I feel the vibrations caress my fingers.

"I fear it...but it leads to the most spectacular of orgasms." Color flushes her cheeks. "I hope I never get used to it."

Me too, Red. Me too.

I loosen my grasp, only to sink my fingers into her hair and coil the glossy strands around my fist.

I tug her head back, exposing her throat.

"You belong to me, Red." I glare at her. "You are mine to knot, to take, to fly with over the wind currents. You are mine because you give me the choice to own you, break you, and put you back together in a form that mirrors every single aching pulsing cell in my body."

She squeezes her inner muscles around my dick and her wings snap out.

The light shines on the delicate feathers, lighting them up again. I am sure my life has changed forever.

52

Alice

I race up the beach, and snap my wings out. They stretch behind me, the air currents seethe under them, and I lift off, just a few inches from the ground, only to land back with a thump.

My knees bow and I manage to take the weight of my body, i.e. I manage not to stumble and fall... again.

I set my lips in a pout. It's not that easy to fly, so why do birds and dragons make it seem so effortless.

Of course, none of the other Fae in this city have wings.

I am the first to exhibit this particular trait, thanks to Nolan's dragon blood. Not only do I fit in with my people...I have something many of them covet. And I am not only talking about my wings. I snicker to myself.

"Red."

I turn around to see the object of my thoughts materialize near me.

My heart begins to race faster, the blood thudding at my veins. "I wish you wouldn't do that." I scold him.

"What?" The outline of his body fades in and out, then solidifies. He stalks toward me.

The breath leaves my lungs, and surely, it's because of the mechanics of teleportation, eh? It has nothing to do with the harshness of his jaw, the way his nose hooks, the way his thin upper lip stretches even as that obscenely thick lower lip juts out in the resemblance of a sexy pout. I want to lean in and sink my teeth into that beautiful flesh. On cue, my gums tingle, my canines stretch and try to break through the surface.

Pain twinges across the surface, moving down my throat to meet the ball of heat in my chest that thuds steadily. *Steady.* He reaches me and his gorgeous features light up. One side of his mouth curls. That wicked smirk of his...liquid lust squeezes my belly. He leans over me, all seven feet of his big body. My breath catches.

"Answer me," He glares and I shiver.

My pussy melts and I all but throw myself at that broad chest and climb him right then.

"What...what was the question?" I wave my hand in the air and his fingers wrap around my wrist. Those thick warm fingers of his dwarf my smaller bones.

To think he'd once been a small boy, vulnerable and hurting from what his father had done to him. When Nolan had revealed what he'd been through, something had clicked. A boy who'd faced so much pain, enough to put him off of relationships, any kind of intimacy, he'd needed the same edge of pain to peel away the walls he'd built around himself, to expose the sensitive soul inside who'd do anything for the one he loved. Me.

It made sense in a warped kind of way.

Not that Nolan would accept it. He wasn't using the excuse of his childhood experiences to justify his kinky tastes. He says it's who he is. A sadist. I say that he is mine. Any which way.

"Do I still make you nervous?"

"Yeah." I wheeze out a breath.

He leans in closer and that dark scent of his flows over me, mixed with the salt of the sea breeze and a tang of something else. Desire? Lust? A heady cocktail that makes my head spin. My knees buckle and I stumble, only to fall against that hard chest.

His arms come around me, holding me close. "You okay, babe?"

"I am now." I rub my cheek against the strip of skin bared by the collar of his shirt. The thud-thud of his heart sinks into my blood and mirrors the pulse that flutters in my belly. *My belly?*

My shoulders tense.

"What is it?"

I can't answer. All thought goes out of my head. I drop into myself and reach inside, to the source of the emotions coursing through me. Love. Possessiveness. Mine. Something that belongs to me and to him. The child we created. *When did that happen?* Probably one of the many times he knotted me, over the past week.

But it's too early to tell, isn't it?

Or is it my heightened senses that confirm that it's true? *It is.* I am carrying his child. I swallow and a tremble shivers over my skin.

"What's wrong, Red?"

I shake my head. Heat flushes my cheeks and I squeeze my eyes shut.

"Tell me." A blue energy reaches out from him through the bond, flooding my veins, heading straight for my womb. He guessed it. *Is that possible?* I lean back in the circle of his arms.

"Is it what I think it is?" His face pales.

I burrow closer and he scoops me up in his arms. I squeak. "I was trying to figure out how to fly."

"Not until the baby is born." His arms tighten around me and I gasp.

"How...how do you know?"

"I see you, Red. I sense you even when you're not with me. We are bonded in more ways than one. Don't you sense that?" He raises me until I am at eye level with him.

"Of course I do." But still, this level of connection, where he can sense what I am thinking, feel what's happening to me, maybe even before I know? "So... you're okay with my falling pregnant?"

His jaw goes solid.

Okay, not that we'd discussed babies or even the future together. With Doc... the best form of communication is on the physical level.

When he touches me, I know he wants me.

When he spanks me, it's a sign that he cares for me.

When he makes me orgasm over and over again...? I know he wants to give me the world.

But when he stares at me with those blazing blue eyes, fixing me with his complete attention, my heart flutters. Goosebumps rise on my skin. "You still didn't say how you feel about..."

He comes to a halt so fast that my breath catches in my throat.

He raises me up until he's holding me up and my belly is at level with his face and he peers up into my face with a strange look. His iris' flash vertically and I shudder.

When he does that... the intensity of what he's feeling is writ large on his face. The bond in my chest lights up and blue and gold bleeds down our shared connection.

He hauls me in close, then presses his lips to my womb. Sweet. So sweet. So not what I expected. Yet so Doc. Harsh and soft at the same time. Dominant and possessive, yet so caring. He doesn't need to say it aloud; I can sense what he's feeling and it's... beautiful.

He tips his head up, "The child is mine. You are mine. I love you both, Red."

A tear trickles down my cheek. The words wrap around me, cocooning me as he rights me in his arms and wraps me closer.

He starts walking up the beach. "A mating bond goes both ways, so you can sense the unsaid with me too."

"It's pretty hot, I admit, being so in sync."

"There's no way I can let you out of my sight, you know that, right?"

I gnaw on my lower lip. Not that he had been easy before. I had barely managed to convince him to let me go for a walk... had been hoping to fly and surprise him...instead the kind of surprise inside me had floored me completely. *Huh?*

"Where are you taking me?"

"The Fae Corps are catching up to decide about Gabe."

I haven't seen him since the Dare between him and Doc. Not only because we needed time together to come to grips with everything that had happened between us, but also because Doc is way too possessive; he doesn't care that Gabe's my brother. As far as he is concerned, no male is allowed to see me. Not unless it's in Doc's presence.

He walks up the path leading away from the beach, to the courtyard in the center of the Fae Corps headquarters.

His steps slow and I look up to find Hawke approaching us. "You're late."

He jerks his chin at Doc. Nolan doesn't answer. He simply walks around Hawke and toward the center where the rest are milling around. "You okay, Doc? You look shaken."

"Speak for yourself," Doc tosses a glance over his shoulder, then keeps walking. His arms tighten; nervous tension spirals off of him. I don't need to look up to know what I'll find. "Gabriel."

He sidles across the courtyard to come to a stop a few feet away. His gaze swivels to me, then back to Doc. "So it's done then?"

He jerks his chin, his eyes soften, and I swear he knows that I am pregnant. But how is that possible?

I swivel my head from Gabe to Doc, who is staring straight ahead. "You two had a discussion, about me?"

"We agreed that if you got pregnant, he'd relinquish all claim on you and leave," Doc thrusts out his chest.

"Nolan, I don't understand."

He looks down at me, "I had to protect you at all costs. Gabriel has a proposition and I wanted you to have no part of it."

"I am not sure what you mean."

"It wasn't enough that we were mated...I knew that the only way to get Gabriel to move on from involving you in his plan was if you fell pregnant."

"So you kept me all but imprisoned and... ah..." *knotted me over and over again until I couldn't move, until I'd been out of my head with the need to stay with him, burrow into him, lose myself in him and consolidate the bond completely, until I fell pregnant.*

Doc glances down at me. His features are pale. The skin across his cheeks stretches.

"Guilty as charged." He holds my gaze, doesn't look away. "I found you. I couldn't lose you. I knew you'd help him all over again, unless..."

"I fell pregnant." I lean into him, let my body relax.

I mean, I should be angry with him. I should be...upset that he'd plotted all this. But I am not. This level of possessiveness, if that's what Doc needs to feel secure, so be it. Besides, I want a child, my own family. My space in this world. Mine.

Warmth fills my chest.

My heart stutters and the mating bond lights up, green, blue and a flash of gold that swims through between us. It's beautiful. "You're gorgeous and possessive as hell, and I should be angry with you." I reach up and press my lips to his.

"But you're not?"

"A little." I peer up at him from under my eyelashes, "Fact is, I don't want to leave you. There's nowhere I'd rather be than with you. Whatever we do next, we do it together. The three of us."

"Together." His lips curve up; his eyes light up.

"Is everyone here?" Dante's voice booms around the space.

My gaze clings to Doc's; he doesn't look away. The chemistry ratchets up in the space, and I feel him shift his weight to widen his stance. His arousal throbs in his pants, pushing into my hip, and he smirks. His lips brush my lips, "Yeah, we are all here, can you tell?"

I chuckle.

"Doc and Alice... if you can stop eye-fucking each other for just a few seconds, perhaps we can get on with the reason for this gathering."

"Oh." I redden and look away.

Doc glowers, but turns his attention to Dante.

"Right then." Dante holds out his arm and Gia steps in closer to him. Dante pulls her into his side.

Is that how Doc and I look together?

Happy, content, yet excited to be in each other's company.

Dante looks around the small crowd. "Gabriel helped Doc and Alice escape from Boris. Thanks to the three of them, Boris is no longer a threat."

Claps sound around the space. I look around to find Tristan grinning and Jess smiling back at me. Hawke glowers, then thumps Doc on the back.

Doc shoots him a glance, then angles his shoulder to hide me from Hawke... Again, not complaining.

The man's holding me close enough that our skin is all but fused, but honestly, I find it hot. Maybe it's because I feel as strongly about the new life in my belly that I am more than happy for my mate to take care of us completely.

Charley walks to stand a safe distance from Hawke. Lily is next to Charley and Gabriel's gaze immediately seeks her out.

His features harden, and he draws himself up to his full height. He can't take his eyes off of the girl who looks at him, then looks away, biting her lip.

I stiffen and Doc leans down, I sense a touch on my forehead and look up, "Did you just brush your lips over my forehead?"

Color flushes his cheeks.

Wow. "And you blushed?"

He shuffles his feet, but doesn't reply.

"You did blush, admit it," I whisper.

His lips turn up in a smile. "I may have," he concedes.

The sound of a whistle blows through the space and we look up and back at Dante who stands at attention, Gia smirking a little at his side. "Settle down people, just a few seconds to let Gabriel have his say, and then I promise you can all bugger off to whatever you were doing."

He narrows his gaze at me and Doc.

A giggle slips from my mouth and Doc chuckles. "Behave or Dante may have a cardiac," he mutters.

I bite the inside of my cheek.

Gabriel steps forward and a silence sweeps over the group.

"Thank you for hosting me the past few weeks." He nods at Dante, then lets his gaze wander across the group. "It's enlightening to see how the Fae Corps have found a way to set down roots, balance duty with family, and also set up your own community."

His voice is smooth, his features hewn from rock. His tone is sincere... too earnest? He sounds almost bored. *Huh?*

He catches me staring and his eyes gleam.

There are so many secrets to my half-brother. I wish I could spend more time with him.

As if reading my mind, he tips his head. "I regret I can't stay but duty calls."

Doc half angles his body, partially hiding me from Gabe. I slap at his shoulder but he doesn't move. I peer around him. "Next time Gabriel, stay with us."

Doc growls under his breath and I place my hand over his chest. His heart beats steadily and his muscles relax.

Gabriel cants his head, then takes another step forward, and another. He moves sideways and closer to Lily, who wraps her arms around her waist, then raises her head to meet his scrutiny full on.

Dante straightens; he slides his bulk in front of Gia, shielding her from Gabriel. "I have considered your proposal of teaming up with us to take on the Vikings, and after much deliberation with the other Fae Corps members, we have decided to decline."

Gabriel stiffens and the tension in the area ratchets up.

Doc steps around in front of me.

Tristan does the same with Jess.

Hawke inches closer to Charley.

"You are making a mistake." Gabriel's voice is low.

"I understand you need reinforcements to take on the Berserkers, but we have a lot at stake here. Our duty is first and foremost to this city and to our families. Boris is dead, thanks to you and Doc; our score is settled. We don't want to take on the Vikings, and bring their attention down on our city. We are still recovering from the damage that Boris dealt to our economy and our community. We don't want to destabilize the progress we have made."

"I see." Gabriel says in a tone that implies he doesn't.

His nostrils flare and his biceps seem to swell. His gaze falls to mine and those green eyes seem to grow darker until they resemble black pools of intent.

The fine hair on my nape hardens. "No, Gabe, don't," I step around Doc, but he yanks me back.

Gabriel moves so fast his feet don't seem to touch the ground.

He grabs Lily just as Hawke pulls Charley out of the way.

Charley screams. Gabriel hauls the struggling Lily over his shoulder.

"Perhaps now this fight will be yours. If you want her, come after me, and I promise I will repay your hospitality...if you track me down, that is."

Doc prowls forward, "Don't do this, Gabe. We are on your side. Don't make enemies of the Fae."

He peels back his lips and his canines drop. "You're a good man, Doc." His ears flick back, "Take care of Alice."

Still holding Lily across his shoulder he turns around, then races toward the sea. Doc sprints forward, as do Dante, Tristan and Hawke.

Reaching the edge of the waves, Gabriel glances over his shoulder with a mocking grin. He raises an arm in farewell, then turns and leaps into the air.

Black wings snap out, massive, the widest leathery wings I have ever seen, they span out at least twenty feet on each side, seeming too big for his body. He takes off into the air.

HANG ON, THERE'S MORE. CLICK HERE TO GET GABRIEL AND LILY'S STORY. ALL YOUR FAVE ALPHAHOLE FAES WILL MAKE AN APPEARANCE IN KNOTTED BY THE FAE - DANTE AND GIA, TRISTAN AND JESS, DOC AND ALICE, HAWKE, CHARLEY AND HEY GUESS WHO ELSE IS PREGNANT? CLICK HERE TO FIND OUT

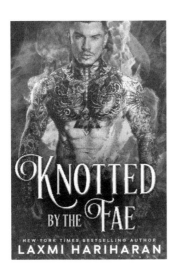

Lily

He'll make me his plaything...

Hot, surly, growly Fae male,

Gabriel, kidnapped me to get the attention of the Fae Corps.

He soul bonded me.

Mated me without my consent.

He demands I obey him.

I am determined to resist him.

He will not stop until he's tamed my spirit,

I will not succumb to his seductive charms,

...The pleasure he wrings from my body.

I cannot, will not give in to him...I *hope*

INTENSE FAE ABDUCTION ROMANCE, STARRING ONE FEISTY VIRGIN HUMAN AND THE FAE MALE STRONG ENOUGH TO MAKE HER HIS! 1-CLICK NOW

LOVE ANTIHEROES? MEET ZEUS IN TAKEN BY THE ALPHA. LUCY WAS SENT TO ASSASSINATE HIM AND NOW HE WILL NOT STOP UNTIL HE'S RUINED HER IN TAKEN BY THE ALPHA.

"ONE HELL OF A PRIMAL READ. THIS ALPHA IS A SEX GOD." - USA TODAY BESTSELLING AUTHOR LEE SAVINO

READ AN EXCERPT ...

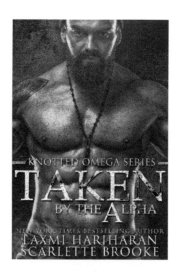

Zeus

"Boo!" I bare my teeth.

The soldier cringes, and sweat beads his forehead.

"Really, Z?" My second-in-command narrows his gaze.

"Okay, a bit over the top." I raise my shoulders then let them drop. But, hey, cut me some slack, okay? I like to play with my prey.

Besides, I have a flair for the dramatic, one of the few redeeming features I inherited from my bastard of a father. Except, oh, wait, I was the bastard in that relationship, given he'd never acknowledged me... not until I had my fingers around Golan's neck and recognition had dawned in his eyes. Too late, Pater. Thirty years too late.

The soldier's skin is stretched so tight over his cheekbones that I expect it to crack any moment. The scent of piss stinks up the warehouse. The fool, clearly a beta by the way his shoulders are hunched, has wet himself.

I yawn aloud. The sound of my jaws cracking seems to snap the man into action, for he staggers forward, followed by his partner. They haul a rolled-up carpet between them.

Loose threads trail from the edges to sweep over the wooden floor. The patchwork on the outside of the carpet is peeling. The fabric seems so innocuous, so unassuming, it's precisely that which sends all my instincts on alert.

A sliver of awareness ripples over my skin. *Thud, thud, thud* my heart-beat accelerates. The fine hair on my neck rises.

What the bloody hell? I can't take my gaze off that damn rug. "Unfurl it."

The edge of impatience in my tone must have signaled the impending flare of temper, for Ethan, my second, moves forward—not that the soldiers will dare try anything. The stripes on their vests mark them out as emissaries of the Leader of Scotland, and Kayden doesn't have the balls to put them up to breaking into my stronghold. I drum my fingers over my chest. Nah! It's exactly the kind of move I'd expect that twat to try to pull off.

Adrenaline laces my blood. I curl my fingers into fists.

That piece of shit wants me out of the way so he can take over my position. Well, he and most of those gathered here. Don't everyone rush all at once. I snicker.

The Scot nearest to me pales.

He expects me to kill him. The body count I've left behind in the past year ensures that most fear me. But just this once, I might spare these men. Just to keep them guessing.

I lean forward on the balls of my feet.

The sudden movement draws a gasp from the beta. He bends and places his side of the rolled-up fabric on the floor. The other man follows.

I take a step forward. Honestly, I don't make any other sign of threat, I don't even peel back my lips, or speak... well, okay, I glare at the soldier on the right.

With an audible gulp, he turns and scampers down the big hall toward the still open doors. His partner blinks then scoots after him. My gaze is already on the piece of fabric left behind.

"I don't think it's wise to open it, General," Ethan warns.

Since global warming unleashed tsunamis and wrecked the earth's sub-layers thirty years ago, trace metals all but vanished. Electronics can no longer be powered up and technology collapsed, leaving no means of communicating. It means the only way to check what's inside that carpet is the old fashioned way. To open it.

"Consider yourself heard." I crick my neck from side to side. "You've done your duty, Second, so can we get this charade over with?"

Sure, his concern is genuine, and yet it doesn't sit easily with me.

Not since he'd betrayed the ex-General, AKA my dear departed father by aiding me in killing the old man.

"Allow me, sir." Solomon, my third, grabs the open seam of the curled-up piece of fabric. He heaves, but it doesn't budge.

Ethan moves to the other side, and together they tug at it. The cloth unfurls... and flattens out into a pool of turquoise and green.

The light from the solitary skylight far above floods over it. The entire rug shimmers, as if made of liquid sunshine.

My pulse races. The breath catches in my throat. My heart hammers as if it's going to rip out of my ribcage.

The next second, a figure springs up from the carpet and launches at me. Head bent, dressed all in black. There's a blur of movement, and a blade whines through the space.

I slide aside.

The breeze displaced by the stranger shimmers over my neck. A flash of pain cuts through me as the blade nicks my skin.

I thrust out my leg, and the intruder goes sprawling to the floor, only to turn in a move which should have been near impossible.

It calls attention to the lithe lines of the body that is wrapped in that jumpsuit. The figure launches itself back at me, and I bend my knees and throw the stranger over my shoulder.

There's a thump behind me, and I hear the sword skitter across the wooden floor.

I swivel around and close the distance to where the intruder leaps up from the center of the carpet.

The colors fade, the room shrinks around me. My vision narrows in on the face, to where the dark cloth has unraveled from around the head of the stranger. Eyes of shattered green blaze at me.

The hair on my nape rises.

It's her, the woman from my dreams.

A strand of dark-red hair slinks free.

The scent of rain on cool dawn air bleeds through the space interlaced with that sugary scent of slickness.

Blood rushes to my groin.

Every instinct inside me goes on alert. "Omega," I rasp.

Lucy

I lift my chin, then farther up, then all the way up, to meet his gaze. To call the General massive is an understatement. He is a monster. A man-mountain, the biggest, most powerful alpha I have ever seen.

His blue eyes blaze at me.

A ripple of fear mixed with something else—lust? Anticipation?—tightens my stomach.

His face is all hard planes and dark angles. Long black hair flows to his shoulders. His lower lip is full, obscenely so. It should have softened his looks, instead it only heightens the feeling of danger that clings to him like a rich coat.

It's the exact opposite of the faded vest that clings to his torso.

His clothes strike a jarring note in the middle of the most prosperous pocket of this city, which is where we are; but it suits this alpha. Declares exactly what he is: an asshole who doesn't give a damn about anyone else.

Who takes pleasure in surprising his friends and outwitting his enemies —no, he doesn't have friends… doesn't need friends… or lovers or… how would he be as a lover? A dominant? A male who'd take without mercy? That feminine, omega core of me quivers in anticipation.

A pulse flares to life between my thighs.

An age-old instinct deep inside awakes and insists that this alpha will make sure I am pleasured. He'll bite me, lick me, suck me… and a piercing wave of desire twists my stomach.

Heat flushes my skin, and yet I feel cold, so cold.

I try to take a step forward, and it's as if my feet are weighed down.

The alpha lifts his chin, thrusts out his chest and the force of his dominance crashes over me. My breath catches in my chest. I can't move. Can't think. Can't do anything but stare at his face, drink in his features. Open my heart and absorb every last particle of impact that his sheer charisma has on me.

I want to trace that long, hooked nose of his. To close the distance between us and bite his square, pronounced jaw. Lick it, nibble on it, then pull his head down between my thighs and make him rub his hard whiskers across my sensitive core.

Heat floods my skin.

My nipples tighten.

I don't need to look down at my breasts to know they're be thrusting out, the sharpness of my arousal a palpable outline against the material.

He must know the effect he has on me, for the strong cords of his throat ripple. His sculpted chest seems to widen as he straightens and plants his arms on his trim hips. His powerful shoulders block out the sight of the room. His entire presence sucks up the air in the space.

The strength of his personality is a visceral force that crashes into me and threatens to overpower me.

I want to reach for the throbbing space between my legs and relieve the pressure that is building in my womb. What is happening to me?

"Do you know what I do to those who cross my path?" He growls.

The rich sound grates over my sensitized nerve endings and shudders straight to my center.

My thighs quiver, my stomach trembles, and I thrust my pelvis forward in blatant invitation. It's as if my body has already arrived at a decision and the rest of me is struggling to catch up.

I grit my teeth. "I am sure you are going to tell me." I am not sure where that need to stand up to him comes from, I confess I am not thinking straight. Not when my heart pounds in my rib cage, my pulse thuds in my veins and the beat between my thighs seems to echo the fear.

Anticipation stretches my belly.

It's as if there is this instinct inside me that is tuned into him.

He growls again, and the sound tugs at my nerves, rolls over me and surrounds me. It's like nothing I have ever heard. Moisture pools in my core. The scent of slick bleeds into the air. I gasp. No, not now. I can't be heading straight into a heat cycle, not when I am here on a mission. Is it the adrenaline of the attack that has brought on this sudden wave of need?

His lips, those sensuous lips, tighten. A pulse ticks to life at his temple, and his cheeks flush, as he looks down at me from his superior height.

I should feel emboldened that I am having an effect on him, the most powerful alpha in all the land, but all I feel is a writhing need to challenge. To ask. To submit to his every demand. And that confuses me.

I am an omega but am not a submissive: the warring of the two sides of my personality is a fact of life for me. One that has made me an anomaly in this world where genetic mutation brought on by climate change has divided the human race into three sub-species. The same mutation had equipped the alphas with the ability to knot the omegas in order to increase the chances of breeding from a single copulation. Nature's way of trying to compensate for a rapidly declining world population.

That I am omega was established by the heat cycles that puberty brought on. I'd managed to hide myself away during the worst of them.

Heat suppressants have been outlawed in an agreement between the alphas of the most powerful countries in the world. Even black market supplies of the precious chemicals had been tracked down and burned.

I should have felt more bitter about it, except that I have never felt even the remotest interest to lay with any alpha, so far. Not until this monster.

I need him, yet I want to fight him.

I must show him he can't just take. Not without paying a price first. Not without begging, pleading, making me scream. The images in my head are so vivid that my knees quake, and I push my boot-clad feet into the dirt for purchase.

He angles his head and peels back his lips. I am sure he can see every single emotion, every nuance of feeling that trembles over me right now.

There is so much cruelty in his look... so much lust... so much everything.

The hair on the nape of my neck rises.

Every single emotion that I have fought against my entire life, denied myself, all of it drips from his gaze.

I can't look away.

It's as if I am watching everything unfold in front of me from a distance.

I clench my fingers, my muscles strain, and I try once more to move. It only sends another pulse of pain through me. It is as if simply being in this particular alpha's presence is weighing me down, making me feel like I am already in his control.

How is that possible?

The General takes a step forward, and his scent slams into me. Earthy, woodsy, and liberally laced with pheromones.

My belly clenches. My womb spasms. Slick pools between my legs and slides down my inner thighs.

Setting my jaw, I square my shoulders, only for another burst of pain to radiate out from my center.

I arch my back, thrust my breasts out at the keening need that grips me.

I wrap my arms around my waist and cannot stop the groan that ripples up my throat. Even to my own ears it feels more like an invitation, a call to the alpha to do what he was born to do to an omega. To mate me, knot me, and make that pain inside me go away.

To fill that emptiness that is once again writhing, gnawing, and tearing at me; growing inside me with every passing millisecond until it feels like I am just one big mass of yearning that will not stop. Not until he slams into me, and no, no, no! This can't be happening.

I'd starved myself of food for days to make sure my libido was at an all-time low; I'd also calculated the time of the month to make sure I was between heat cycles… I hadn't counted on the proximity to this particular alpha sending me straight into one.

My head spins with the overload of endorphins that my overwrought nervous system is dumping into my blood. All brought on by his presence. Him. He's the reason why my body is responding with such primal need. The omega in me recognizes him. Only him.

My pulse thuds in my head; my vision blurs.

Pain cramps my womb, and I double over.

Over the years, the shortage of omegas has led to alphas exploiting them, taking them at will. As he no doubt intends to overpower me now.

I will not let him do that. I straighten in time to see the General stalk toward me. His masculine presence tugs at my nerves, pushes down on my skin, sinks into my blood and makes my head spin.

Heat sweeps over my skin and heads to my lower belly. My core weeps.

All my life I have tried to hide what I am. An omega. The receiver, the nurturer whose insides are starved of an alpha's touch, who has been deprived of the sensory stimulation that only comes from an alpha's rut. Now, his scent, that concentrated testosterone, sinks into my blood, forcing a reaction.

My womb cramps, and a fresh burst of slick gushes down between my legs to wet my pants. I don't dare look down, don't dare acknowledge the liquid pooling under me.

I should be mortified, ashamed at my public display of what I am... an omega meant to be mated and bred, who cannot physically hold back her reaction, not in the presence of this prime male specimen, and yet the survivor in me says I need to fight. Fight! My shoulders shudder, and I straighten my spine.

The General growls.

It's a long, drawn-out purr that seems to emerge from the very depths of his masculine body.

The hair on my neck stands on end.

Liquid need radiates out from my womb, bleeds through my skin, and flares up in the surrounding air.

The General slams his fist to his chest, "Leave us." He roars. The aggression comes off him in waves, surrounding me, cocooning me as if he's trying to shield me from the sight of his own men. My knees threaten to give out from under me.

Around me I hear murmurs, footsteps sound, then fade away.

The doorway to the warehouse slams shut.

"You scared?" His voice murmurs through the space.

I shiver, I don't speak, I *don't* need to speak. The scent of my fear is so strong I am sure he can smell it. "What do you think?" I intended to snarl at him, but the words come out a groan. I try to stagger away from him, trying to put space between me and that lethal, coiled, powerful male, only for my feet to tangle in the carpet. I go sprawling on my back and stay there.

"Get up." He snarls.

I blink, then slap my palms onto the carpet for leverage and stagger back to standing. Thrusting my chin forward I meet his gaze. Those startling blue eyes burn into me. Concentric circles of aquamarine, teal and a wild blue, draw me in, and make me want to lose myself in them.

"Kayden sent you to kill me."

It's not a question, but a statement. And not one that demands a response.

My chin quivers and I ball my fists at my side.

His jaw firms. "I should kill you right here, Omega, for daring to burst into my stronghold and trying to assassinate me."

"But you won't." Yeah, that would be too merciful of him. He's a monster and I don't expect any pity from him. But every alpha has an ego. And this predator has more ego than anyone else I have met. Perhaps it's that I need to appeal to. The thoughts skitter through my head, and I force my brain cells to knit the words together in a coherent sequence.

He tilts his head. "Feisty, aren't you?" His voice is soft, almost casual.

My stomach churns. Whatever he has in mind for me, it's not good.

"You bet," I set my jaw.

His gaze narrows.

My stomach twists and not just with arousal. My heart hammers and a bead of sweat trickles down my spine.

"You are a big powerful alpha; me, I am just a helpless omega." I flutter my eyelashes and fuck, I am overdoing this, but what the hell, I keep going. "Why don't we make this more exciting for you?"

He cants his head.

What do you know? He bought it. A flicker of hope sparks in my chest.

Then, his lips widen in a smile, and it's so predatory that I almost lose my will to resist, almost. I straighten my spine.

"I agree."

"Huh?" I blink. Why am I having this conversation with him? Just delaying the inevitable, that's all, but what the hell, I have to try, have to.

His nostrils flare, "Run. You have until I count to ten to get a head start."

"What do you mean?" I swallow.

"You are losing precious seconds."

No, it can't be. This is not exactly what I had in mind when I had suggested to make things more exciting. Not.

"Nine."

The alpha is toying with me? He's going to hunt me? My palms begin to sweat. It can mean only one thing. He wants to increase the anticipation of whatever is to come. There is only one ultimate conclusion to this game, and it's not going to be in my favor. I close my fist so tight that my nails slice into my skin. The scent of copper leaks into the air.

"On the other hand, perhaps you'd rather we conclude this farce right now?" His eyes gleam.

The bastard no doubt thinks that I don't have a chance of outrunning him. It's that which makes me square my shoulders and thrust out my chest. I will not submit, not so easily.

His gaze sweeps over my breasts, down to my core and he stares at the space between my legs. There's no mistaking the anticipation that laces his features.

It makes me want to scratch that look of satisfaction off his face, to deny that my insides tremble in response. More moisture gathers between my legs. What is wrong with me? I am here to kill him. Not to mate him. Not. To. Mate. Him.

I turn and race to the exit of the warehouse and throw myself against the doors.

Want to know what happens next? Get this passionate, action and suspense filled Dark Romance here

Read the RONE Awards nominated, AMAZON top 200 bestselling,
BONDED TO THE DRAGON (Dragon Protectors 1), HERE.
"★ ★ ★ ★ ★Primal, sexy and so very satisfying! Sizzles from page one with toe curling and tummy tingling heat!" -InD'tale Magazine, Crowned Star of Excellence

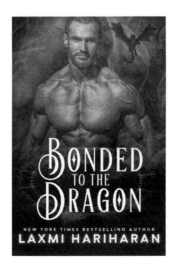

Read an excerpt...

Hope

Twenty-four hours into her break from being a sentinel of the dragons of Mauritania, Hope had walked into that bar.

She wasn't supposed to be in Bombay.

The dragons had flown under the radar for so long. They'd kept away from people until they had all but faded from memory.

She was taking a major risk by being in that city, but she hadn't been able to resist.

The city had always called to her, and for once, Hope couldn't soothe her dragon out of the urge to visit.

A few weeks more, and she would be bonded to a fellow dragon shifter. She was looking forward to it.

Liar.

Sweat trickled down her spine. The scents of the shifters, vampires, and humans in the bar, entwined with the smell of her desperation.

She tightened her fingers around the glass. It shattered, the liquid splashing onto the bar counter.

As one of the seven born to the dragon who'd founded her clan, it was her duty to mate with another dragon and continue her bloodline.

No other species could survive the psychic impact of bonding with a dragon shifter. She was screwed.

Likely, this was her last night of freedom, and she had to make the most of it.

When she was out flying through the air or winging through the seas on her boat, she could be herself. She felt free to do what she wanted, without fear of letting down her family.

It was also the reason she kept breaking the rules of her clan.

It was childish of her, but these occasional bouts of rebellion were what kept her dragon sated. Enough to allow the woman to stay in control in human form.

"Non-alcoholic ambrosia, please." She peered up at the bartender from beneath lowered eyelashes.

The man's eyebrows flew so high they disappeared under the hair that fell over his forehead. "Let me guess. You're a dragon shifter, the only species who don't like alcohol."

A jolt of fear ran through Hope. The heat of the enclosed space inside Alex's bar weighed down on her shoulders. Had she been found out?

Then she saw the teasing glint in his eyes.

She relaxed and raised her fingers to her mouth, pretending to yawn. "Do I *look* like a dragon shifter?"

The bartender looked over her features, down her chest, to her waist, then back. "Hmm. You're curvy and tiny and too sexy to be one."

She recognized his harmless flirting and decided to play along. "What does a dragon shifter look like, anyway?"

"Large, fire-breathing, with wings." He flapped a palm in the air. "Never seen one. They're almost extinct, right?"

"Right." She flashed a smile.

Had the satisfaction of seeing him blink.

Oh, he was interested all right, and cute and friendly. Only… she wasn't looking for any complications.

"By the way, it's not like dragon shifters don't like the occasional alcoholic drink. But when you're a fire-breather, alcohol tends to add fuel to the flames. Know what I mean?"

Hope clamped her lips shut. Hell! She shouldn't have said that. But her dragon had insisted she set the facts right.

Dragon 1. Woman 0.

Stupid game! But it was so much more fun to keep her dragon and woman in balance this way.

Her animal was too damn close to the surface. She never had managed to rein it in. Very early, Hope had realized that unlike the others, her dragon took a lot more to control.

The bartender didn't seem to hear her muttered comment. He was too busy shaking up a concoction.

A crash from the other end of the bar had her turning that way. The hair on the back of her neck prickled. Both dragon and woman were riveted.

The clinking of the glasses, the conversation of the couple next to her... all of it faded. All she saw was him.

The man who had her attention rose to his feet, only to stumble.

She didn't even realize she was moving until she found herself next to him.

The feel of the rock-hard muscles of his shoulder bunching under her fingers sent a thrill of awareness rippling through her.

She was in so much trouble.

To find out what happens next, get Bonded to the Dragon here

FREE BOOKS

DRAGON PROTECTORS BOXED SET (8 BOOKS + EXCLUSIVE PROLOGUES AND EPILOGUES)
INCEPTION (HOPE AND AARON)
OBSESSION (EVE AND CAIN)
DECEPTION (PANDORA AND RAGE)
FORBIDDEN (FREYA AND AXEL)
SEDUCTION (NEO AND TRINITY)
ASCENSION (MIRA AND ZACH)
REVELATION (ARJUN AND NAYA)
TEMPTATION (VANCE AND SERENA)

MANY LIVES SERIES
AWAKENED (RUBY AND VIK)
FERAL (MAYA AND LUKE)
TAKEN (JAI AND ARIANA)
EXHALE (FREE)
REDEMPTION (MIKHAIL AND LEANA)
CLAIMED (KRIS AND TARA)
MANY LIVES BOX SET (6 BOOKS WITH FREE BONUS SCENES, PROLOGUES AND EPILOGUES)

MANY LIVES ORIGIN STORIES
ORIGIN (FREE)
CHOSEN

CONTEMPORARY ROMANCE
LOVE, CAUTION (JACE) - BAD BOY BILLIONAIRE ROMANCE

GET ALL LAXMI'S BOOKS HERE

ARE YOU STALKING ME?
Why not? You're missing out on all the fun!

NEWSLETTER – Claim your FREE book. If you want to get in on all bonus content and public giveaways, Join my list here
➔BookHip.com/WFVDWA

FACEBOOK PAGE – I am here a LOT➜ http:// laxmihariharan.com/LaxFBPage

BOOKBUB – If you want to be notified when I have FREE BOOKS and new releases follow me on Bookbub HERE➜ https://www.bookbub.com/ authors/laxmi-hariharan

AMAZON FOLLOW – If you want Amazon to automatically notify you via email with a link every time I push publish, click the yellow tab under my author picture here ➜ https://www.amazon.com/Laxmi-Hariharan/e/B007M6E542/

INSTAGRAM - Follow my walk on the wild side London life on IG ➜ http://laxmihariharan.com/IG

PRIVATE FAN GROUP –This is where I chat with readers and run private giveaways➜ http://smarturl.it/TeamLaxmi

TWITTER FOLLOW - I tweet about special deals, giveaways, and my writing progress on Twitter, follow me here ➜https://twitter.com/laxmi

CONNECT WITH ME ON MESSENGER➜ http:// laxmihariharan.com/ManyChat

BUY BOOKS – If you want to buy my books, or just see what I have available, CLICK HERE➜ https://readerlinks.com/mybooks/950

ABOUT THE AUTHOR

Laxmi is a New York Times Bestselling Author. Happily married, she lives in London.

PS. She insists that you call her Lax :)

CONNECT ON MESSENGER

FOLLOW LAX ON AMAZON HERE

FOLLOW LAX ON BOOKBUB HERE

ON GOODREADS

JOIN LAX'S READER GROUP FOR EXCLUSIVE SNEAK PEEKS

CLAIM MORE FREE BOOKS BY EMAIL HERE

ACKNOWLEDGMENTS

Thanks to my awesome beta readers Lenka and Li, I couldn't do this without you!

To everyone on my FACEBOOK page who cheers me on.

Thanks to my editor Elizabeth aka The Marginatrix who whips my manuscripts into shape! :)

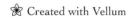 Created with Vellum

Made in the USA
Monee, IL
13 September 2020